in the
BAG

Previously published Worldwide Mystery title by
EMERY HARPER

PERSON OF INTEREST

in the
BAG

EMERY HARPER

W RLDWIDE®

TORONTO • NEW YORK • LONDON
AMSTERDAM • PARIS • SYDNEY • HAMBURG
STOCKHOLM • ATHENS • TOKYO • MILAN
MADRID • WARSAW • BUDAPEST • AUCKLAND

As always, to my men: Alan, Collin, Aaron, Reed and Zac—love y'all.

Recycling programs
for this product may
not exist in your area.

In the Bag

A Worldwide Mystery/October 2017

First published by Carina Press

ISBN-13: 978-0-373-28429-0

in the
BAG

ONE

"You got an anonymous birthday card."

I looked up from my second cup of coffee. I really needed three so early in the morning to be human, but Levi Weiss was my very best friend, so I'd give him the benefit of BFFdom and not take it out on him when he was trying to engage my not-fully-caffeinated brain. Not to mention he's my child's honorary uncle, so if I chucked my mug at him, I'd have to explain it to Paige.

"It's no big deal. Besides, it was addressed to Mrs. Celeste Eagan. All formal and…" *Strange.* I shrugged. "Like I said, no big deal."

"No big deal? Sweets, when was the last time you got a random birthday card?" He pulled out a chair at the kitchen table and sat. "Could it be from…?" He trailed off and waved his hand.

"Muldoon?" I chuckled. "No." My on-again, off-again dating interest Detective Shaw Muldoon had been more off-again lately. He was extremely dedicated to his job and didn't let his personal life distract him. Which is great if you're a resident of Peytonville, Texas, but sucks if you want to go out to dinner with the man. "It's probably one of those sales gimmicks. Maybe from the dealership where I bought my Outlander."

"Without any kind of advertising? Don't think so." Levi waved off my suggestion. "So. Someone else sent it." His blond brows shot upward. "Someone from work?"

I frowned at him. I was a principal actor and recently promoted to manager at the Peytonville Playhouse. No one there would be so mysterious. Hell, I was more like a mom to the troupe—though the card did have a puppy on the front—so they wouldn't have left it unsigned. Plus, those guys were more likely to send an e-card, being all digital and technophile twenty-somethings. "Not a chance."

"Yeah." He snorted. "I didn't think so. Who?" He snagged a leftover pancake from the plate.

"You're making it way too mysterious."

"It's exciting." He ripped the pancake apart piece by piece and polished it off in four bites. "When did the card come in?"

"Yesterday." I took a long sip from my pink Best Mom mug. "Why? What difference does that make?"

Levi tsked. "This is why I'm here. You don't know these things." He used finger quotes around *things*.

"I know plenty of *things*." I matched his quotes and threw my balled-up napkin at him.

It smacked Levi on the chest and landed in his lap. "You know *things* about as well as I know quantum physics." He scooped up the napkin and dropped it onto the table. "If it weren't for me, you'd lose your girl points. Daily."

I started to argue, then looked down at the outfit he'd picked out for me. I would never have paired the camel blazer with the navy striped top—it did look pretty good. I was rocking the knee-high brown leather boots he picked out, too. But when it came to men, I was not ready for his tutelage. "Look, been there. Done that." And, yes, I was a little gun-shy. First, I'd been with my ex, Colin Eagan, for fourteen years. And it wasn't that

I was stuck on him—hell no, we were so over—it was that I was so out of practice. I didn't really know how to date. Second, Colin had been instrumental in getting me involved with crimes I'd had no business nosing around in. "The ex-hubby got my car blown up."

Levi waved away my comment. "That was after you were divorced and it wasn't his fault per se."

"You're defending him now?" I'd been sitting on the car bumper only moments before. Had a quick-thinking detective—one Shaw Muldoon as it so happens—not pulled me away, I'd have gone kablooey along with the car, my purse and cell phone.

It was difficult not to take it personally when your belongings were wired for detonation. But I wasn't going to let it occupy my mind any longer. I snapped my fingers. "Focus, man. Birthday card. Meaning of post office efficiency."

Levi snagged another pancake and tore it in half. "If you get a card two weeks before, it's an empty gesture. They know they have to send it and just get it out of the way. If you get it the day of or the day before, it's a guilt-ridden gesture. Again they know they have to do it and waited until the last possible moment—maybe they're considering not doing it but in the end they did even though it could be delayed and get to you late. Guilt."

I wasn't sure I was buying any of what Levi said.

"And five days before?" I flipped the envelope over and studied the post office cancellation stamp. It was mailed from one of the Fort Worth branches. The address was computer printed, as were the salutations inside. It was as much intriguing as it was unnerving to receive a strange birthday card.

"The person timed it well. They wanted to make sure you got it in time to know you're in their thoughts."

I stared at him for a long moment then scoffed. "You're so full of crap."

Levi huffed. "Fine. What's your theory?"

"I think someone is trying to sell me something or butter me up." I looked him square in the eye. "If it's not you…"

He shoved half the pancake in his mouth. "Not me," he said with his mouth full.

"Gross, Levi." I swatted his shoulder and pushed the pancakes far away. "If it's not you, then I'd guess Colin is warming me up for another favor. And if he's going to this much trouble, I'm almost afraid to hear what it may be."

"Maybe he needs a maid of honor for his bride of Frankenstein."

"Far as I know, he's hasn't popped that question yet. I can't imagine her being low-key if it happens."

"If? Are there chances that he won't ask?"

"Don't know. Don't care." Only a half-truth. I mean, really, I don't care if my ex remarries. And I'd swear to it on a stack of caramel macchiatos. It was the *who* he was possibly going to marry that rankled. Naomi Michaels rubbed me the wrong way. Ten times over. It wouldn't be so bad if I didn't have to share Paige with her every other weekend. Okay, so I really only had to share Paige with Colin but as long as he was with her, she'd be around my—our—daughter. Luckily, I no longer worked with Colin and Naomi. But we all still lived in Peytonville. The suburb of Fort Worth was by no means small, but when you, your ex and his…skank all lived, shopped and shared a kid within the city limits it could be stifling at times.

"Unless or until I get a diamond necklace or a seventy-inch TV to go with that birthday card, then it's just a waste of effort." I tossed the card atop the mail pile.

"So you can be bought."

"Absolutely." I smiled at Levi though inside I heaved a sigh. It's not that I *wanted* it to be from Muldoon… We barely had enough time on our own much less for the two of us. I did not know how adults with busy lives dated.

I drained the rest of my coffee. "Shouldn't you and Paige be headed to her meet about now?"

Levi taught my daughter karate. Paige loved the rules and discipline and I loved the fact it kept her active and her nose out of a book for a few hours a week. Eventually she surpassed his tutelage and they both joined the same dojo. The two of them had entered several tournaments over the past few months, but thanks to a knee injury—Levi tripped trying on leather pants at a department store, though he would deny it ever happened—he'd been sitting out the recent tourneys.

"Yes, Mother." He pushed up from the table. "You'll be on time, won't you?"

"Yes, Mother," I mimicked. One time, ten minutes late and he wouldn't let me live it down. I got lost. It's not like I was shopping or anything—though when I saw the adorable little boutique I'd gotten a little distracted, missed my exit and was blocks away before I realized it.

"Paige, sweet pea, y'all are leaving any minute."

"Okay," she called from the back of the house.

"Do you need me to bring anything?"

Levi pulled up short. "No. And please leave the air horn at home. You'll get her disqualified."

"Air horn?"

Levi arched an eyebrow.

"Whatever."

Levi ran, yes, ran, from the kitchen and down the hall. "C'mon, Paige. We gotta book."

I refilled my mug. Third cup's a charm. Sufficient sugar and creamer added, I all but moaned when I took the first warm sip.

Moments later the front door slammed. I closed my eyes, took a deep breath and called Colin's cell to remind him about the tournament. She-Devil herself picked up after the second ring, and I rattled off the information Levi'd written down for me. "Please pass..."

She hung up. I growled low in the back of my throat. I was pleasant to her. I never called her names...to her face. I made sure that I was kind toward her around Paige. Most of the time.

I shook off all thoughts of Naomi, cleaned out my bag for the tournament, setting the air horn aside for a special occasion later. After checking email and calling the theater to check in with Annabelle, I glanced at the clock on the microwave. "Crap." I was going to be late again. I should have just gone with Levi and Paige but I needed to head to the theater afterward.

Snacks gathered up for after the meet, I ran to my car, the fairly new Mitsubishi Outlander I'd bought when I had to replace my sedan. Just as I popped the lock with my key fob, a dog barked and I stutter-stepped. A tow-headed teenager was wrestling a large dog down the sidewalk. It looked like the dog was winning. The teen's hushed commands fell on deaf ears as the dog dragged him from one bush to the next. Once, the kid looked back. If he was hoping for assistance, he was sadly barking up the wrong tree. I did not mess with dogs. They'd scared the crap out of me since I was five.

I wrenched the door open and tossed my bag inside into the passenger seat. A white slip of something tucked under the windshield wiper caught my attention. I leaned back out and grabbed it. A note. Levi was probably reminding me to leave the noisemaker at home. "I did, Levi," I said aloud and tucked the note into my hip pocket. I didn't have time to read it if I wanted to make the beginning of the meet. I'd gotten the message earlier.

At the Will Rogers Auditorium in Fort Worth, I had to park ten rows away from the building due to the crowd. I shouldered my bag. If I race-walked, I'd just make it in time. I tried not to show how out of breath I was when I found my friend Kellen in the stands.

Kellen Schaeffer was a reporter with the *Peytonville Gazette*. We'd met while he was working on the story of my former boss's murder. Since then, we'd had coffee from time to time and as a way to thank me for an exclusive on facing down a killer—that won him numerous awards—he offered to personally write up all of Paige's matches. Kind of a human interest piece. Personally, I thought he had a wee bit of a crush on me and hadn't worked up the nerve... Maybe he sent the card.

I glanced over at him dressed in his pressed khakis and starched navy oxford. He spent more time in front of the mirror primping his blond curly hair than I did with my own copper mess—case in point, my hair was pulled up in a lopsided doubled-over ponytail—all the rage, if you were fifteen. I shook my head. He didn't strike me as the kind of man to send a sappy card with a puppy dog.

"You're late," he leaned over to me and whispered.

"No, I'm not." I dug my cell from my purse. The clock

on the cell was never wrong; it was like a law of the universe to keep people on time, right? "See." I waggled my phone in his face. "11:15. Right on time."

Kellen's gray eyes narrowed at me. "Eleven. It starts at eleven." He laughed. "Don't worry. They're running late. Something about a last-minute substitution." He patted my knee. "Relax. Take a deep breath."

I sucked in a deep breath and released it.

"Feel better?"

"Eh." I dropped my phone back into my purse.

"Talk to Muldoon lately?"

He asked me every time we saw each other. "No, you?" Which was my standard comeback. "The man's busy with work."

As he always was. I didn't begrudge him. Really. He was a damn good detective and took his job seriously. I frowned. He'd actually been busier than usual. Which was weird because I hadn't heard of any more crimes than usual.

I looked around the auditorium for Paige and Levi. The rest of their group was sitting next to the floor, but I didn't see either of them. "Have you seen Paige or Levi?"

Kellen frowned. "Huh. No, now that you mention it."

"What about Colin?"

"Yeah. He was at the bottom of the bleachers about ten minutes ago. I checked my cell but he was gone when I looked back up."

I scanned the crowd. No Colin. No Naomi either—not that I would complain about missing her. "Hmm. I'll be right back." I shouldered my purse and wove back down to the bottom of the stands. Paige's instructor was speaking with a young girl I didn't recognize.

He paused when he saw me. "Celeste?"

"Where's Paige?"

"Didn't you get a call? She got hurt. Levi took her to the children's ER."

"What happened?" My heart stopped and I waved frantically at Kellen to come down.

"One of the other contestants was warming up and smacked her in the face."

"Is she okay?"

"Her nose was bleeding. I'm pretty sure it's not broken. But Levi wanted to take her in just in case. Her father left about a minute after them." Jarkard glanced over his shoulder when a buzzer went off. "I'm so sorry no one informed you. We have to get started. Please give her our best."

Kellen arrived at my side in time to hear what had happened. "I'm sure she's okay."

"Why didn't Levi call me?"

"Maybe it's the blood thing?" A smile curved his lips.

Blood. Ugh. I shivered.

Kellen rubbed my shoulder. "He was probably in a hurry to get her to the ER."

The children's hospital was only a couple of miles from the auditorium. I ran out to my car. Kellen offered to meet me there, but I told him he didn't need to. They probably wouldn't let him in anyway.

I was lucky I didn't get pulled over. I'm pretty sure I was driving like a maniac. I'd been thrown in jail several times last year—none of which were really my fault, they'd let me go each and every time, not a single charge pressed—still, I was not ready to see the inside of a jail cell anytime soon.

I found the ER lobby and asked the woman at the desk for Paige Eagan's room.

"And you are?"

"Her mother."

The young woman frowned. "Her mother came in with her father."

Really? I clinched my teeth. "I am her mother. That was her father's girlfriend."

"Sorry." She typed a few things into the computer. "Around the corner. Go straight back, then make a left. She's in the third cubicle."

"Thanks," I called over my shoulder. I was halfway down the hallway when a loud scuffle echoed from around the corner. I didn't know exactly what I expected to see, but it sure wasn't Levi being dragged away by two hospital security guards. "Hey. What's going on?"

"Celeste! Thank God you're here. Can you tell these goons I did not hurt Paige?"

"What?" I pulled up short. "Of course you didn't."

A man clad in full doctor's garb stepped out from a curtained cubicle. "May I help you?"

"I'm Paige Eagan's mom. I just heard about her accident. From her karate instructor. She was hit by another contestant warming up."

"That's what I told them," Levi said at the same time Paige did from behind the curtain as the doctor frowned and said, "Her mom? I thought…"

Naomi stepped from the cubicle. "Oh, you're here." She crossed her arms and shoved her pointed nose toward the ceiling.

"I'm her mother. Where else would I be?"

The doctor volleyed his gaze between me and Naomi until Colin stepped out, too. "Celeste, she's in here." He held back the curtain and I got a quick peek of Paige with an ice pack to her face. Already black circles colored the edges of her eyes.

"You okay?"

She gave a quick solemn nod. "Yes."

"I'll be right in. I need to talk to the doctor." I waved at Colin to release the curtain. Once he did I shoved my hands on my hips and turned to the men holding Levi. "Can you tell me why you're detaining my friend?"

"I'm sorry. There was a misunderstanding. Mr. Weiss brought the child in. When her father and her, er, um, her father showed up, Mr. Weiss was instructed to leave. He refused. Oftentimes with abuse—"

"Are you kidding me with *abuse*? She was at a karate match. Anyone happen to notice her gi?" I thought of the uniform, probably bloodied. Wooziness crept in around the edges, but I held it at bay not actually seeing it. "You both knew what happened." I narrowed my gaze at Colin then Naomi. "You were there. Why didn't you tell them Levi didn't hurt her?"

Colin blushed. "It happened so fast. Got out of hand."

I looked at the security guard. "Can you let him go now? It was a misunderstanding."

The larger of the two men looked reluctant but did release his hold of Levi. While Levi was rubbing his arm, two uniformed officers came around the corner. One of the security guards walked over to wave them off.

"They called the police." Levi shook his head and slumped his shoulders—it wasn't out of defeat. No, the man was pissed and ready to charge like a riled-up bull.

"I'm so sorry, hon. You okay?" I patted Levi's back.

He had murder in his eyes as he glanced over at my ex. "Yes, no thanks to you," he snarled at Colin, then shoved past him into the cubicle. "I'm gonna go now, sweet pea, since your mom's here. I'm sorry you didn't get to compete."

"It's okay, Uncle Levi."

He kissed her forehead, then did the same to me. "I'm headed out to a couple of my properties. Might as well get some work done."

"I'm so—"

He waved his hand and cut off my words. "I'll call you later."

I nodded and watched him leave. Once he was out the door I turned on Colin. "How could you? I know you don't like him. But Paige loves him and he's been a part of her life since she was born. That was just plain spiteful on your part."

Naomi eased closer to Colin. "You don't have any right to talk to him that way." Big talk for a woman who hid behind her beau.

"You better stay out of this. Telling them you're her mother—you're lucky I don't—"

"Mom?"

Paige only called us Mom or Dad when she was scared or hurt, it was usually Celeste this or Colin that. "Right here." I pushed into the cubicle.

"I broke my glasses." She held up the two separate pieces.

"It's okay. We have an old pair at home and we can get you an appointment first thing Monday to get a new pair. Okay?"

Her chin quivered slightly but she didn't cry. Then she sucked in a deep breath. "When can I go home?"

"I don't know. I'll go check." I glared at Colin as I passed him on the way over to the doctor. And if I growled a little, making Naomi scurry away like the rodent she is, I had every right to. I was angry at the crap she and Colin had pulled.

The morning stretched into late afternoon by the time we made it back home with a prescription of rest and ice for the remainder of the weekend. I fixed Paige a huge bowl of strawberry ice cream—her favorite—set her mega-favorite movie in the DVD player and got her cozy on the living room sofa.

Then the phone started ringing. Nonstop for about an hour. All Eagans. Colin, his mother, two cousins and an aunt called to check on Paige. Feeling a little guilty, I called my parents in Kansas. Well, my mom. Dad was not home, she'd said. I let her know that, yes, Paige was just fine now but she'd been in an accident. Though my mother didn't come right out and blame me, she implied it was all my fault for letting my child—my girl child—participate in a barbaric sport.

Please, the child in question had been doing it for four years and other than a bruise here and there had never once been hurt. But you couldn't correct my mother. Oh, no. If you tried, you'd think the world had come to an end. She was that dramatic. I honestly think that is where I got the acting bug from. I'd learned from the master. It was also why she lived in Kansas and I and my precious child in Texas. Absence made the heart not want to scream and pound your head against the wall.

Once all the other phone calls were out of the way, I snuggled up with Paige.

She settled her head on my shoulder. "I can't understand why the doctor thought Uncle Levi hurt me."

"I don't know either."

"It was stupid Naomi's fault." She sighed. "She's an uppity snob."

"That sounds like your uncle Levi talking."

"Still, I have to agree with him." She tilted her face up toward me. "How bad is it?"

"Marcia Brady bad."

"Huh?"

"Never mind. It's pretty swollen and your eyes are all bruised up."

"That's just great. Caleb and I have lab next week."

"Sweet pea, I know you like him. But he's too old for you."

"Now." Paige was only eleven but already in the seventh grade. Not a problem until you threw in thirteen-year-old boys who were surrounded by thirteen-year-old girls and Paige. She'd had a crush on the boy for the better part of a year now. "My father is two years older than you are."

"And you can see how well that turned out." I wanted to bite my tongue the minute the words left my mouth. If nothing else good came from the marriage, Paige was enough to make it all worthwhile. "Give it time. There's no rush now."

"I know. It's frustrating though. He already thinks I'm an egghead. Now I'm a busted-up egghead."

I kissed her forehead. "You're a special busted-up egghead."

She snorted then moaned and settled the ice pack back on her nose. "I'm still mad they thought Uncle Levi did this."

"They just don't know your uncle Levi like we do. He couldn't hurt a fly. Why don't you…?" The phone rang again. I tried to think who I'd missed in the phone-tree of calls as I scooped up the receiver.

"Celeste. How's Paige doing?"

"Hey, Levi, we were just talking about you. She's good. Bummed about this boy—" I waved away my words. "Never mind. I'm—"

"Good. Listen, I need you to do me a favor. I'm at my property on Lancaster. Do you think you can run over here real quick?"

"Paige still isn't feeling great."

"Call your ex. I need you."

The level of edge in his voice had me getting up from the sofa. "Give me ten minutes."

TWO

"I'M HERE." I walked into the living area. Sawhorses and crates—one full of tile squares, the other with several ceiling fans—were set about almost like furniture. Where a sofa might be was a stack of lumber. A stainless steel sink sat off next to the fireplace.

"In the back. But don't come all the way in."

"Why?" I wove through the building equipment. As I was about to round the corner to the back room, my foot caught on something. I almost yelped like a little girl. I thought it was a small animal. "Omigod, omigod," I squealed like a big girl when I realized it was a Bassani handbag. The designer du jour at the moment. Very trendy. Very in. And my very best friend in the whole wide world called me over to surprise me with a brand-new handbag for my birthday. "You shouldn't have left this just lying on the floor."

"Not my intention, I promise you."

I tucked the leather bag onto my shoulder. "Levi, you shouldn't have." I rounded the corner and found him standing slump-shouldered over a red heap on the floor. His blond eyebrows were pulled down into a tight V.

"What are you—"

"Freeze."

I jumped at the sharp command behind me. And I recognized the deep timbre immediately. "Muldoon?" I frowned. "If this is some kind of weird surprise party, it really sucks."

"Back up, Celeste." Muldoon gave me one of his patented glares. "Levi Weiss, you are under arrest."

"Arrest?" I scoffed. "What the hell kinda joke is this?"

"Murder is no joke." Muldoon skirted a large crate, accompanied by two uniformed officers. "Celeste, you need to move back."

"From what?" I looked at Muldoon as if he'd gone crazy—because that was pretty much all I could figure, that he'd gone stark raving mad. Then I looked to Levi to see if he was going to let me in on the joke. He was shaking and gripping something in his hand. A hammer. The one I'd gotten him on his last birthday. I could see half the engraving above the handle. The other half was obscured by something red. A red droplet rolled down the neck of the hammer onto Levi's balled hand, then fell off onto the heap at Levi's feet.

The heap. My eyes widened. It was not a what, but a who. "Dead body?" I gasped. I tried to back away but one of the uniformed officers was right behind me, blocking my exit.

"Hold it." He snagged my arm.

"You don't understand." I tried to force my eyes away, but I couldn't stop staring at the heap—body. There were red stains blooming from several places and slashed across his face. "I'm going to…" The world went black.

"WAKE UP." A sharp stench burned my nostrils.

"Sweets." I heard Levi. He sounded far away.

It was kind of hard to tell. My ears were ringing. "Ugh." I swatted at the ammonia scent engulfing me.

"Is she faking?"

Faking? Faking what? Why was I lying down? I peeled open an eye. A uniformed officer stood over me, ready to shove a little white packet under my nose again.

"No," I heard Muldoon answer.

"Celeste, you need to get up." The urgency in Levi's voice spurred me to come out of my little stupor. I had a little—okay, more than a little—issue with the sight of blood. Okay, so a big issue. I faint. Have since I was a little girl. My father swears there's a story behind it but damned if anyone has ever shared it with me. It was something I had controlled quite manageably until last fall. It had been months since it'd made me faint though. Still I avoided it at all costs.

"He's covered up now, Celeste." Muldoon squatted in front of me. "You okay?" There was a little bit of concern as well as annoyance tinting his voice.

"Yeah." It croaked out as I sat up fully. I scanned the area for my friend. "Levi?"

"We're taking him in." Muldoon stood and held out a hand to me. I let him pull me to my feet despite the dour expression on his face. When I wanted to hang on to him a little longer to steady myself, pride slammed my hands down to my sides. One of the uniformed officers pulled out a pair of cuffs, and Muldoon stepped between us.

"She wasn't here earlier. She arrived just before you did," he told the officer. "We need to interview her, but don't cuff her."

I stood with my mouth hanging open. I finally remembered walking into the house, then Muldoon barging in yelling at Levi to freeze. "Cuffs" and "arrest" were just not computing despite the now-covered-up heap.

"Who…" My gaze shot to Levi just as Muldoon turned him toward the wall to frisk him. Levi thrust his hands onto the wall in front of him. I tried to step closer to Levi, was all prepared to get between him and Muldoon, but the officer stopped me. "Stay."

"Stay? I'm not a dog." I was all indignant and rigid, but I did, in fact, stay. "How'd you know to come here?"

None of the sworn officers bothered to answer, but Levi said, "I called him."

I blinked several times. "You did?" I frowned. "Because…"

"Duh, I found a dead body."

"Shh." Muldoon looked back over his shoulder to glare at me.

"He called it in. Why are you arresting him?"

Muldoon patted down Levi's legs one at a time before he answered. "Dead body, probable murder weapon."

I rubbed at the aches that came with hitting the floor in a dead faint. "Come on."

"We gotta take him in to sort this out. You know how it works."

"You don't have to arrest him. Or cuff him," I said as he slapped the manacles onto Levi's wrists, "to sort this out. You can simply interview him."

"I know how to do my job." Muldoon walked Levi back through the house to the front. "Don't let her see the body again. We don't want another…incident."

I'd swear that Muldoon was holding back a grin. Me fainting at the sight of blood was not funny, though I really had no idea what I looked like when I crumpled to the floor. Maybe it was hilarious. Thank God no one had ever videoed me going down.

"Celeste, you're a material witness." Muldoon paused at the door. "You need to stay put until you're told otherwise."

"Fine. Whatever." Still, I hustled and tried to keep pace, which was not an easy task as I was also avoiding the officer trying to corral me. "Levi, don't worry. We'll get this sorted out. I'll meet you at the station." The officer snagged my elbow and escorted me toward a squad car. "And it looks like it's not going to be my choice."

"HE CALLED ME to come over," I said for the tenth time.

Detective Bush, who I'd met the previous year, held my gaze for a long moment, then jotted something down in the notebook in front of him.

"Why?"

"Moral support? It's not easy walking in and finding a dead body." I knew firsthand.

Bush was less than sympathetic. I didn't think he liked me much. I couldn't imagine why. I was likable. But the man sneered whenever he came within sneering distance. Hell, he'd all but accused me of blowing up my own car last year. Which I did not. Thankyouverymuch.

"You've been involved in several crimes over the past six months."

"Crimes that were not my fault." I fought off the urge to fidget. I didn't really know interrogation etiquette, even though I'd been through this several times before. I was so worried it would go in my permanent record that I couldn't sit still. Maybe it signified some kind of tell of guilt or something—not that I had anything to be guilty of. I would hate for that to get notated. I could only imagine what was in there already in the few short months I'd accumulated a record.

They'd kept me waiting for over an hour before they'd even started questioning me. Not once had Muldoon come back to check on me. I guess I should thank him for not getting handcuffed as the two officers at the scene clearly wanted to do. They both kept giving me a strange side-eye look on the ride from Levi's house to the station. I'm sure it wasn't every day that a detective told them not to cuff a potential suspect.

Gaw.

That chapped. Me a potential suspect. I was no more capable of killing someone than Levi was. And Muldoon knew that. He knew Levi, too. How could he ever think Levi could or would commit murder? It was so ludicrous it was hard not to laugh and call him out.

"Trouble seems to find you anyway."

"Is there a question here?" I was torn between anger and fear. Because he was right. But it wasn't like I was looking for it, I couldn't exactly stop something I had no control over. I hadn't had anything to do with this crime other than being there for my friend.

"Tell me what really happened."

I stared at him. Confused.

"Mr. Weiss was cutting out the competition?"

My mouth fell open. I was speechless—which almost never happened.

"Let me try. He calls you over to help him get rid of the body but before you can, the police show up." Detective Bush examined his fingernails, scooped up his pen, clicked it open then closed, and waited. But only for a moment. "Did they fight? If they fought, he might have a claim for self-defense. You could help your friend out here by talking to me. If not…" He tilted his head to the side. "You could be charged as an accessory."

"Are you insane?" I slammed my hands down on the arms of the chair. I'd had enough. "Where is Detective Muldoon?"

"Doing his job."

Well, duh. I knew that. I didn't think he was out catching a ball game. Nor did I expect him to interview me himself. He would never jeopardize a case. I wasn't even wanting preferential treatment. I just didn't want Levi to get railroaded into this. I knew he didn't do it, but the PPD wouldn't take my word on that.

"Would you help Levi?"

Hell, yes, I'd help him. If he did anything, I wouldn't even think twice about it. At first. I might get that hinky feeling once I'd done something wrong, but for my friend, I do anything.

"You seem like the type who would," he said as if reading my thoughts. "It's loyal. But it can lead you into some trouble that maybe you didn't ask for. Are you willing to go to jail, leave your daughter, for a man who killed someone?"

I narrowed my eyes and was opening my mouth to invoke the end-the-interview word *lawyer* when Bush's cell went off.

When Bush looked up from his phone, he said, "You're free to go. For now."

"But don't leave town, right?"

I TWEAKED MY messy ponytail as I walked out of the Peytonville Police station interview room. I spied my quarry at the end of the long counter that kept the public away from the public servants. He had his nose buried in a folder and was making notes as he flipped page after page.

"Muldoon." I rapped my knuckles on the countertop between us. "I'm here for Levi Weiss." I was tired, irritable and hungry and so ready to get home. I'd half expected Levi to be waiting on the bench by the door. "Hey." I snapped my fingers when he didn't immediately look up. "I'm ready to go."

"Then you're free to leave." The raven-haired detective shuffled a few papers on the countertop. There were dark circles under his ice-blue eyes and a day's worth of scruff covered his chin. His white shirt looked like he might have slept in it.

I wanted to ask but my friend's situation was more pressing. "I need Levi. This has been a hell of a day." I was ready for this cosmic joke to be over. Get to the gotcha already. "It's not every day my BFF gets jailed." I was trying not to be flippant but I was afraid it was coming off that way as well as bitchy and snippy.

"With you two, there's no telling what the next adventure is." Sounded like someone else was being bitchy and snippy, too. He walked around the end of the counter to stand next to me, still engrossed in the folder in his hand. His usual calm demeanor was nowhere to be seen. His shoulders were stiff and his breathing was heavy.

The refrain "this is not good" shot through my head, and nerves skittered through me.

"Celeste." Muldoon's tone was sharp. His frown deepened. "Levi's in real trouble here."

"You don't honestly think he killed that person?" I tried to get him to look at me, but he kept his gaze glued to the papers in front of him. "Or that I'm an accessory. To murder. Detective Bush asked me to confess my part. To help."

That got his attention. To a degree. A muscle ticked in his jaw. He was grinding his teeth—which he did when he was frustrated. I should know. I'd caused him to be frustrated several times in the past six months.

"Who was it that Levi supposedly killed? I couldn't tell."

Muldoon ignored my question. As I expected. He had to be the most dedicated police officer in all of Peytonville. Probably all of Texas.

"Fine. Whatever. I'll find out as soon as the news hits." It wasn't that I could be so blasé about death. Quite the contrary. Finding my boss dead in his office back in November had keyed me in to how very real death was. The killer coming after me had given me a front-row seat of the entire process. But it was easier to be matter-of-fact about it than to let it freak me out or worry. Yet.

"What's the bail? I'll just pay it and get him out." The times I'd been arrested—unjustly of course—I'd been let go free and clear. Bail had never been an issue, much less set. I didn't know the current rate, not that I thought Levi was guilty at all. No matter what, I couldn't let him sit in lockup while everything was sorted out. I reached into my purse for my wallet. Did Discover pay you back when you used your card for bail?

"Bail hasn't been set."

"What? Why not?" I blinked rapidly.

Muldoon leaned back over the edge of the counter and grabbed a pen. "It's Saturday. Right now he has a no bail hold. Then there's going to be a hearing to set bail." He wrote something out and handed it to me.

He'd scribbled the address to a bail bondsman with a crude map at the bottom. Did that mean it would be more than my Discover could handle? "Puh-leeze. Levi didn't do anything. He couldn't hurt anyone. You know him." I dropped my wallet back into my bag.

"The courts take murder pretty seriously."

"Who is he accused of killing?" My curiosity was

off the chart. Was that bad? "Can you please tell me that much?"

He leaned against the counter. He gave me his cop stare, which lost its scary effect about the third time he'd ever given it to me. I knew it meant he wasn't going to say another word, though.

I sighed and dialed a number in my cell. When Colin's cousin—Peter Cosgrove, or as we liked to call him, Coz—and a damn fine attorney answered, I said, "Hey, Coz. Can you meet me at the Peytonville police station?"

"Celeste? What is it now?"

"Not me, I swear." Well, not exactly, I didn't add. My gaze darted to Muldoon's. For the first time, a smile curved his lips. He'd been the bane of my incarceration issues. Now he'd apparently moved on to locking up my friends. "Levi needs your help."

"Be there in ten. Fifteen tops." Coz hung up.

Muldoon sighed. "Calling your lawyer isn't going to change anything."

I stared at him for a long moment. "Levi said he called you, right?"

Muldoon shifted. A slight grimace tugged at his lips. "He did."

"And…you think someone who just committed murder is going to call the police and say, 'Hey, come get me'?"

"I don't know how criminals think."

"Levi is not a criminal." I had tried many times in the past to give Muldoon my best intimidation-stare. Don't get me wrong, I was scary to recalcitrant actors who tried to pull a diva act, but to the man used to dealing with hardened criminals, I was afraid it fell flat. Still I gave it my best. Shoulders squared, left eyebrow arched in ire with narrowed eyes. I thrust my hands on my hips for good measure, but he did nothing more than sigh.

I could stand there all evening—well, not the entire night. Colin was still with Paige—luckily he'd left Naomi at home, or I might have had to kick some serious skanky-ass and then I could talk to Levi through an adjoining cell. I wanted to help my friend out, but I did need to get back to my daughter. "C'mon, who did he allegedly kill? What else do you have on him?"

"More than him standing over the body holding a bloody hammer?" He shook his head. "You know I can't give you that information this early in the investigation."

It wasn't ten, more like an hour and a half when Coz came through the door. He wrapped a long, lanky arm around my shoulder in a quick hug, then morphed into lawyer mode. "Sorry, got stuck on an upcoming case. What's up?"

"Levi is being charged with murder." I held on to the edge of his sleeve. "Not that he killed anyone. Not Levi. And I can't bail him out. They're holding him under, what did you call it?"

"No bail hold." Muldoon went on to describe the phone call—from Levi—that led them to his jobsite. "She should know, she got there before we did."

I opened my mouth to point out to Muldoon that he, himself, knew exactly when I'd gotten here. He'd apparently been waiting for his backup to arrive and saw me go into the house.

But before I could utter even a single syllable, Coz abruptly shook his head. "No." He shifted to put himself a little between Muldoon and me. "They have every right to hold him for up to seventy-two hours while they look through evidence to tie him to the crime."

I tensed up. "So I can't get him out until Tuesday?"

"Thursday," Muldoon said and stepped back. "Time starts on Monday morning."

"Gaw, this is insane. First the damn hospital security guards try to manhandle him, now this."

"What?" Coz and Muldoon asked simultaneously. Coz continued, "When Paige was in the ER?"

Muldoon frowned and said, "What happened to Paige?"

The two men talked over each other. I held up my hands to quiet them. "It's okay. She's fine," I said to Muldoon. "She got hurt at her karate meet this morning. Got a bloody, but thankfully not broken, nose. Levi took her to the ER and when Colin got there, Security tried to make Levi leave—by unnecessary force—thinking he hurt her because Colin didn't correct their assumptions."

"When was this? Which hospital?" Muldoon pulled his ever-present notebook from his pocket.

"Just before noon. At Cook Children's Hospital downtown. I tried to call you," I said to Muldoon. "But I just got your voice mail."

He paused for a moment. Was that guilt that skittered across his face? Or was I projecting all sorts of anxiety? I shook off my *Dr. Phil* moment. Wrong place, wrong time. "Why?" I arched an eyebrow upward.

He mumbled something.

"Beg pardon?"

"Nothing. Don't worry about it." He finished writing and put the notebook up. "And don't read anything into my questions. Until the coroner establishes a time of death for the vic, it doesn't mean anything."

I nudged Coz as he tapped away on his cell, taking notes. "Can we see him?" I asked.

Muldoon played the hard-ass much better than I did.

"C'mon, Detective." He hated it when I called him Detective. "It's not like I'm going to slip him a file or something. I'll even leave my purse." I set my new designer bag on the counter—it was mostly empty, just my wallet and keys—which they'd given back to me when Detective Bush was done with his ridiculous interrogation.

"I'd like a moment to speak with my client." Coz tucked his cell in his bag. "And I need Ms. Eagan with me to clarify a few points."

"Fine. This way." Muldoon led us back to the holding cells.

Levi jumped up from the small bench when he saw us. He white-knuckled the bars. "Thank God you're here."

"Is there someplace we can sit and talk with him in private?"

Coz actually knew the answer to that, but as Muldoon was not too quick on cooperating it was the impetus he needed to show us to the interview room at the end of the hall. I wasn't sure why he was being such a jerk. But I wasn't going to ask. At least not while Levi was still locked up.

"How are you holding up?" I patted his hand.

"I apologize for any and every time I mocked you when you were locked up last year." He visibly shuddered and rubbed his hand over his face. "Just ghastly."

Coz settled his briefcase onto the table and pulled out a notepad. "What happened? Go through your day up until the police arrived."

"She told you about Paige, right? Of course she did." He waved away his own comment. "Did she tell you about the security guards?" Levi gave Coz a quick rundown of everything from when he picked Paige up at the house, up to when he brought her to the ER and until he left.

"I'm sure they'll remember," I jumped in. "And Colin and what's-her-face witnessed it all, too. Hell, it was their fault for not setting the doctor straight on how Paige got hurt." I dug into my wallet—Muldoon hadn't made me surrender it again. "Here's the receipt for her co-pay. It has a time stamp to get you a ballpark." I handed him the small slip of paper.

"After I left the hospital I was in a little bit of a snit." Levi rolled his eyes and took a long breath. "I wanted to work off the full head of steam I'd built up so I went to one of my properties. We're tearing out a wall between the kitchen and the dining room."

Coz frowned for a second.

"Levi flips houses," I said. "I told you about it last year when your sister was looking for a new house."

"Right. Sorry, go on. What happened when you got there?"

"I worked there for an hour, hour and a half, then headed over to my other property. On Lancaster."

"That's where they picked him up."

Levi made a face at me.

"There's no electricity at that house, so I walked through, pulling up some of the blinds. When I got to the dining room, the window was open. Which it shouldn't have been. I'd locked up everything when I left a few days ago." He shifted in his chair and turned to face Coz more squarely. "I went to see if the window glass was broken out. Kids will throw rocks and whatnot to bust the windows on unoccupied houses." He rubbed at his wrists as if the handcuffs were still there. "I didn't see him at first. We'd set up a couple of workstations in there for a teardown on Monday. He was between the workstation and the window. Bleeding all over the floor. I checked for a pulse but got nothing. He was cold." Levi shuddered again.

I leaned closer to him. "Who was he?"

"Arnie. Arnie Showalter."

I sucked in a breath.

"What?" Coz's gaze snapped to mine.

"Arnie is one of Levi's biggest competitors." I rubbed at the pain throbbing at my temple. "They go to public auctions and buy houses. Fix them up and sell them. Arnie has accused Levi of bribing the auctioneers."

"To do what?" Coz frowned. "It's a public auction."

"Exactly." I raised my hands in a who-knows gesture. "He's a nuisance, but doesn't, um, didn't have anything to back up any of his accusations."

"Okay." Coz tapped his pen on the pad. "You found the body how?"

"Like I said, he was lying at the base of the window. I immediately pulled out my phone and called Celeste."

"Wait, what? You called her first?" Coz pointed his pen at me as he tsked. "Why would you do that?"

"Habit? Comfort? I don't know, I wasn't really thinking straight. I called 911 immediately after. I debated doing CPR on him but you could tell that he was gone." He rubbed his mouth. "I set my hand on the sill to stand back up and knocked something off. It was a hammer. My hammer." He looked at me. "The titanium one you gave me for Christmas."

"Yeah, I saw that. Don't worry. I'll get you a new one."

Coz scribbled something on his pad. "How do you know it was your hammer?"

"It was engraved with his name," I answered for him.

His blond eyebrow arched. "A hammer?"

I narrowed my eyes at Coz. "So says the man with an engraved Sirius Black wand."

"Uh, yeah. Okay." He blushed slightly.

"The hammer was covered in blood. And damned if Celeste and Muldoon didn't show up the minute I grabbed hold of that sucker. Did y'all ride together?"

"No." I snorted. "Didn't you hear him getting all, 'Don't cuff her but detain her, she just got here, too'?"

Levi shook his head. "I was a little too preoccupied freaking out to notice much of anything else."

"Was the window broken?" Coz jumped back into the conversation.

"No. It looked like someone opened it as they were leaving."

"How could you tell?"

"Bloody handprints on the outside edge of the sill. Like they gripped it and jumped out. It's not a huge drop from the window. About four feet."

"Who has keys?"

Levi hung his head. "Just me."

"That you know of," I added. Maybe I watched too much TV—I mean, I really did love my DVR—but how many times had a bad guy copied keys without the owner ever missing them?

Coz closed up his notebook. "Until the coroner comes up with a time of death, there's not a lot I can do to persuade them to let you out sooner than they have to."

Levi looked so grim and dejected. I could only imagine the tension rolling through him. Despite my brush with holding cells across the metroplex, the arresting officers had never intended to keep me there long. Once was to prove a point, the other time was to verify my identity.

I reached across the table and grasped his hands in mine. "Levi, can you think of who would want to hurt Arnie?"

"Oh, no. No, you don't." Coz stood and grabbed my elbow. He pulled until I released Levi's hands and was on my feet, as well. "We are not going to have a repeat of last fall."

"Did I say I was going to do anything? This is information you can use in your defense."

"If the timeline pans out then that won't even be necessary."

I tried to shrug off his hold, but he was damn strong for a skinny fellow. "But until then…"

Coz looked down his long pointy nose at me. "Celeste, we talked about this, remember? You swore after last year you weren't going to go butting your nose into anyone else's business."

A phantom shoulder ache from the fall blossomed, as if I needed a reminder.

"I appreciate the thought, but he's right. You don't need to do anything." Levi's mouth said the words, but his eyes pleaded with me to snoop away.

At least that's what I told myself. "Fine." I raised my hands in surrender. "Are you going to be okay?"

Levi barked a quick sarcastic laugh. "I have a choice?"

I managed to give him a quick hug before they took him back to his cell.

Before we left the room, I pulled Coz to the side. "Um, one more thing."

He groaned and shifted his briefcase. "I'm thinking your retainer just doubled."

"Really? Fine. I'll send you a check." I smiled for a sec then it slid away just as quickly. "I was interviewed, too. The detective was strongly suggesting I get Levi to say it was self-defense. To spare me from getting charged as an accessory."

Coz lowered his eyelids and rubbed the bridge of his nose. "They didn't charge you though, right?"

I held out my arms. "I'm on this side of the cages."

"Okay. Don't worry. They're just trying to scare you into incriminating Levi."

"He didn't—"

"I didn't say he did. I'm telling you their tactics. We'll deal with that if/when it happens." He wrapped an arm around my shoulder. "You good for now?"

"Yeah. Thanks. You're the best."

Coz chuckled. "You only say that when I'm bailing your butt out of trouble."

"Then it gets said a lot." I nudged him in the ribs and he released me and checked his phone. "We'll talk soon." He waved his cell and left to go meet with the district attorney, who was a friend of his from college—small world, right?

Muldoon was waiting for me up front. We stood in awkward silence by the door. It was our first conflict. Well, at least since he'd locked me up last year. If you didn't consider three broken dates conflict. Or him pulling away a little bit at a time. Or me being so busy with the playhouse that I often forgot to call… Maybe we had more conflict than I'd ever really thought about. I should have just left, walked right out the front door, but some perverse quirk kept me rooted in place. Standing. Waiting.

"Paige is okay?" he asked finally. The haggard expression on his face softened.

"Yeah. Massive nose bleed and a little Marcia Brady."

"Bummer." He knew the reference. Then he frowned. "How did you, um, hold up?" He reached over and rubbed my arm for a brief moment before he tucked his hands in his pockets. He was fishing for information whether or not I fainted then, too. I'd never done it twice in one day.

"Ha, yeah, no. Levi was with her and he got her to the hospital—hence his alibi." I looked at him expectantly but he didn't give away anything. I sighed. "By the time I'd gotten there she was swollen and iced. No blood. We'll have to get her some new glasses. They got busted." I shifted from foot to foot. Looked up, down, anywhere but at those piercing blue eyes, then finally swallowed. "I should probably go." I motioned to the door. "Colin's at the house with Paige."

Muldoon didn't have much of a response. He was distant. Not so much physically, but definitely emotionally. I think the conflict just grew a little more.

"Hey, Celeste."

"Yes?" So my heart pitter-pattered a little bit faster.

"Do me a favor." He had one of his rare smiles plastered on his face. "Please don't go poking your nose into your friend's case. I've pretty much used up my favors in the surrounding precincts."

"I'LL SHOW YOU POKING, Detective Smarty Pants."

After I got home from the police station, I sent Colin home and pulled out my laptop. I had Google pages burning up the internet looking for information on Arnie Showalter.

Unfortunately, there wasn't a show-me-only-the-dirt link. I waded through his social networking pages as well as all the websites that advertised his business. Nothing screamed out as a reason to murder the man, then frame Levi. As a matter of fact, for all intents and purposes it looked as if the man was alive and kicking. Nothing of his death had been reported yet.

I could have called Kellen and asked what he'd heard, but if the police hadn't even released a death notice, I didn't want it leaked through me. By ten that night my eyes were crossing and the words started swimming so I decided to call it an evening. I didn't stop poking because Muldoon told me not to, nope.

Sunday morning to cheer Paige up I offered to take her to Dunkin' Donuts, but she didn't want to be seen in public with her shiners and swollen nose. She was moodier than usual but under the circumstances, she was excused. I still wanted to pamper my baby so I ran out and bought a dozen of her favorite donuts. We had a late morning pig-out fest.

Afterward we watched several of her favorite movies. The entire time I worried about poor Levi sitting alone in a cell. Twice I called up to the station but Muldoon wasn't in—which was hard to believe as I was convinced he kept a cot in the back and slept there when he wasn't working.

I called a few of the guys who work with Levi. One of the handymen who was helping with the teardown didn't recall anyone snooping around—that would be too much to hope for, I guess—but another man, Guy Bueller, had come by looking for Levi.

I sat at the kitchen table and looked over a few notes. "Guy? Guy Bueller? Where do I know that name from?"

I tapped a spoon to my lips, then stirred raspberry chocolate creamer into my coffee. "Hmm."

"Christmas party." Paige came up behind me and set her head on my shoulder.

"What's that, sweet pea?"

"Mr. Bueller. He was at Uncle Levi's Christmas party."

"How do you remember?"

"I thought it was funny. A name like Ferris Bueller. Except he acted more like Ferris's friend Cameron."

"In what way?"

"He was all uptight and—" she tilted her head back for a moment "—pent up. That's what Uncle Levi called him. Said he had a stick firmly implanted in his—"

"Yeah, I get it." I patted her copper mane. I remembered the man, sort of. He was trying to start out in the business and kept asking Levi question after question about vendors and shipments. It'd driven Levi nuts. Later, I'd seen him cozied up to several other men at the party.

I couldn't remember if Levi ever mentioned if he'd gotten his business up and running.

"How are you feeling? Can I get you anything?"

"May I have a snack?"

"Sure. Why don't you go lie back down and I'll bring it to you?"

She went back into the living room. I cut up some fruit and set it on the tray. I added a glass of milk and one of the iced donuts from breakfast.

"Is Uncle Levi going to be okay?" Paige sat up and let me set the tray onto her lap.

"He's going to be fine." If I had anything to do with it. I patted her head and went back into the kitchen. It took me a couple of clicks through links to find a number for Guy Bueller. The man answered on the third ring. I quickly introduced myself.

"I remember you," Guy Bueller said. "You're Levi's girlfriend."

I frowned at the phone. "Just friend."

"Is it true? What I heard on the news?" he asked. "Levi killed Arnie."

Seriously? It was already making the rounds that Levi was a murderer. This could kill his business. I slapped my palm to my forehead. Kill, gaw. I needed to watch what I said when Levi was released. People needed to know the truth, too. "He was arrested. But he didn't kill anyone."

"Yeah, no." He cleared his throat. "That's what I meant. What can I help you with?"

"I spoke with Levi Weiss's foreman and he mentioned you'd been by looking for him the other day. I was wondering if you'd by chance seen anyone hanging around his properties."

"Anyone like…?"

"I don't know, someone who shouldn't be there."

"I'm sorry, but I don't know Levi's workers very well. I wouldn't know a worker from a stranger."

"Sure." Duh, the man was a potential competitor of Levi's. Much like Arnie. "Oh, okay. I guess I should—"

"Why are you asking so many questions? Shouldn't the police be doing that?"

"Well, yeah. But Levi's my friend and I want to make sure every possible scenario is explored."

Guy chuckled. "You sound so official."

"Just trying to help."

"Who have you called? I may be able to point you in the right direction."

"You'd do that?"

"Sure. No one's working today, but tomorrow we can check in with some of the vendors and suppliers Levi uses."

"I'd appreciate that. Thanks."

"Are you free tomorrow? We could meet for lunch?" He named a restaurant in downtown Peytonville.

I had a couple of errands I was going to run, but could push them back. "I could do that."

"Good. Make a list and I'll make one. We can compare notes to see who to talk to first."

"Super. See you then."

MONDAY MORNING I already regretted making plans with Guy Bueller. By lunchtime I was considering calling and cancelling outright. I was dragging someone else into something I was supposed to be butted out of anyway. Not that I really knew what I was looking for. But he was willing to help, which was unusual for me, so I stuck to the plan and went to the restaurant. I picked a table on the patio so I could make a hasty exit in case the meeting was horribly awkward. Considering he was already fifteen minutes late, I might not have to worry about it anyway.

Tired of waiting for Guy to show up, I forked a piece of lettuce off my plate. I could just leave, I considered as I chewed. No harm no foul. I could barely remember what the man looked like, so there was a good chance he'd never even know who I was if I got up and walked past him to leave.

I racked my brain. What did Bueller look like? I'd only met the man once. At the Christmas party. It had been filled with people Levi worked with. Most were what you'd expect house flippers to look like. Men who worked with their hands and weren't…fussy. There'd been one man there who stood out. He looked like he belonged at a country club, in tennis whites, rather than someone who performed manual labor. And he was walking toward me now. His light brown hair was slicked back and the man was wearing an—I swear to all things java—ascot under his navy blazer and crisp white shirt.

I waved at the man. "Mr. Bueller?"

He smiled and held out his hand. "Guy."

"Thank you for agreeing to help me." I shook his hand and motioned to the seat across the table from me.

"It's the least I can do." He dusted off the chair with a handkerchief he produced from his coat pocket.

Sweat popped out on his temples despite the shade covering the table.

"If it's too hot out here, we can take a table inside."

He dabbed at the sweat. "No, no, I'm fine." He offered a weak smile. "So, you're looking into matters to help Levi out?"

"*Looking into* makes it sound so formal." I toyed with the straw in my water glass. "I'm just making sure we know all the facts."

"And you don't think the police can do their jobs?"

How many times had Muldoon asked me the same question? I believed he was one hundred percent capable of doing his job. Once again doubt filled me. I should be at the playhouse looking through headshots rather than asking another potential competitor of Levi's to help me sort through the world of home flipping.

"You know, from what I hear, Arnie Showalter was pretty unscrupulous when it came to his employees."

I arched my eyebrows upward. "I've heard that."

"Now, I know you said Levi didn't—"

"There's no way." I held his gaze.

"Okay." He held his hands up in front of him, defensively. "Do you have any theories?"

"No. I was hoping you might." I took a quick sip of water, then leaned my elbows onto the table. "I called some of the men I know who've worked for Levi. I was checking to see if anything hinky had been going on, but from what they've told me it was business as usual. The house where they found, um, the body was in the beginning of its renovation. It looked like it had just received its shipment of supplies."

"Was anything missing?"

Strange question. "I have no idea. I was only inside a few minutes and I have no idea what should have been there."

"Did Levi say if anything was stolen? Had Arnie—I mean Mr. Showalter—maybe been looting the place?"

Had Levi been talking to Bueller about the issues he was having on his sites? "Levi suspected him of it in the past, but considering he was dead, I doubt he ended up with anything."

Bueller nodded solemnly. "Makes sense." He reached into his coat pocket and pulled out his cell phone. "Sorry. I know this is rude. Excuse me just a moment." He stood and walked a few feet away from the table.

I glanced at my watch. My lunch break was nearly over and I hadn't found out a single shred of info from the man. I rubbed my temple. It was almost like he was probing me for info. I frowned. That made no sense.

"I'm so sorry," he said when he came back to the table. "I have an important meeting I need to attend to. I hate to eat and run…"

Eat and run? He never even ordered anything.

I pasted on a smile. "No problem." I lifted my new handbag into my lap to pay for the salad I'd barely touched.

Bueller's step stuttered as he started to turn to go. "Maybe we can try this again. I will ask through some of my contacts and see if anyone has heard of any bad blood working up with Arnie."

"I appreciate that, but you don't have to." I tossed enough money to cover the bill, tip and then some, not wanting to hang around any longer. "Thank you for your time. Bye."

I didn't like the vibe the man was giving off. And if Muldoon found out I was snooping again... Not that I would necessarily stop snooping, but I didn't want Guy Bueller privy to anything more than he needed to be privy to.

THREE

TUESDAY MORNING I was still just as far along—or not as far along, as the case was—in my investigation. I'd found zilch to help clear Levi. And ostensibly me. "We need to get moving, sweet pea." Paige was usually motivated to go to school, but with her swollen and bruised nose she'd been sluggish. I would have thought she'd be over it by now. The swelling had gone down and the bruising was fading.

Yeah, when I was her age, I'd have crawled up under the covers and refused to come out until it was completely gone.

Maybe she was picking up on my mood. I wasn't much more enthusiastic to get to the playhouse. I'd stayed up into the wee hours of the morning—again—trolling the internet. Curiosity was always a downfall of mine, so I've been told. And I gained nothing but gritty eyes and a crick in my neck for the third morning in a row. "Paige?"

"I'm coming." She walked down the hall without her extra little bounce. She even dragged her backpack behind her as we walked to the door.

We hadn't gotten a foot away from the coffee table when the doorbell rang. "A little early for morning callers."

"Is there such a thing as morning callers?"

I ruffled her hair and chuckled. "I don't know."

Paige stayed right beside me as I went to answer the bell. I opened the door and my mouth fell open.

"How are my two best girls?"

"Daddy, what are you doing here?" I said as Paige jumped into my dad's arms and yelled, "Grandpop!"

"My, my, those are quite some shiners. Gives you character." He twirled her around. When he finished his last rotation, he looked at me and said, "Can't a man come see his baby girl on her birthday?" He bent down and gave me a peck on the cheek.

No, I wanted to say, not when you live in Kansas. I leaned past him and looked at the front porch. "Where's Mom?"

My dad set Paige back down. "In Kansas. I left her."

"He showed up on your doorstep, just like that?" asked Annabelle Paulk, the playhouse owner and my boss, as we waded through some newly donated costumes.

I set down a heavily brocaded coat. "Yep." I'd filled Annabelle in on Paige's accident—I did, however, leave out all of Levi's woes. I didn't have the mental capacity to deal with it on top of my father's so-called split from my mother. "I called my mom on the way here. As far as she's concerned, Daddy needed to blow off some steam, and he'll be back in no time."

"Did he say what had made him pick up and go?"

"No. But between needing to get into work and Paige standing right there, I didn't have time to press the issue." I made a note on the coat's tag and hung it up on the rack behind us. "More than likely she drove him insane. It's the only thing that explains him showing up on my porch unannounced. I can't blame him. I escaped Doris Abercrombie as soon as I could."

Annabelle shook her head. "You're the only person our age whose parents are even still together anyway."

I shuddered. "So in other words, it's about time."

"I guess so." She set aside a pretty green dress she was examining. "Oh, I forgot. Lookie what I got." She crossed the room to her desk and pulled out one of the largest boxes of chocolates I'd ever seen. She held it up and shook it.

"Who's the big spender?"

"You remember that man I met last month at the grocery story?"

"The good-smelling one or the bad comb-over?"

"Bad comb-over. His name is Ronnie. He went to the barber and shaved it all off. He's a knockout."

"Who knew?" I laughed. She went through men like I went through coffee. She'd joined the Beau of the Month Club and as far as I could tell, she was making good on the title. She'd met Bad Comb-over, though, back in March. "Is it getting serious?"

"Maybe. He's taking me to dinner tonight." She named off a new hot spot in downtown Fort Worth.

"Ooh-la-la. I'm jealous."

She waggled the opened box. "Want one?"

I waved off her offer. "Thanks, maybe later."

"When you're ready." She set the box atop her desk and went to check on something on the stage.

The room deflated with her absence. I dropped my head to the pile of clothes and closed my eyes.

The quiet didn't last long when my cell rang.

"Hey," I said when Colin said hello.

"Is everything okay?" he asked. "Paige said your dad just showed up this morning."

To tell the truth or not? "It's been a while since he's

been down. He can't sit still since retirement." Not. There was no point in letting Colin say I told you so. He and my mother got along only slightly better than his mother and me. Mama Eagan and I could not stand to be living in the same city—we tolerated each other for the sake of Paige.

"Oh, well, tell him I said hello."

"You can stop by after school if you want. Say hello for yourself." The two had gotten along well enough when we were married.

"Maybe I will." He paused. "How's Levi holding up?"

"I haven't been able to speak to him again, but hopefully he's okay." I picked a string of lint from the hem of a pair of slacks. "With any luck the medical examiner will get through the autopsy today and will prove the time of death. You know, if you and Naomi hadn't been jerks and tried to throw him out of the hospital, he wouldn't have had as strong an alibi. He told me to tell you thanks."

I hung up before Colin could comment.

"DADDY, PAIGE, I'M HOME." It was a little past six, later than usual for me. When we didn't have a show in progress, we pretty much worked a regular nine-to-five workday, though as we zeroed in on our next production, the days got longer. I dropped a couple of scripts and costume books on the coffee table—the theater had just wrapped a show and Annabelle tasked me to figure out next year's lineup. "Guys?"

"In here."

"Levi?" I dashed into the kitchen. Levi, my dad and Paige were making cupcakes. "You're out early?"

"I told big bad Muldoon to release me or face the ire of my sweets. He was quaking in his boots."

"Whatever." He scooped me up in a bear hug. When he finally put me back down I asked, "So what really happened?"

He waved me over to the corner of the kitchen and away from Paige. "They went ahead and set bail this morning. Sympathetic judge."

"Why didn't you call me?" I frowned. "I would have been there to bail you out."

"The bail was a little high."

"How high?"

"One million."

"One…" My mouth fell open. "Holy…"

"I know, right."

I wasn't sure if it was pride or horror that rolled across his face at the steep amount. "Where'd you get the bail money?"

He hesitated. "A friend."

"You have a friend who can loan you a million dollars, just like that?"

"He only needed ten percent," my dad piped up from the counter.

"That's still a hundred grand." I waited for an explanation but Levi just stood there.

"Mom," Paige called, "come taste the chocolate cupcakes."

"She called me Mom." I glanced up at Levi. "We'll talk later," I warned him.

"Banner day for us all." He wrapped his arm around me. "Let's have a cupcake."

We all sat at the table with our chocolate confection and coffee for the adults and a huge glass of milk for Paige. "Your nose is looking better."

Paige rolled her eyes. "I look like Marcia Brady."

I cocked an eyebrow.

"Internet." She pointed to her tablet. "I found the episode on the computer."

I laughed and hugged her.

"I keep forgetting to ask." Dad added a heaping spoonful of sugar to his coffee. "Did you get my card?"

"For?"

"Your birthday."

I swear it almost sounded like there was an inaudible duh on the end of Dad's statement. I frowned. "You sent me a card?"

He took a sip. "Yes."

I closed my eyes for a long moment. The news wasn't sitting quite right. "Did it have a puppy dog on it?"

Dad smiled. "Yes. Didn't you recognize it? It was just like the one you gave me when you were just about Paige's age."

I hadn't recognized it. I'd been a little too preoccupied by the fact that it had been postmarked in Fort Worth. I stifled a slight gasp. That meant Dad had to have been in town for close to a week before he came to my front door this morning. Stranger still, I'd spoken to my mother a couple of days ago and she hadn't let on that Dad hadn't been there. Hadn't acted like a single thing was amiss.

"That's sweet, Daddy." Levi and I shared a glance. He had to have been thinking the same thing I was.

Levi leaned over. "Well, I was right about one thing."

"That the person cared enough. Why do I feel like I'm twelve and my parents are splitting up?"

He rubbed my arm. "It's just something different than what you're used to."

Dad dusted crumbs from his hands. "So when do I get to meet this detective I keep hearing about?"

It was a good thing I hadn't been drinking or the other side of the table would have been drenched in coffee. I was nowhere near the point of telling my parents about Muldoon. Truth be told, I'd be okay if I were to keep the two worlds from colliding until sometime south of say a first year anniversary, assuming we ever get that far. Was that bad? That I would prefer whoever I'm with not to meet my mom and her all kinds of crazy. God forbid the man wonder if it was genetic or inheritable. I ground my teeth to keep from saying any of that aloud. "Pardon?"

"Paige was telling me all day about the detective who you were helping out with his case last fall. And Levi was going on and on…"

The rest of what Dad said was drowned out by Levi's loud and obnoxious throat clearing. "Gil, why don't we go take a look at that…thing you brought." Levi stood and pushed away from the table.

"Oh, no, you don't. Sit." When Levi obliged me, I twined my fingers together and leaned forward. "I'm sorry, Daddy, but you have the wrong idea."

"Aren't you dating the man?"

"We had a couple of dates. But we've broken more than we've kept." Both of us. For one reason or another. I was pretty sure we both liked each other, but neither of us was willing to put the rest of our life on the back burner long enough to really make time for the other. "Before Saturday, I hadn't even spoken to him in over a month."

Dad frowned. "I just thought, with you helping with a case and all…"

"The case I helped with nearly got me killed."

My father blanched a little. I hadn't told him or my mother many of the details. And I'd well underplayed my injuries. Thankfully not all the news from Fort Worth was relevant up in Kansas.

I gave my friend a very pointed look. He didn't even bother to look abashed. Some days he was worse than my interfering mother with the matchmaking ideas. He'd have the wedding china picked out if it were up to him. Luckily, his own social life kept him plenty busy most of the time. "If you want some juicy tidbits, maybe we should ask Levi why Arnie Showalter was at his house?"

"Not fair." Levi tried to look affronted but it came across as more of a childish pout.

"Better you than me," I whispered.

He examined his fingernails, picked at invisible lint on his jacket and ran his finger around the edge of the table.

"Who's Arnie Showalter?" Dad asked.

"One of Levi's competitors. And the murder victim who landed Levi in jail."

Levi made a face at me. "I don't know for sure why he was there. I suspect he's been stealing equipment and supplies. Damn, that makes me look even guiltier."

I sat back in the chair. "Yeah, it kind of does."

He widened his eyes briefly. "That's why I didn't tell Muldoon."

I opened my mouth to tell him that was stupid, that Muldoon would find out, he always found out, but I didn't want to kick the man while he was down.

"I don't have proof. Things go missing all the time, but it seemed like he was always at one of my sites when stuff disappeared."

"Your men?"

"I trust them completely. Most of them have been with me for years. You know that."

"Sure, but you have to consider everyone and everything."

He sighed and rubbed a hand down his face. "Yeah."

"Can I go watch TV?" Paige stood and pushed her chair in.

"We didn't mean to bore you."

"You're not. But I found where they show *Brady Bunch* reruns on one of the cable channels."

Oh, boy, I'd created a monster.

When Paige left the room, Levi stood and got a glass of water. "I've heard Showalter will use illegals to get his work done. And he pays them squat. If they balk, he threatens to send ICE after them."

"That's awful." I wrapped my hands around the coffee mug. "Why hasn't he been caught?"

"It's hard to prove. From one job to the next, hell, one week to the next, he has a different crew. Seems pretty moot now."

"Too true." I picked at the cupcake in front of me. "So how was your stay at Club Muldoon?"

"See." Levi nudged my dad. "I knew it would get back around to the detective. It wasn't so horrible. The drunk tank was the next cell over and the people coming in and out of there were quite interesting. Did you know Councilwoman Williams likes to tie one on?"

I couldn't imagine the five-foot-zero owner of a chain of yogurt shops drinking, much less to the point to end up in the PPD drunk tank. "Did you try to sell her a house?"

"You know me too well." He smiled. "It was a no-go. She was pretty much passed out the entire time."

"Maybe she was faking it so she didn't have to talk

to you," Dad said. He kept a straight face, but I burst out in laughter.

Levi gave an exaggerated sigh. "Story of my life." He put the cupcake batter bowls into the sink—he was like having my very own wife. If we wouldn't kill each other inside of a week, he'd have moved in years ago. "Where are we at?"

"Sorry?" I ducked my head.

"Now, don't give me that. I know you well enough to know that you've probably been working on who might have killed Arnie."

"The police think you did."

"And you know it isn't me. Until they clear me you will stop at nothing to prove me innocent."

I smiled. "You think very highly of yourself."

Levi leaned over and kissed the top of my head. "And…"

"I spoke with Guy Bueller."

"Why?" Levi asked at the same time Dad asked, "Who's Guy Bueller?"

"Another sort of competitor of Levi's."

"You've got the most interesting life," Dad said under his breath as he poured himself another cup of coffee.

I turned my attention back to Levi's question, "What do you mean *why*?" I swiped up the crumbs into my hand and got up to drop them into the sink. "He knows some of the people you know. He's in the business."

"Barely. When he's not too busy in a tanning booth or trying to start up another new venture. He won't last in this business."

"Oh, well. Hmm. He and I met for lunch this afternoon."

Levi frowned. "Why would you do that?"

"He said he could help me get through to some of the people y'all know."

Levi tsked. "He should be so lucky to know who to talk to." He took a sip from his glass. "Did he give you anything useful?"

"If anything, it felt like he was fishing for info."

"From you." When I nodded he added, "About what?"

"Hell if I know."

"Huh? Weird." Levi cleaned off the rest of the table—he was such a good wife—and got it ready for dinner. Not that I'd even had one inkling about dinner. I'd been thrown off all day between Dad showing up and my strange visit with Bueller.

"I did look online myself." I racked my brain for anything interesting to point out. "I couldn't find anything." I scrunched up my nose.

"Why does that bother you, Celeste?" Dad set his cup in the sink.

"Those who did talk about him had nothing nice to say. I think people were too afraid of him."

"I'm doomed." Levi leaned his hip against the counter.

"No, you're not. We'll figure this out." I stood and pushed my chair in. "I can call Kellen and see if he can help us figure out what's what."

"Wait, wait, wait." Dad waved his hands. "First, who's Kellen? And second, why do you have to do anything? Levi has a lawyer. There's no reason for you to get involved in anything at all."

"Kellen is a new friend who works at the local paper." I ignored the second part of his question.

My father's eyebrow quirked up. "You have all sorts of new friends."

"Yep. Last year was an interesting one." I stood next

to my dad and wrapped my arm around his waist. "Even though I don't quite get what's going on with you and Mom, I'm really glad you're here."

The doorbell rang. By the time I got to the foyer, Paige was swinging the door open. "Sweet pea, you shouldn't... Colin, hi."

"I couldn't stop when I dropped Paige off after school."

Because Naomi was with him and she'd have a fit. "Dad, there's someone here to see you."

"Your mother better not have..." Dad pulled up short. "Colin. How are you?" He hurried over and greeted my ex.

The bell rang again not five minutes later. "Grand Central tonight." Paige at least listened to me and didn't rush to answer the door. I gripped the knob and hoped to high heaven that Naomi hadn't followed her man over to my house. She had no reason to want to see my dad; she'd only met him once, briefly, when my parents had come for a visit.

But it wasn't Naomi. "Muldoon?" I blinked and wondered that my eyes weren't maybe deceiving me. But, no, the detective stood on my front porch. "I wasn't expecting to see you."

He lifted a manila envelope. "You didn't sign your statement."

"That was days ago."

"It still needs to be signed."

"You could have called."

He nodded. "I could have, yes."

Muldoon looked just as haggard as the other day, but he looked a little more upbeat.

"You going for the lumberjack vibe?" I reached out

and scrubbed the day-old beard on his cheek. I dropped my hand and softened my voice. "You look tired. You need your beauty rest, Detective. It keeps you sharp and focused and wrinkle free."

A smile crept into his eyes. "I do what I can."

"And you have to eat right. Are you getting your veggies?"

"Well, look who we have here. The good detective." Levi twisted up his mouth. "Did the neighbors complain about the party?"

What little smile that might have tipped the corner of Muldoon's mouth fell away.

I cleared my throat. "We're not having a party. My dad's in town. Colin came over to see him." I leaned toward Muldoon and in a stage whisper said, "If you hadn't noticed before, Levi tends to hold grudges. You threw him in jail so..." I tsked. "He'll get over it. Eventually."

"You don't owe the detective any explanations." Levi grabbed my elbow and tried to pull me along with him.

"Stop it." I pried Levi's fingers from my arm. "Come on in and join the non-party, Muldoon." I held the door open wider and motioned for him to go into the living room.

"Should I call my lawyer?" Levi turned up his nose and sniffed with all his uppity pride.

"I'll go." Muldoon took a step back.

"No." I snagged the envelope from him. "Levi, cool it. Now." I waved the papers. "You need this, right? Come in a sec, let me sign it, then you can go."

I didn't know why I was pushing it. I didn't even know if it was some kind of conflict or just bad form to invite your best friend's arrester in to an impromptu family get-together.

Paige sat on the sofa between her dad and my dad. All three looked up when Muldoon entered the room. My wish to keep my worlds from colliding was certainly not granted. I hope that didn't mean the wish to win the lottery and world peace were shot to hell, too.

"Daddy, I'd like to introduce you to Detective Shaw Muldoon. Muldoon, this is my dad, Gil Abercrombie. He came in from Kansas for a visit. You know everyone else."

Muldoon walked over and shook my dad's hand. "Gil Abercrombie? *The* Gil Abercrombie?"

My dad's polite smile morphed into a chest-thumping beam. "You've heard of me?"

Muldoon sat in my club chair. "I spent all four of my college years playing your video games."

Colin snorted.

Muldoon shot him his patented scary, shut-the-hell-up frown.

Colin cleared his throat and quietly finished whatever he was saying to Paige.

"It's a pleasure to meet you." Muldoon volleyed his gaze from me to my dad. "I didn't know you were Celeste's dad."

"You mean all those times you threw her in jail you didn't do a thorough background check? I'm surprised you don't know who her third grade teacher was either." Levi brought two kitchen chairs out for me and him to sit on. "Mrs. Rowe by the way." He smirked as he sat.

"Be nice." I patted Levi's knee. "He tends to get a little testy when he's held on murder charges."

"Unlike you, who takes it like a walk in the park." Muldoon dug a pen from his jacket pocket and held it out to me.

"How did you get into my dad's games, Muldoon?"

He shifted back in his seat and crossed one leg over the other, letting his ankle rest on the opposite knee. It should be nothing, the fact that he was so relaxed around my dad. I didn't think I'd ever seen him so laid-back. It was as much disconcerting as it was totally hot. I gave myself a mental headshake. I so needed to focus on my houseful of family and former family and not if or how much the detective turned my insides to mush.

"My roommate broke his leg two weeks into the school year and his mom sent him a care package once a week, to pick up his spirits. One of the times she sent 'The Planet Guardian.' I think we spent three straight days on his computer playing that game."

"One of my favorites." Dad tucked his arm around Paige. "Celeste was the inspiration for Queen Fraz."

Muldoon's eyes widened for just a moment. Queen Fraz was an ass-kicking nymph-warrior hybrid who shot fire from her fingertips. I'm sure it was a stretch for him to picture sweet little old me as her.

"She was fifteen when I started."

I stuck my tongue out at my dad.

"I have four sisters. I completely understand."

I stuck my tongue out at Muldoon. Which earned me a laugh. "My cousin Lucy was the inspiration for the toad." I've never liked Lucy. We competed in everything growing up. Everything from the schools we went to to the dance classes we took. She was one year older than me and lived one town over.

"Be nice. She's a good girl."

As opposed to what I was. I always got in trouble and she always shone like a brand-new penny. Pretty but not worth squat.

Muldoon laughed. And laughed harder.

I frowned. "What? Inside joke or something?"

"I just realized. Queen Fraz's downfall."

I moaned. He was definitely a tried-and-true Guar-head.

Levi and Dad laughed, too. Queen Fraz was an ass-kicking hemophobe. One drop of blood and she was a goner. Her weapons cauterized wounds. To keep them from bleeding.

"What?" Colin volleyed his gaze around the adults. "What's so funny?'

Muldoon sobered and straightened his shoulders.

"He's never played the game," I said to combat the look of confusion on Muldoon's face.

"Never?"

I did a half headshake. "Nope."

"Cooter, how could you be married to her for so long and not play?" He cleared his throat. "Sorry. None of my business."

Colin shifted at the mention of his high school nickname. "I'm not that into role-playing games."

Levi leaned toward me and whispered the nickname. I'd learned it when I'd first met Muldoon. Considering that Colin'd gotten it for his skirt-chasing ways, I didn't feel the need—oh, hell, who am I kidding. I'd plain forgotten about it until Muldoon said it again. I whispered back, "I'll tell you later."

"So, Detective." Levi scooted to the edge of his seat. "What's in the envelope?"

"Celeste's statement."

"The one that says you and your men jumped to all sorts of conclusions?"

I patted Levi's knee again. "Chill."

"I called you guys, for goodness' sake. Y'all must think I am a first-class dumbass to kill someone and make sure you come to the scene and see me with not only the dead body but the murder weapon."

Muldoon didn't even blink. "Look at it from Showalter's family's point of view. What if you're guilty and we don't explore every possibility? You get away with murder. The truth will come out. It always does."

Levi sat for a moment, then burst out with a quick and loud bark of laughter. "That's the biggest crock of—"

I gave him a swift blow to the ribs with my elbow.

He glanced over at Paige, who had a huge smile on her mouth. She loved it when Levi got on a roll. "Hooey."

Colin snorted. I glared at him and he shifted uncomfortably, then pulled his cell phone from his pocket. "Oops. I've got to get moving." He kissed Paige on the top of the head and leaned around her to shake Dad's hand. "It was good seeing you again, Gil."

As Colin stood, Muldoon did, as well. "I should be going, too."

"Yes, you should," Levi said under his breath.

If Muldoon heard, he didn't react. I quickly signed the document and walked the two men to the door.

Colin paused at the door. "Happy Birthday, Celeste." He leaned closer for a moment like he was going to try to kiss my cheek or something, but thought better of it at the last moment.

"Thank you. You better get moving before she comes over here looking for you," I said, guessing it was Naomi who texted him. I couldn't help but wonder if he'd lied and said he was going to the store or something rather than telling her the truth—that he liked and wanted to see his ex-father-in-law. I'd bet a week's worth of coffee there were some sort of groceries in the back of his truck. Whatever it was, as long as she didn't show up on my doorstep, I didn't give a rat's big fat booty.

Colin frowned and turned and left without another word.

"It's your birthday?" Muldoon rubbed the back of his neck. "I should have remembered."

"No reason for you to." I pasted on my best smile— thank goodness I was an actress or he might see how much that truly hurt. I was glad I hadn't assumed that the card was from him and done something stupid like thank him. "Colin only mentioned it so I wouldn't squeal on him to the skank. He's not allowed to hang out over here. I should tell her just for fun."

"I would hate to get on your bad side."

"Arresting Levi didn't do you any favors." I gave him a wry smile. "So, be honest. How much trouble am I in? Detective Bush won't really charge me as an accomplice, will he?"

Muldoon took a deep breath and released it slowly.

My settled world had tilted on its axis and gone wonky again. It was starting to feel like last fall all over again. Me on one side, Muldoon on the other.

He tucked the signed papers under his arm and shifted into his cop-stance. "It doesn't look good."

"You know Levi didn't do anything." I all but pleaded Levi's case. He couldn't really think my best friend was capable of murder or that Levi would be so stupid as to commit a murder and then make sure he was caught literally red-handed holding the murder weapon.

"Like I said, the truth will come out." Muldoon was unmoved, unfazed and uncompromising.

Once again, the two of us were back to sniffing

around each other—I liked him, I wanted to spend time with him—but there always seemed to be something, someone standing between us. This time it was Levi— and possibly me. Again. Where did it leave me though?

I did understand. "I get it. You have a job. A responsibility."

Levi leaned his shoulder against the wall separating the living room from the foyer. "Careful, Celeste, you don't want the detective to think you're trying to sway his opinion in the case. He could arrest you for interference."

Muldoon cleared his throat. "On that note, I should go."

LEVI'S PHONE CHIRPED and he walked off into the hallway.

"You should have invited the detective to stay for your birthday dinner." Dad lifted one of the table chairs and headed back toward the kitchen.

"He had to go, Daddy." The man probably ran away from here as fast as he could. There were times—like the past ten minutes—when I would if I could.

Dad walked back out of the dining room. "So did you have anything special planned for dinner tonight? It's not any ole day when my one and only daughter turns thirty-seven."

Thirty-seven. I waited for the twinge of pain that came with every new birthday age, but there wasn't even a twitch. I guess after coming so perilously close to death, another birthday was a wondrous thing. "What would you like to do?"

"I'm glad you asked." He clapped his hands together. "Levi picked up some steaks on his way over here and I thought we could grill out."

"That sounds great." Exhaustion pulled at me. I would

much rather make a quick sandwich and crawl into bed, but my dad seemed so excited about the idea of cooking out.

"And I don't want you to lift a finger. You go sit with Paige and chill."

Chill? I figured it out. An alien had come and taken over my father's body. It was the only thing that could explain his odd behavior and using words like "chill."

"Grandpop's acting weird, right?" Paige asked as I sat next to her.

"You can see it, too? I thought it was just me."

"I'd say he's having a midlife crisis, but he's a little long in the tooth for midlife."

And the alien brought a friend to inhabit my little sweet pea's body. "Don't worry. I'm sure it's just a phase. As long as he doesn't go out and buy a sports car, I think we'll be fine."

Paige didn't look convinced but didn't comment.

"Everything okay?" I asked Levi as he joined us in the living room.

"What?" He glanced down at the phone in his hand. "Yep."

"You didn't have to pick up steaks for dinner. But thank you."

"After my time in the joint, I needed some real food."

I walked over to my friend and wrapped him up in a bear hug. "I love you. I'm sorry you're going through this."

He sighed. "I know." He hugged me back a little longer and with a little more oomph than he had in a very long time. "Okay, okay, okay. Enough of this morose behavior. It's time to celebrate your birthday." He released me. "I have something for you."

"For moi?"

"You know jail or no I would not come here empty-handed." Levi reached for a bag behind the sofa and handed it to me.

I yanked out the oodles of tissue paper and found a turquoise cable-knit sweater. "I love it, thanks. But you didn't have to get this, too."

Levi opened his mouth, closed it on a frown, then said, "Too?"

"Yeah, the Bassani handbag. I found it when...um, the other day. At your flip house." I walked over to the foyer and grabbed the bag where I'd left it sitting by the front door. "Didn't you get this for me? I thought that's why you called me over the other day. I thought you were throwing a surprise party."

"And what, I decided to use Arnie as a piñata?"

"Levi." I slapped my hand over my mouth to keep the shock and laughter at bay—I would not laugh at that. That was horribly wrong.

"I didn't mean that." His eyes widened. "I swear."

"I believe you," I said through my closed fingers.

He ran a hand through his hair and sighed. "Let me see the handbag." He traced his finger across the stitching that separated the green leather from the red and blue stripes. He gripped the rolled top handle, examined it. "Where'd you find this?"

"You really didn't get it for me?"

"Sorry, but no." He had the bag up to his nose and was smelling the tassel hanging down the side.

"What are you doing?"

"Trying to see if this is real."

"Of course it's real." I snatched the bag out of his hands and petted the small satchel. It took a lot of effort but I didn't croon, *My precious*. Though I really wanted to.

"Uh-huh. Because folks leave a two-thousand-dollar handbag just lying around a house under construction. Makes sense."

"Don't be rude."

"Not being rude, being practical. Tell you what, after dinner we'll ride out to see a friend of mine. She'll know for sure."

FOUR

"WHO'S THIS FRIEND? Why have I never heard of...?"

"Beetle." Levi pulled into a lot behind a dilapidated warehouse.

"Beetle? That's...interesting." And not the least bit illuminating. "And you met this bug person where?"

He doused the lights and drove another fifteen feet before he parked. "Now listen, when we get inside, don't make any sudden moves. Some of these people can be a little jumpy. And whatever you do, don't make eye contact with Beetle."

"What the..." I had my hand on the door handle. "Yeah, I think I'll just stay in the car."

"Don't be a baby. C'mon." Levi was halfway to the door before I got up the nerve to get out of the car.

"If this goes sideways," I said when I caught up to him, "I'll get even somehow."

"Sideways? What the hell do you think's gonna happen?"

"I don't know. But what if I can't resist the urge to make eye contact. You can't just tell me not to do something. It's all I'm going to want to do." I grabbed the back of his shirt so he couldn't get too far ahead. "Are you rolling your eyes? I feel like you're rolling your eyes."

"Sweets, where's your sense of adventure?"

"I think I lost it last fall. This shouldn't be an adventure. We're just getting a purse authenticated—which I didn't even know was a thing."

Levi chuckled. At least I think he did. I felt it against my fingers more than heard it. He knocked once on a thick metal door, then walked on in. "It's Levi. We're here."

There was a small spotlight on a good twenty feet away that lit up next to nothing.

"Maybe we should go. I don't really care that much about the bag." Which was a total lie and we both knew it.

"Quick question." Levi turned and faced me. "What was the one thing you asked me never to do?"

"Sing in public."

He rolled his hand. "The other thing."

"Please tell me you—"

"Surprise!" Lights came on and a bass-heavy song blocked out whatever pittance of an apology that Levi might have attempted. Though by the smug smile on his face, it wouldn't be anywhere near sufficient.

The small warehouse was decked out in streamers and balloons like you might see at a tween's party. There were several food and drink stations. A little DJ stand was tucked into one corner—I knew where Levi was headed as soon as I released my death grip on his arm.

There were half a dozen actors from the playhouse, several friends Levi and I had made over the years, and a few folks I hadn't gotten a good look at yet.

The music leveled off low enough to have a conversation, so I asked, "So no Beetle here to tell us about this?" I lifted my arm.

"You think I know someone named Beetle? You are so gullible." He patted me on the head like a toddler.

"When did you have the time to plan this?" I asked as I saw how much effort had gone into creating such a fun party.

"It's been in the works for weeks. Your dad showing up just helped keep you distracted."

My hand fell away from his arm. "All the stuff with the police station?"

His smile fell. "All real."

I guess it was too much to hope that the death on his property was an elaborate ruse to get me to the party unaware. He tried to walk off and I snagged his sleeve one more time. "This is not over," I said in a singsong voice as Annabelle approached me.

"She did it." He pointed at my boss and took off toward the DJ station.

She wrapped me up in a huge hug—that was one thing about Annabelle, she gave the biggest and best hugs. "I hope we surprised you."

"No doubt about that. I hadn't suspected a thing." I'd been so preoccupied by Levi and Dad's arrival, they could have been talking about a party right in front of me and I probably wouldn't have noticed.

Dad and Paige stood next to a table loaded down with cakes in several forms: cake pops, cupcakes—that looked suspiciously like the ones she'd been making when I got home from work—and mini Bundt cakes. There was even something that looked like mini pies on sticks. I loved mini pies. "How did you guys get here before us?"

"Birthday magic. Happy birthday, baby girl." He gave me a peck on the cheek and handed me a soda. "We're only going to stay for a little while, then we'll cut out so you can have some grown-up fun. Plus, it's a school night."

"Thanks, Daddy."

One by one, people came up to give me their well wishes. After half an hour, my dad took Paige home, left the grownups to play.

A familiar face came into view. "Rachel."

My former officemate from my time teaching at Peytonville Prep handed me a glass of champagne.

"You brought booze. You're a godsend." I traded the soda for the bubbly.

"The playhouse must be agreeing with you." She nudged my elbow with hers.

"Yeah." I missed my students but the playhouse was my dream job. "How's the new theater teacher working out?"

"She's barely older than the kids, but she's getting there."

"Who else from the school is here?" I glanced around the room.

Rachael took a long sip—too long—of her drink before she said, "Only two."

"Two? Two." It hit me who else might be here about the same time I heard her voice. "He didn't."

A hand clamped down on my shoulder. "I can't believe you let Levi throw you a party."

I downed the entire drink in my hand—to steady my nerves. "One doesn't let Levi do anything," I said as I turned to my ex-husband. "You knew about this...earlier?"

He gave a very noncommittal head tilt and I narrowed my eyes in something akin to *I'll get even somehow.*

I pasted on the fakest smile I've ever pasted on and shifted to his companion. "Naomi. Thanks for..." I waved my hand to encompass the roomful of people.

"Yeah."

Wow, so that was about as nice as we were going to get to one another.

"O-kay." I turned to talk to one of the actors from the playhouse, but Naomi latched on to my arm.

"You did not." She was a little shrill and breathless.

I flinched and jerked my arm free. "What the hell are you doing?"

"Where did you get that purse?" Naomi reached for the bag on my shoulder.

"Naomi." Colin pushed between me and his skank. Maybe it was the look that said I was about to coldcock her. Maybe it was Levi bearing down on her from across the room. Either way, Colin made the wise decision. He glared at the crazy woman, gave her a look that one might give to a spoiled child.

"I'm sorry." She said the words but there was little to no sincerity in it.

"We're going…" Colin wrapped his arm around Naomi's waist and walked her toward the exit a few feet away.

"The entertainment portion of the night is over. Everyone drink up. It's a party." Levi waved his hand to encompass the group.

People went back to their conversations, every now and again glancing at Naomi and over to me.

Levi kept a smile pasted on his face and whispered to me, "What the hell was that about?"

"She freaked out over the purse." I lifted my shoulder and wiggled the bag.

In the corner, Colin and Naomi were getting a little animated in their conversation and her voice rose on every word. "Why are you still paying her alimony if she can afford a two-thousand-dollar bag?"

"It was a gift," I hollered over to the pair. "Not that it's any of your business."

She scoffed. "From who?"

I started to advance on her, but Levi held me in place. "Why did you invite her?" I asked.

"I didn't exactly. Paige wanted Colin here and Naomi walked in when they were talking about it." Levi glared over at my ex. "Paige was afraid this was going to happen."

"Too bad she didn't get to see Naomi's little hissy fit." I snagged Levi's glass and slugged down the little bit left in the bottom. "To hell with her. The both of them."

Colin gave me a quick wave and escorted his lovely— eck, I couldn't even think nice things about her—date out.

Every time I had an encounter with her it left me a little shaken and angry. Why did I let her push all my buttons? Who Colin chose to spend time with was none of my business. I just wish he'd quit throwing it in my face every time I turned around. I sauntered over to the libation station, as the sign above it said, and poured myself another glass of champagne.

I looked around the room at all the guests. There was one person I didn't see. "Muldoon?"

Levi mumbled something and looked away.

"Come again."

"I didn't invite him." Levi poured himself a drink. "He didn't even remember it was your birthday."

"Neither did I."

He rolled his eyes, but said, "I'm sorry. I should have.

But Annabelle said she invited…" He tilted his head to a point over my shoulder.

"There you are," Annabelle said from behind me. Two men stood with her. A tall, distinguished bald man and a man closer to my modest five foot four. "I want to introduce you to Ronnie." She motioned to the taller of the two.

He smiled. "Thanks for letting us crash your party."

"Sure."

"And this, this is Jack."

The friend who Annabelle'd been wanting to set me up with. I shook hands with Jack and Ronnie and gave my friend a very pointed look that screamed *no fair*, to which she just smiled broader. She knew I wouldn't duck out on my own party so I would have to talk to Jack.

"Thanks for making it out here tonight, I appreciate y'all coming. Help yourself." I motioned to the snacks and drinks. "Excuse me a moment."

I snagged Levi's sleeve and feigned interest in the chocolate cake pops. "I have a blind date at my surprise birthday party? Really?"

Levi sucked in a breath and let it out slowly. "Not the best timing, but it can't hurt, right? Give the man a chance."

Give the man a chance? I had a perfectly good man I was interested in. He was so tied to his work he couldn't take time to have a personal life. I was okay with that, sort of. My friends were not, however, and it left them thinking it was okay to go setting me up on a blind date without even cluing me in. Super. At least I got a great party and a kick-ass purse out of it. Except…

"So, you really didn't get me this purse? You're not screwing with me because of the party."

"No, I really didn't."

"And your friend who knows handbags?"

Levi gave me a deadpan look. "Who would I know that can authenticate a purse?"

"I don't know. Until yesterday I wouldn't have thought you had a friend who could post a hundred-thousand-dollar bail."

Levi blanched slightly, but didn't elaborate.

"No worries, we'll sort it out. Tomorrow." I finished the drink in my hand and took Levi's. "Tonight we have fun."

"STOP THE CAR, stop the car." I moaned and Levi pulled over to the curb.

"Seriously?"

"I have to pee."

"Can't you wait?"

"Nope."

He popped the locks on the doors. "Hurry. Before someone drives by."

I ran off into the shrubs that lined Gateway Park and did my business. A black-and-white cruiser drove by as I was walking back out. I waved at the patrolman inside. "Nothing here to see, Officer," I said to myself. "That was close," I said once I got back into the car. I had a full case of the giggles. "Omigod, I haven't laughed this hard in a long time."

Levi snorted and put the car in gear.

"Thank you for the party, if I haven't already told you. You are the very best friend a girl can have." I set the bag in my lap and petted it like it was a puppy. "Do you think I should turn my new precious over to the police?"

"Why?"

"It's not yours so maybe whoever killed Arnie could have left it there."

"You just want to talk to Muldoon again."

"Maybe I do. Is that a bad thing?"

"Bad, no." Levi slowed to a stop at a yellow light, then tapped his fingers on the steering wheel. "A wasted effort..." He shrugged.

"He likes me. He does," I said when Levi rolled his eyes. "It's not the booze talking, I swear." I leaned my head against the headrest and twisted to look at him. "Let's go by his house."

"It's two in the morning."

"The man never sleeps." I dug my cell phone out and lifted my arm to see it. My head was too heavy to lift. "We'll find out." I found Muldoon in my phone. My finger hovered over his name for a long moment.

"No." Levi reached for my phone. The car swerved in its lane.

"Stop." I swatted at his hand.

"Celeste?" A tiny voice echoed in the car.

"Did you hear that?" I asked.

"It's the booze talking."

"No, I heard something. Stop trying to grab the phone."

"Celeste?" the tiny voice asked again.

"There it goes again." I looked around the small area. The radio was off.

"Sweets, the phone."

"What about it?"

"Answer the phone."

I set the phone to my ear. "Hello? Who is this?"

"You called me." The voice was groggy and a wee bit irritable.

"Muldoon? What are you doing calling me so late?" I giggled again.

"Have you been drinking? Are you driving?"

"I have a chauffeur." I rubbed my nose. "Whatchya up to?"

"Sleeping."

"You sleep? I would never have guessed you know how." I nudged Levi with my elbow. "You want some company?"

"How much have you had to drink?"

"You already asked that." It came out a little sing-songy.

"And you didn't answer me."

"It was a party. I had three."

"Try five," Levi mumbled.

"Whoo-hoo. It was five. I'm a party animal. Who knew?"

"You're going to feel it in the morning." Muldoon sounded more wide awake.

"You missed my birthday party." I stuck my lower lip out in a pout, not that he could see me. I could Face-Time him.

"I wasn't invited."

"I know. I can't believe Levi didn't invite you. He knows I like you. I mean like-you like you." I slapped my hand over my mouth. "Did I just say that aloud?" I snickered. "I shouldn't have. It was a secret."

"Not so much a secret," Levi mumbled.

I turned to my friend. "If you have something to say just come out and say it." Back to the phone, I said, "Let's pretend I didn't say that. You aren't supposed to know. Uh-oh."

"Uh-oh what?" both men asked at the same time.

"Pull over, pull over."

Levi didn't hesitate or ask why. He pulled the car over to the curb.

"You don't want to hear this." I pushed at the buttons on the phone and hoped like hell I hung up before the five drinks made a reappearance.

"I'M DYING." I smacked my dry lips together. "Someone put me out of my misery, please. It's all I ask for my birthday."

"Your birthday was yesterday." Dad set a plate in front of me, but I couldn't pick my head up from the table.

"It feels like I'm dying."

"You're not."

"This is so embarrassing. I don't even remember half of last night."

"Which half?"

"Pretty much everything after Colin and the She-Devil left."

"What's wrong with Celeste?" Paige asked as she entered the kitchen.

"Your mom's just getting old."

I tried to give my dad the stink-eye, but even my eyebrows were sluggish. It took some doing but I finally pushed myself up on my elbows. The room didn't spin nearly as bad as it had when I walked in. "You about ready for school?" I rose from my seat and grimaced.

"Yes, but I'd rather have Granddad drive me if it's all the same to you."

I dropped my head back to the table. "Sounds like a plan." I gave the pair a quick thumbs-up.

"Eat." Dad nudged my shoulder and pushed the plate closer to me. "It'll make you feel better."

I didn't want to feel better. I just wanted to crawl into a hole and die a quiet, pleasant death. Was that too much to ask?

The front door shut with way more force than necessary. "Not cool, guys." I rubbed my temples and willed the pain back. The maddeningly loud peal of the doorbell set my teeth on edge. It took all my strength to push myself up from the table and go to the door. I was a little nauseated by the time I was turning the knob. I wanted to scream and yell at whoever was standing on the other side. I yanked open the door and everything in me stilled.

"What are you doing here?"

"I come bearing gifts." Muldoon held a bottle of some suspicious red liquid.

"Why?"

"I thought you might be feeling a little worse for wear this morning."

"And you know this how?" I eyed the sofa to my right. "Can we sit?" I didn't wait for Muldoon to answer and walked over and sat heavily. "You weren't even at the party," I said once I settled into the heavenly soft cushions.

He sat in the club chair across from me. "You're kidding, right?"

"Kidding?"

One dark brow arched upward and he plucked his cell phone from his pocket. "Last night…"

"Last night what?" The nausea increased. "Please tell me you didn't show up to the party. Did I do something terrible?"

"I wasn't invited."

"Stupid Levi," I mumbled. "Did you crash it?"

He was tucking his cell phone back into his pocket

and the teasing smile fell away. "You really don't remember last night?"

"It's a blank from about nine-thirty on." I narrowed my eyes. "What's on the cell phone?" He didn't think I'd noticed.

"Nothing."

"Tell me."

"Here, drink this. This really will help." He handed me the red mixture.

"What's in it?"

"You don't want to know. Drink."

I tipped the cup up. It tasted like a cold tomato soup. Not horrible. "Thanks," I said after I managed to drink down several sips. When my stomach didn't revolt, I drank about half. "So. Now...tell me what happened last night. You didn't think I'd forget, right?" I tapped my temple. "I only forget when there's copious amounts of alcohol involved." I don't even know how much I drank so that probably constitutes copious amounts. Crap. How bad could it have been? Levi was my designated caretaker for the evening, or so he'd said several times. "What'd I do?"

"You called me. No big deal."

"Oh. Is that all? Why'd you make it seem like I drove by your house and flashed you or something?" As I took another sip, my cell phone went off.

Muldoon shot up from his seat. "I'll get that for you. Where's it at?"

I frowned. "No need." I dug the offender from the pocket of my sweats. "It's Levi." I clicked the little green phone icon. "Hey, hon."

"Wow. I wasn't exactly expecting you up. How's your head?"

"Still attached, so pretty good I think."

"Good, good. Do me a quick favor."

"Sure."

"Okay, don't ask questions when I tell you this. But as soon as we get off the phone, go into your photos and delete everything from last night. Don't look at them, just delete."

My hand paused as I was raising the cup up for another sip. "Why?"

"I told you not to ask."

I narrowed my gaze at Muldoon. He squirmed a little. "Will do. I gotta go. Call you later? Okay, bye." I hung up while Levi was still speaking. "Strange call," I said to Muldoon as I set down the tomato drink. "It was Levi."

"I got that. Trained detective." He pointed at himself. "I, uh…"

"He wanted me to delete some photos from my phone."

"Weird."

If I didn't know Muldoon better, I'd swear he was nervous. I'd only ever seen him nervous once and he'd squirmed way less then.

"Celeste, maybe you should listen to Levi."

I have never been good at doing what I should. That's why when I didn't listen to Levi I shouldn't have been surprised that I had, in fact, shown up on the doorstep of one Detective Shaw Muldoon. And apparently took selfies. "Omigod. Omigod. I… I… I'm so sorry." I couldn't look Muldoon in the eye.

The only good thing I had going for me was the fact that at least I hadn't flashed him. "I kept my clothes on, correct?"

"Yes."

I swiped one photo after the other. Me on Muldoon's front porch. Me leaning provocatively against his Camaro. Oh—and the best one—the best one was when Muldoon apparently opened the door, his bedhead hair sticking up everywhere, and I smooshed up against him and snapped away not one but three pictures.

"You think I'm crazy, don't you?"

He chuckled. "No more than usual."

FIVE

THE NEXT DAY, my dad still hadn't spoken to my mom. She hadn't called once. It was a wee bit unnerving for my parents to not be talking—unnatural even. Mom bossed, Daddy acquiesced. That was the way the Abercrombie household had run for as long as I could remember. But now… It wasn't right. I had lain awake every night fretting over it. I might as well be some Southern belle the way I was getting all worked up.

And while I have no clue how Dad occupied his time while I was at the theater, I never once saw him pick up the remote or a book. Did he just sit alone in the quiet house doing nothing? That would drive me bonkers.

That afternoon I was dragging by the time Paige and I walked in the front door after our days. No amount of coffee had perked my droopy lids open. Worse, I had a nasty case of the jitters from all the caffeine.

Guy Bueller had called a couple of times. Gave me a name or two to contact—which I said I would, but never got around to—he was still trying to be helpful, I guess. The PPD had yet to charge me with anything. I hadn't even heard from them again, so I wasn't even sure where I stood with being charged as an accomplice to my best friend's murder charge.

I just wanted to prop my feet up and relax.

"What's that smell?" Paige covered her nose with her arm.

Ugh. "Daddy, tell me you didn't?" I dropped my bag onto the coffee table and hurried into the kitchen. My worst fears were realized with one sniff of the concoction on the stove. My father had cooked his specialty.

"It'll do you good, baby girl." He glanced up from the table.

"Grandpop, what are you making?" Paige pinched her nose.

"Haggis, dear grandchild." Dad put on a heavy burr. "You've never made it for the wee lass?"

"No." I breathed in through my mouth and tried not to gag—not so much from the smell as the memory of being subjected to it every year when my own grandfather came to town for a visit. It was the only time my mother tolerated Daddy in the kitchen. And only then because it kept him and my grandfather occupied and not getting in her way—so she said.

"What's in it, Grandpop?"

I nudged Paige toward the door. "You don't want to know."

"A wee bit o' love, tradition and a special touch my da taught me as a laddie."

Paige tried to stop me as we closed in on the door. "Why's he talking so strangely?"

"It's part of your heritage, lass."

I rolled my eyes. "Dad, you were born in Milwaukee and so was your dad."

"Yes, but our ancestors hail from Glasgow."

"Go get started on your homework." I handed Paige an apple and pushed her along. "I guess you found the grocery store okay."

"Not that it did me any good. You know they don't carry most of the ingredients for this."

"You don't say."

"Levi came over and we found a gourmet market clear across town."

"Remind me to thank him." In my own special way, I added to myself. "If it's all the same to you, I think I'll order a pizza for me and Paige."

My dad shrugged. "Your loss."

As great as an impromptu visit from my dad was, I needed to find out what was going on with him and Mom. I didn't think I could take much more of this. "So, when are you going back?"

He rinsed his hands off in the sink. "Back where?"

I widened my eyes. "Kansas. Topeka."

"I kind of like it here. Was thinking of maybe relocating." He cleaned off the table. "I wanted to talk to you about that detective of yours. He seems like a really good guy. I know you're probably a little gun-shy after Colin, but you shouldn't close your heart to your future. Shaw is a good guy, I like him. And it's obvious that you two are smitten with one another." With that parting comment, he left the kitchen.

It took a full minute before I picked my chin up off my chest. What was stranger? Daddy giving me relationship advice—did he or did he not just leave his wife of forty years?—advocating for a relationship with Muldoon or the fact that he was considering moving here and hadn't mentioned my mother. As I wasn't prepared to contemplate my love life, I scooped up the phone and dialed a number by rote. My mother answered on the third ring.

"Twice in one week. To what do I owe this honor?" Mom sighed into the phone.

"What happened, I mean really happened, between you and Daddy?"

"Not a thing."

"He drove several hours away. And it was over nothing? I don't get it." I didn't want to say anything about what my dad just told me. Who knows if it was just talk or if relocation was something he was seriously considering.

"Married couples have their spats. If you were married, you'd know that." The end of the line clicked.

"Mom? Mom?" I stared at the receiver in my hand. "She hung up on me?"

"Who's that?" Levi came in and dropped his arm over my shoulder.

"You have a lot of nerve showing your face around here." I elbowed his ribs and hung up the phone. "How could you?" I pointed to the pot on the stove and scrunched up my nose again.

"What was I supposed to do? He'd already called to confirm they had what all he needed. Hell, he'd printed out a map." Levi inched closer to the pot and sniffed, then gagged. "I suppose I could've told him no and let him schlep himself all over town and hope to high heaven he didn't get lost. And then have to deal with you because it was my fault. Yeah, I don't think so."

I picked the phone back up and shoved it at him. "I want cheese, sausage and pepperoni."

"I'M GOING TO BED, baby girl." Dad kissed the top of my head.

"Okay. Love you." I flipped through the magazine in my lap, but didn't really see the pages in front of me. My cell was on my knee. Annabelle and I had been texting about the new script possibilities and I'd been too lazy to get up and put it back in my purse. Some small part of me kept trying to work up the nerve to call Muldoon. But after the other morning, I didn't think he'd want to talk again for a while. It's one thing to make a total ass of yourself in front of someone. It's another thing entirely to be so drunk off your ass you don't remember any of it. Gaw. I hope he didn't leave anything out. I hope I didn't say something embarrassing because when he left, he had this strange—almost disappointed—look on his face.

What the hell was that about?

When I pressed him on it though, he just said he needed to get to work. I frowned. It was pretty much his MO. When things got moving between us, he had work. There were days when I should take it personally, but, well, I'd gotten too busy for a couple of our dates and had to back out, so it evened out really. Neither one of us had up and walked away. We were both hanging in there.

Something my parents didn't seem to be doing—hanging in there. Hell, my mother was in denial and holding so tight she was all but strangling everyone around her, and my dad, he was plain running away and landing on my doorstep. But every time I tried to wrap my brain around my parents, my mind would roll back to what Dad said earlier about me and Muldoon.

Was I holding myself back? Closing off my heart? I hadn't meant to. Granted I also hadn't expected to meet a man because I was his number one suspect, so I really couldn't prepare for that. I'd met Colin by accident. And by accident, I'd hit him with my car one afternoon. He hadn't been hurt. Badly. We'd gotten to know each other rather quickly as I ensured he was okay.

We fell in love and out of love in a reasonably short amount of time and in the middle of all that we'd had

Paige. We were amicably enough divorced and both adored Paige. There'd been a man here and there, but none who made my heart zing. Not 'til Shaw Muldoon waltzed into my life. He and Colin were so different, but they both started out similarly. They went to the same high school. They both went to college on football scholarships and they both took their jobs very seriously.

Maybe that was why I kept myself back just so far. Maybe I was afraid anything with Muldoon would end just like it ended with Colin. "But you'll never know if you don't try," a little voice whispered in the back of my head. It sounded very similar to the "Go ahead and have one more" voice, so it was a little suspect.

The big question was…could I take that chance?

I set down the magazine and tapped the phone.

My knees knocked like I was in the tenth grade again about to call Dustin Hawser. I'd sat on the floor of my closet all night with the cordless phone in my hand. By the time I'd worked up the nerve and called, his mother yelled at me—it was half past midnight and I'd woken up the entire house. Thankfully it was before caller ID was a household staple and she'd had no clue who I was. Needless to say though, I never worked up the nerve to call back and I never had a date with good old Dustin.

As if to mock me, the darn contraption vibrated and nearly sent me rocketing off the couch.

"Hey, Coz. What's up?" I said. I tried to hide the disappointment in my voice.

"Sorry to call so late. Today's been crazy."

"No worries. What's going on?"

"I heard from the medical examiner today. Showalter's time of death was not definitive enough to put Levi in the clear."

"But…but…" I gripped the arm of the chair.

"I know. Not what we were expecting."

"Levi will be okay, right?"

"We're working on it."

I hated to ask. It shouldn't be about me, but… "Am I going to be okay?"

The was a long pause. "We're working on it." He gave me a few words of encouragement, reminded me to keep my nose in my own business and said goodnight.

Keep my nose out of it.

How was I supposed to do that when Levi and I were both potentially getting fitted for orange jumpsuits? Levi did not look good in orange.

Yeah, my nose was already twitching for something to dig into. I could not, would not, sit idly by.

I called Guy Bueller and left a message when he didn't answer. I'd misplaced that number he'd left me. Maybe a little on purpose but now I needed it again. And I needed to find the notes I'd started. In search of my other notepad, I pawed through the top layer on my desk. It couldn't be too far down.

"Ah-ha." It was hidden under the credit card bill. I skimmed my previous notes—I had very little information at all. I made a note to call Levi on my lunch break the next day and get some more names to look into.

A heavy yawn caught me before I could stop it. Sleep was a tad more tempting than making any more lists. Especially when I didn't really have a jumping-off point to go with. I was walking back to my room when a strange noise echoed from the guest bedroom/office. I knocked on the door. "Daddy? Is everything okay?"

He didn't answer. He could be asleep, but the sound

was annoying. And not something I'd heard before. What if he fell? Or had some kind of attack?

I knocked again. "Daddy, I'm coming in." I opened the door and just stared. The screen for the window sat inside on the carpet. The widow was open a crack and the wind was sucking the blinds out over the sill and back—hence the unusual racket, as the screen has never once been off before.

"What the..." I hurried over to the window. "Daddy snuck out of my house?" Why would he do that? Where'd he go? I ran back into the living room and immediately dialed Dad's cell number while I checked for his car. Sure as shooting it was gone, too.

A little tinkling sound echoed from the coffee table. It was Dad's phone.

He left without his cell phone.

I ended the call and had Muldoon's number punched up and ringing before I'd even given it a thought. Once my brain engaged I quickly hung up—hopefully before it'd rung through completely. It was so inappropriate to call the man for every little thing. Though I wasn't sure if my dad sneaking out was a little thing or a big thing.

It was definitely a new thing.

My phone vibrated in my hand almost immediately. Muldoon's name popped up on the screen.

I closed my eyes, took a deep breath and answered. "'Lo?"

"Did you just call me?"

"I, uh...butt-dialed." I paced behind the sofa, my gaze kept darting back to Dad's room. "Sorry. Won't happen again."

"Celeste?"

"What?"

"Butt-dial?" I could almost hear a smile in his voice. "Did you need something?"

Was that the window creaking open? I race-walked back to the bedroom to check. Nope. No one there. I reached over and closed the window and made sure the lock was engaged.

"Hey. Is everything okay?"

"Huh? Oh, yeah, sure." I'd all but forgotten Muldoon was on the phone. "I'm fine."

"You don't sound fine."

"It doesn't matter."

"It mattered enough for you to call in the first place."

"Butt-dial."

"Come on, Celeste. We're friends."

"Are we?" I didn't mean it to sound so peevish, but tension built in my shoulders and neck and was creeping its way through the rest of me.

"Always." His voice softened.

"Dad's missing."

"What do you mean missing?"

"He snuck out of the house. Out through a window."

"Did you try his cell?"

"He left it here." I glared at the contraption sitting silently on the table as if it was at fault. "Can I file a Missing Person Report on my dad?"

"He's a grown man."

"Who climbed out through a bedroom window. Who does that? A damn grown-assed man. Can't he use the front door like a normal freaking person? Nope. Did he think I wouldn't let him go somewhere?" I kicked the corner of the coffee table and regretted it the second my big toe hit the curved wooden leg. "Where the hell could he go anyway? He's from freaking Kansas. He doesn't know anyone here but me and Levi. Should I call Levi?" I waved away my comment. "No. He had a date. He'll be out for hours." I took a deep breath. "Why aren't you doing anything?"

"Are you finished?" There was a little too much humor in his voice.

"Muldoon, this is serious."

"When did you see him last?"

"When he went to bed an hour ago."

"Are his belongings still there?"

I mentally retraced my steps. Had I seen his things? "Yes. His bag and at least a shirt or two are on the floor. Gaw." I plopped down on the sofa. "Why would he sneak out?"

"I don't know. Do you want me to come over? I can't file a police report. The man hasn't even been gone a few hours, and even then had he taken all his stuff I couldn't do much."

"You'd do that? You'd drop what you're doing to come over here?"

"In a heartbeat."

Oh, the Muldoon-flutters—that's what I called the little butterflies I got from him—were back and stronger than ever. "That's okay. You don't have to." My voice shuddered.

"I'll be there in ten minutes."

SIX

"I SEE YOU took my advice."

Muldoon and I were sitting next to one another on the sofa, going over places Daddy might have gone. "Daddy? Where have you been? Why did you sneak out?"

Dad was wearing jeans and a sports jersey—who knew he even had a sports jersey? He reeked of cigar smoke and some sweet scent I couldn't quite place. "You noticed." He ducked his head.

"You thought I wouldn't?" I blinked several times, thinking that any second the situation might morph into something I understood. Something that made sense. Not a scary bad version of *Freaky Friday* where I became the scolding parent and my dad the furtive child. "Why did you sneak out?"

At least the man had the decency to blush a little. Then he frowned. "No reason. I didn't mean to worry you. I'm going to bed." He turned to go.

I moved to follow but Muldoon reached across the sofa and grabbed my arm. "Let him go to bed. You can talk to him in the morning when you're not so upset."

"I don't think that will happen." All said and done, Dad had been gone maybe two hours, but still, I couldn't understand why he had to be so covert. "Why couldn't he just leave through the front door like a normal person? And would he even have told me he'd left if I hadn't noticed?"

Muldoon ran his hand across my shoulder, massaged the knot at the juncture of my neck. "He's home now so that's something."

I heaved a sigh. With Dad home, Muldoon probably wanted to leave and get back to whatever it was he did when he was home. Work from home? I'd once accused him of not being able to shut down, but he was bombarded with his duties morning, noon and—I glanced over at the clock on the mantel—five minutes to midnight.

"I need to ask you something." Muldoon pulled my attention from the little brass pendulum swishing back and forth.

I turned on the sofa to face him fully, pulled my feet up in front of me. "Ask away."

He looped his arm across the back of the cushions, scratched at the crisscross pattern with his thumb. "You haven't been going around to work sites asking questions, have you?"

To the work sites? "No. Why?"

"No reason." His gaze shifted down to the square of cushion separating us.

"Nuh-uh." I snapped my fingers in his direction. "You can't drop something like that and say it's for no reason."

"Some woman's been going around harassing some of Showalter's former jobsites and a few current sites."

"And naturally you thought of me. How sweet."

A smile ticked up the corner of Muldoon's mouth. "You do have a penchant to…um…"

"Annoy people?"

"That's not what I would say."

"Not in so many words, no." I poked his thigh with my foot then tucked it back up under me. "In what way is this woman harassing people? And I guess the better question is why?" I let my gaze zone out and spoke my thoughts aloud. "If Levi is the one being accused of Arnie's death, then there'd be no reason for someone to be looking into anything. Unless she knows something. Like who might have really killed Arnie." I glanced around to see if I'd left my notepad close. I needed to write this down before I forgot. "What type of questions was she asking?"

"No."

"No what?" My gaze focused back on Muldoon.

"This is exactly what I was afraid of. I should have known it wasn't you."

"Why?"

"You'd probably have caught the killer, or had him chasing after you by now."

"Ah-ha. So you admit that Levi's not the killer."

"I admit nothing." The tips of his ears reddened. "I didn't really think it was you."

"You thought enough to ask me about it." Where was my notepad? My cell phone had a note app. I could type it into my phone. I dug my cell from my pocket. "I can't imagine what kind of things she'd be asking."

Muldoon snorted. "Nice try." He made a mock attempt to get my cell phone from me. "There's no reason for you to go looking into Showalter's case, so you don't need any tips."

I couldn't stop the smile that turned up the corner of my mouth. "I wouldn't dream of getting mixed up in your case. I was just curious."

"Uh-huh."

"Out of curiosity, have you found anything out?"

One eyebrow arched up.

"I could call Kellen and ask him." I opened the note

app, labeled it Levi's Defense and plugged in a couple of lines about the woman asking questions.

"You could do that. Assuming he knows anything."

"He's the crime reporter. Of course he does."

"Or not."

My turn for an eyebrow raise. There were two reasons why Kellen wouldn't know—aside from the fact that his father was the chief of police, he had lots of sources. If there were zero leads, there would be nothing for the intrepid reporter to uncover. Or if it was a tad more scandalous and the detective and his department were keeping any and everything close to their vests, they would be very careful what got out.

Hmm. I'd need to think this over—and talk to Kellen, of course—then figure out a course of action.

He said, "I'm—"

"What about—" I said at the same time.

"You go ahead." He leaned forward, put his elbows on his knees and clasped his hands in front of him.

"I'm sorry you had to come over here so late. But thanks."

Muldoon's expression softened. "You know I will help you whenever I can. You don't have to butt-dial me to get my attention."

"I, uh. Sure." I shut off my phone and dropped it onto the coffee table. "I hope I didn't pull you away from anything." Was I fishing? Absolutely.

"Nah. Claire was over. They're fumigating her apartment so she's staying with me a few days."

His sister Claire. One of three sisters. He also had a younger brother—who could be his twin despite the ten-year age difference.

He scrubbed his hand across his face. "It's been a

little chaotic. Between her and…" He stopped abruptly and shook his head.

I looked away. "None of my business." I stood and scooped up a handful of magazines, straightening—or rather pretending to. It was all a total ruse. Anyone who knew me knew I sucked at housework.

Muldoon grabbed my hand. "You don't have to act weird around me."

"Who's weird? I'm not acting weird."

"Come here." He tugged on my hand.

I hesitated a moment then let him draw me down beside him on the sofa. He intertwined our fingers. "How do you always get into so much trouble?"

I flattened my free hand on my chest and feigned indignation. "It was not my fault this time. Totally innocent bystander of sorts, really." Same as the first time technically.

He scoffed. "Innocent?" He looked like he might say something else, but the buzz of his cell phone stifled whatever it might have been. I long ago learned—and admired when it wasn't interrupting my me-and-Shaw-time—that he could no more ignore the little silver contraption than I could ignore a free cinnamon latte. Though it was not life or death if I chose to forgo the java, Muldoon did not have that luxury.

"Sorry," he whispered on a sigh before he released my hand and snatched up his phone from his belt clip.

I held out hope that the interruption would only be momentary until a dark frown crawled across his features. He thumbed through his phone and a low grumble eked out.

"Everything okay?" I set my hand on his forearm.

He jumped a little as if he'd forgotten where he was.

"What? No, yeah. Everything is fine." His expression softened. "I'm so sorry to have to do this again. But I have to go."

"No worries. Duty first." I grinned and hoped it looked genuine. But Muldoon looked distracted enough that I didn't think he noticed one way or the other.

He got up from the sofa and held out a hand to me. When I clasped his hand in mine, he pulled me to my feet and wrapped me up in a knee-wobbling hug. "Mmm, you smell so good." His warm breath feathered over my neck.

I doubted I did with the haggis still in the air, but I would take the compliment just the same.

"I better go now." He set me back at arm's length. He started to speak only to have his phone go off again.

"I know, you'll call me."

DAD WAS QUIET at breakfast. No matter what I said, he replied with monosyllabic grunts and didn't try to initiate conversation. Didn't even ask any questions about Muldoon. That was fine with me. I don't know what I would have told him. If anything the past week made things even less clear than before with Muldoon. He was making moves that one would think meant progress but pulling away even further in the next breath. I swear it could give a girl a complex. So if Dad didn't want to talk about him, I would save that for another time.

Dad's silence gave me time to think. About him and what he was up to. The steadiest man I'd ever known decides to up and leave his life and starts sneaking around, something wasn't right. I wasn't a counselor—and ew, I so didn't want to delve into my parents' relationship—but I needed to figure out what was going on. The quiet time let me build a game plan, which was probably for the best since Muldoon had already accused me of harassing vendors and I had yet to hear back from Bueller.

Figuring out what was up with Dad was my number one priority at the moment. I'd already started. I'd gone out to his car and checked the GPS system after Muldoon left. I wrote down the address and planned to go there at lunch to check it out.

"Paige, you're going to be late if you don't hurry." Every morning it was the same thing. She might be a genius, but lately, prompt she was not.

"I'm not ready yet." She dragged her rumpled butt into the kitchen still in her PJs and robe.

"Sweet pea, c'mon. You've got to get moving. We're both going to be late."

She nodded and ate her pancakes in a few quick bites.

"Did you breathe at all during those bites?" I teased.

She mumbled something with her mouth still full.

"You're developing your uncle's habits, I see." I handed her a glass of milk. "You think you can change and be ready in five minutes?"

After she shrugged and headed down the hallway to her room, my dad spoke for the first time. "I'm here." He looked up from his bowl of oatmeal. "I can take care of her. You go ahead and head off to work."

"I can't ask you to do that."

"Who do you think took care of you when you were little? Your mom is a lot of things. Nurturing is not one of them."

My eyebrows spiked up. I'd never heard such dissention from him before. "Are you sure?"

"Absolutely."

"Thanks, Daddy." I leaned down and kissed the top of his head, then hurried back to Paige's room. She was sitting on the edge of her bed tugging at the tie of her robe. "You feeling okay today?" I didn't quite believe her quick nod, but she also didn't look like she was about to open up to me. "We'll talk when I get home. Grandpop's going to drive you to school today."

"Sure."

Back in the kitchen I shouldered my bag and handed him a sticky note with the address of the school. "Just plug this into your GPS." I waited for any kind of reaction at the mention of the GPS, but got nothing. "Colin will take her home with him after school. It's his weekend with her. I'll see you—" I pointed at him "—this evening."

I WAS COMPLETELY distracted all day at work. Twice, I doodled notes on headshots and during my meeting, when a potential donor sneezed, I jumped up from the table and handed her a tissue. Before I even realized what I was doing, I'd set the back of my hand across her forehead. Luckily, Mrs. Cortland found my attention sweet and endearing and pledged to donate enough to offset our next production.

Unfortunately, she was also a talker, kept us busy straight through lunch and on into the afternoon. I had to resort to eating my emergency candy bar from the bottom of my purse on a "bathroom" break to keep my blood sugar from dropping precariously low—which made me a little grumpy. Not something you want to get with a donor whether or not she finds you charming.

Even after a long day at the playhouse, I was volunteered to drive home one of the actors when her ride didn't show up. I dropped her off at her small house on the far side of town and thumbed through my phone, realizing I was only two blocks from the destination on Dad's GPS.

I drove the two short blocks and pulled up in front of a dilapidated strip mall. Only one store had signs of life in the windows; the rest were boarded up. I could not imagine what my dad would be doing sneaking out to go to a Polish bakery.

I shouldered my purse and shoved my keys between my fingers. I'd seen an episode of Oprah or something where a police officer showed women how to protect themselves with just the contents of their purses. I'd left my Aqua Net at home so the keys were it. Not that there was another soul stirring despite the eight other cars in the lot.

Little bells tinkled over the door. The inside looked like any old bakery with glass cases under the dark wooden countertops. Fresh-baked breads lined the wall behind. On the opposite side of the room, up against the wall, were several wooden booths. Wicker baskets hung from the ceiling. Three very large, very burly men turned from their seats, belly-up to the counter, and stared at me.

"Evening, guys," I said and immediately feigned interest in the double case of pastries. There were several types of cookies, cakes and other desserts that would have you salivating in an instant. If Dad came here last night, he'd been somewhere else, too. It smelled only of baked bread and sugar—a yummy scent I must add. None of the cigar smoke that had rolled off Dad.

The fourth man with red-going-gray hair peeled away from the other side of the counter and wiped his hands on a towel that hung from his waistband. "What can I get for you today, ma'am?"

I pointed to the closest cookie. "Is that apricot?"

He nodded. "And we have raspberry, too."

No point in wasting a trip. "May I get a dozen of each?"

"Paul, get her some kolachkes from the back. They're nice and warm." A man in the corner booth a few feet away slashed his finger across a tablet. He wore a light green button-down oxford. Had he not spoken, I wouldn't have even noticed him, which was a little startling. At first, he looked totally benign. But upon closer inspection, he oozed *don't mess with me*.

"Thank you."

He nodded once.

I squeezed the strap of my purse and gave myself a mental kick in the ass. No one knew where I was. I hadn't the slightest clue what my dad was up to. Peering at the three remaining large men still sitting at the counter, I realized I could get broken in two and tucked away neatly in a food pantry and no one would be the wiser. I could assume, with a whole bunch of hope, that wouldn't happen. However, it was a bakery so I didn't know what I should be afraid of. But glancing at the man in the corner I would almost bet there was something that my dad would have some explaining for.

The man settled his tablet on the table just as Paul brought out a white pastry box. When I stepped forward, I caught a glimpse past him. Four more men crossed from one side of the small kitchen to the other. None were dressed like bakers—they looked similar to the corner booth man. Like your average, dressy casual businessman out for lunch. Even though it was past 5 p.m. and they didn't serve anything besides pastries and coffee.

I frowned. What were they doing back there? Why would Dad come here? At ten o'clock at night?

Paul, still waiting at the counter, cleared his throat.

"Sorry. How much?"

He named off a fee and I dug in my wallet for a few bills to cover it, thanking the stars I had just enough cash. Credit cards would leave them a trace to who I was and... I was working myself up into a full-blown case of paranoia.

He gave me the box and then the change. Of course, I dropped the change at my feet. My mind was rolling all over the place with what-ifs and what-could-bes, not on catching the ones and quarters Paul was handing back to me. As I bent to grab it, the man from the booth swooped down next to me and snapped it up. "Be more careful, Paul," he chided the man behind the counter.

"No, it was completely my fault." I breathed in a mingle of the sweet kolachkes and cigar smoke. The same scent I smelled on my dad the night before. I'd never known my dad to smoke, nor ever to smell of it. Not once. Weird. Realizing I was staring, I gave the man a wan smile. "Thanks."

He grabbed my elbow and helped me stand. Once I was upright and set to go he stepped back and smiled. "Enjoy."

"I will." As soon as I could breathe again and my heart wasn't trying to make a hasty escape.

As calmly and nonchalantly as possible, I walked back to my car. If I was confused before, I was ten times more so after leaving the bakery.

The men in the back didn't look like bakery workers. And they were headed toward...the empty storefront next door.

I started the engine of my SUV and sat there. When I was in high school I worked at a store in a strip mall— I sold stylish yet affordable women's clothing. I wasn't very good at it. I ended up getting fired after only three months when a regular customer came to return a sweater that had a soda stain smack-dab down the front of it. I'd told her she'd do better trying to return stuff if she wasn't such a slob. I got the boot and she got a full refund plus a ten-dollar gift certificate off her next return, I mean purchase.

One thing I remembered though, the back of the stores gave you information the front didn't reveal. I drove around the side of the building and into a small alley to see what I could glean. Case in point, an empty storefront should not produce copious amounts of trash as the empty one next to the bakery had.

I was biting my lip, contemplating what to do next when the back door to the bakery opened and the man in the green oxford waved at me. In fact, he waved me over to him.

I could speed away and be home free and clear. But the way he looked at me, the way he came out like he expected to find me there… That little curious bug had me pulling over and rolling down the window—I wasn't stupid enough to turn the car off and exit it.

He tucked his hands in his pockets. "Boyfriend or husband?"

I frowned. "I beg your pardon?"

"Are you checking up on your boyfriend or husband?"

"I don't…"

"You can play it like that." He narrowed his gaze. "I know you." He tilted his head to the right and looked me over for a minute before his smile grew. "You're Celeste Eagan."

"I, uh." I gulped. I'd bet he could hear it four feet away. "How do you know me?"

He chuckled. "You were all over the paper last fall. You're one ballsy woman."

I grimaced. "Is that good or bad?"

"Depends. Why are you here?" His smile fell slightly. "Let me guess. Gil Abercrombie."

"How did you…?"

"He's new. You're new. It doesn't take a genius. He's a little old to be your husband. Sugar Daddy?"

"No, just plain Daddy." I gripped the steering wheel so tight my knuckles ached. I glanced through the windshield. Light traffic passed by the end of the alley. I was already busted and now had more questions than answers. I might as well tell the truth. "I followed him here. Sort of."

"How's that?"

"GPS. When he came in last night, I snuck out and checked his GPS thingie." I shifted my gaze back to… "You know me, but I don't know you."

He leaned forward with his hand outstretched. "Gabriel Grady. I own the bakery."

I took his hand in a quick shake—okay, I did flinch slightly at first, but I did shake it. When he released it I glanced at the door. "Gradkowski's?"

"My dad changed it to Grady, thought it sounded more enterprising."

I laughed. "I got married to change my name. Abercrombie was just so dang long." I hadn't meant to joke with the man, but he was so affable. "Because I am going to ask anyway, might as well come right out. What was my dad doing here last night?"

"What did he tell you?"

"Not a single thing."

Mr. Grady looked back toward the building, then motioned to the kolachkes. "I own a bakery, Mrs. Eagan."

"Dad didn't come home with any food."

The man looked down his nose at me for a moment. "I guess he ate it all before he got home." He turned and went back into the building, the door shutting behind him, which concluded my half-assed interview.

"Nope, not confused at all now," I said as I pulled onto the street. I headed toward my neighborhood and decided to make a quick pit stop.

Box of kolachkes in hand, I stopped at the front desk of the Peytonville Police Department. "Hey, Jenny. Is Detective Muldoon in?"

The desk sergeant looked up and smiled. "Hey, Celeste. Hang on." She picked up the phone. "There's someone here to see you, Shaw."

Jenny and I had become friendly once I stopped getting arrested. Those times she'd always looked at me with something akin to pity crossed with some womanly understanding. The things we do for family... Afterward, when I came up to see Muldoon, she and I would chat as I waited for him. She has one son close to Paige's age and her ex was a nightmare, too. We bonded.

"He'll be right out," she said just as my phone went off.

"Thanks." I waved to her as I answered.

"Celeste, hi. It's Guy Bueller. I have a lead for you."

"Really?" My heart did a little jig.

"Yeah. There's a place out on the far edge of town.

Arnie would meet some…let's say less desirable vendors out there. I think I can get you a meeting with one or two of them. Maybe they can give you some more info that might point you in the right direction."

"Oh, that would be…interesting." I wasn't sure I wanted to meet with the less desirable vendors the man dealt with. "Let me…"

Muldoon frowned as he rounded the counter from the back. "Celeste, is everything okay?"

I held up a finger to Muldoon, then to Bueller said, "Can I call you back in a bit? I can't talk at the moment."

"Sure, sure. Anytime. Just let me know when I can set it up."

"Thanks." I punched the disconnect button. "Hey," I said as I tucked the phone back into my handbag. "I come bearing gifts." I wiggled the white pastry box as two people came in through the front door and headed over to Jenny.

Muldoon motioned me to follow him to the other side of the small lobby and out of earshot of anyone coming or going. "You didn't have to bring me anything."

Heat tingled up my cheeks. "It's kind of a twofold gesture." I shoved the box in his hand and sat in one of the chairs. "I kind of did something silly."

"Uh-oh." He sat next to me and set the box on his knee. "What did you do? And will I need to call in more favors with another police department?"

I gave a shaky laugh. "Very funny." I leaned in closer and lowered my voice. "I snuck out and checked Daddy's GPS last night after you left. He'd left the address of his destination on there."

Muldoon closed his eyes and sighed. When he opened them again he said, "And you went there." Not a question.

I tapped the box. "Daddy went to Gradkowski's Bakery on 7th last night."

"Celeste…" He set the box on an empty chair, leaned his elbows on his knees and scrubbed his hands over his face. "What did you find out?"

"Nothing. Gabriel Grady—"

"You talked to Grady?"

"Yes. You know him?" When Muldoon didn't comment further, I continued, "He seemed nice enough. Knew who I was thanks to Kellen's piece in the paper last fall." I tucked a lock of hair behind my ear. The squiggly feeling that preceded when I was about to learn something I didn't want to know flitted through my chest. "Mr. Grady didn't tell me anything. Why would my dad be at a bakery so late at night? And feel the need to lie about it?"

"Gradkowski's is a front."

"For?"

"Gabriel Grady is a sports bookie."

SEVEN

"Daddy!" I slammed the front door.

"Shh. Paige is taking a nap." Dad came from the kitchen wiping his hands on a towel draped over his shoulder.

"Why is she here? And why is she taking a nap?" I waved away my comment. "Don't try to change the subject." I'd get back to that little bombshell momentarily.

"What subject? What's got you all fired up?"

"A sports bookie?" My hands shook. Whether I had a right to be upset or not, I was thrown when Muldoon told me that Gradkowski's Bakery was the legitimate side of Gabriel Grady's business—not that they had ever been able to find proof of his illicit gambling ring. "You snuck out of my house to go see a sports bookie?"

His face lit to an alarming shade of red. "How'd…"

"It doesn't matter how." I set my purse and tote bag down. "I have tried to stay out of whatever is going on between you and Mom." Mostly because they weren't telling me anything. I paced the length of the living room. "But when you start sneaking out of my house at all hours—"

"It wasn't all hours. And it was only once." He shoved his hands on his hips.

"Anyone could have come into my home. You left the window wide open."

"This is a safe neighborhood." He ducked his head, not meeting my gaze.

I could argue that not once but twice had a killer sneaked into my house last year. The man had also taken shots at me while I stood on my very own front porch in said safe neighborhood. Granted the man was now behind bars, and it was a somewhat isolated incident, but still… "Regardless. Why? Why are you going to Gradkowski's?"

"Why do you think?"

"Daddy, come on. Why are you sneaking around?"

Dad walked over to the sofa and plopped down.

"It's not for the kolachkes." I sat on the coffee table in front of him and set my hand on his arm. "If it's any consolation, Mr. Grady wouldn't tell me anything."

Dad swallowed heavily. "You spoke with him? You shouldn't have done that."

I tightened my grip. "Are you in trouble?"

He shook his head. "No, no. Nothing like that."

"I don't understand. You didn't place any bets?"

He sighed. "I did."

"Daddy…"

Dad stood and walked several paces away. "I'm not in any trouble. I covered my losses."

"*Losses?* Plural?" My cell phone buzzed in my pocket. Out of habit I pulled it out and checked the screen. It was Colin. He could wait. I hit the ignore button and kept waylaying Dad. "What are we talking here? One hundred dollars? Two?"

"Four…" He mumbled something unintelligible.

The cell phone went off immediately again. Again ignore. "Come again."

"Four thousand."

Four thou… I'd never spent that much on anything. A weird sound came from the back of my throat. It sounded like a cross between a gasp and choking.

"It's not as bad as all that. I had a run of bad luck this week." Dad patted my head. "I was in the middle of fixing some soup for Paige. Hungry?"

"No." My cell buzzed again. "Hang on, Daddy." I stabbed at the green talk icon on my phone. "What!"

"Why aren't you answering my call?"

"I didn't want to talk to you." I thought I showed great restraint not adding, "Duh," on the end of that.

Colin huffed out a breath—we hadn't spoken since the birthday debacle with his she-beast. Like he had any reason to get huffy. "I was worried about Paige," he said finally.

That pulled me up short. "Why?"

"Because I'm her father."

I closed my eyes briefly. When I opened them again, I asked, "What is there to worry about?" I tried again, about at the end of my rope between Dad's escapades and this call from my ex.

"She's sick."

"Is that why she's here?" I needed to go check on her.

"You don't know?" There were accusations tinting his voice. "She missed school. Gil called this morning and—"

"This morning?" I massaged my temple. "Dad, really? You told me you'd take her to school."

"I did, well, started to." He looked like he was about to bolt from the room.

"I'm pretty sure Paige is fine, but I'm gonna have to call you back." I hung up on my ex. I took a deep breath, then another. After the third I was calm enough to ask.

"Why is Paige taking a nap?" I'd wondered about it for a nanosecond when I'd come in and Dad told me but I was on a tear for the bookie thing. "Is she really sick?"

My dad looked away. "Sort of, but not exactly."

"What exactly is she?"

"She's worn out."

I rolled my hand for him to get on with it. "From?"

Dad sucked in a breath, squared his shoulders and began to list off about fourteen different places he'd dragged my daughter to instead of taking her to school. "The batting cages may have been overkill. It wore her out."

"That may have been *just* a little bit of overkill. Not the fact you played hooky with her. Not the fact that you lied to her dad, didn't tell her mom and—"

"Lighten up, baby girl."

"Lighten up?" I frowned. "It's Friday. You could have waited twenty-four hours and done all of this without any crap from me." I ran my hand through my hair and heaved a hefty sigh. "Are you, or are you not, the man who instilled the priorities of school and honesty? Are you not the one who taught me lying was a coward's way out of owning up to your mistakes? What the hell, Dad?" I narrowed my eyes. "This is on top of dropping four grand in a bakery/gambling thingie."

He didn't comment, just stared at me for a long moment, then walked off like lying to your kid and losing a chunk of money was an everyday occurrence for him.

Who knew, maybe it was.

I followed after him. I was not done. "How would you even know where to find a place like the bakery?"

Again the man mumbled.

"Daddy, look at me and answer."

"Levi introduced me to Gabriel."

My eyes narrowed to slits as a red haze washed over my vision. "I am going to kill him."

"WHY AREN'T YOU ANSWERING?" I yelled at my cell phone when Levi's voice mail came on for the fifth time.

Dad had gone to his room and wasn't speaking to me. Paige woke up from her nap all apologies, then promptly puked up an Icee, a pretzel and an entire bag of gummy bears. I sent her back to bed with the last bottle of ginger ale and some crackers.

I needed to run to the store and grab some more ginger ale. I might as well stock up on some quick meals, too. I constructed my list of the standards: bread, milk, cereal and was working up a menu for the next few days. It took me a few minutes to realize I'd gone from groceries to potential suspects in the Arnie Showalter murder when there were several vendors—including the couple of mysterious ones Bueller said he'd connect me with—listed under the oatmeal and bananas. Levi's name was still at the top of the list.

Sitting alone at the kitchen table, I tapped the list trying to figure out how my easy life got turned sideways. Then I felt horrible because I remembered it came at the cost of Arnie Showalter. The poor man might be a little sleazy and a horrible employer, but no one deserved to be bludgeoned to death with a hammer. The news had finally made the paper. Kellen had written up a crime blotter piece on it, but there hadn't been any outcry to find the killer, and the community didn't seem overly concerned that there was a murderer on the loose.

It was like no one really cared the man was gone.

Though someone had cared. Some woman. She'd gone

around asking questions—apparently the kind of questions that I myself would ask since Muldoon thought it was possibly me doing it. I wondered who she was. Or what she might have found out.

I dropped the pencil and stood to stretch out a kink in my back.

Levi was still on the hook for the murder. I knew there was no way he had anything to do with it—and Coz was a damn good lawyer—but if the police didn't find the real killer, Levi could have some hard times ahead. And while he was in trouble, so was I. I didn't blame Levi. He couldn't have known they would threaten to charge me as an accomplice, but damn if it didn't suck being eyed by the police again.

For the briefest moment I wondered if he deserved it for taking my dad to see Gabriel Grady. Pre-karma? Was that even a thing? If it was, then my involvement was pre-karma for thinking it. Gaw. I had to be more proactive.

I picked the pencil back up and separated the grocery list from the suspect pool and grabbed my notes from the day of Levi's arrest. Who had I spoken to? I still needed to call two of his subcontractors.

First on the list was the electrician.

"Marlon, hi. This is Celeste Eagan. A friend of Levi's. We've met a few times."

"Yeah, sure. Whatchya need?"

"You were working at Levi's properties the last couple of weeks, right?"

"Two of them, yeah."

"Did you see anything strange?"

"Strange how?"

"Anyone hanging around? Anything that didn't flow as usual?"

"Nah, it's all been pretty regular. Levi keeps his projects on a pretty tight schedule."

Damn. That was what I was afraid of. That was one of the things about having a Type-A best friend, he likes his routines and schedules. "Okay, well, thanks, I—"

"There was that one thing. A couple of weeks ago."

"What thing?" And why didn't you mention it when I first asked?

"Arnie was over at one of the sites. He was all bent out of shape because someone started to open one of his crates that wasn't supposed to be there. He was yelling and carrying on. Even made me and my guy load the damn crate onto the back of a flatbed."

"Did he often have stuff sent to Levi's properties?"

"Once or twice. I never could figure out why."

"What was in the crate?"

"Don't know. Don't care. That man was a pain in the ass. The less we saw him the better."

"Was there anything on the crate—"

"Look, I don't know why you're asking all these questions, but I don't know what else I can tell you. I gotta go." The man hung up.

"Well, thanks," I said to my cell.

Barry, the lumber supplier, was much friendlier once I explained who I was and why I was calling.

"Yeah, I was there last Saturday. I remember 'cause there was a huge crate blocking the driveway. It was early morning. Before nine. I only had thirty minutes to drop off some of the wood Levi ordered."

My Spidey senses tingled. "Hmm."

"It was meant for Arnie's warehouse."

"How...?"

"Arnie was all apologetic—which was weird. The man never apologized. Said he was supposed to get it to his warehouse. And that he needed to get it before it rained. I remember thinking it was clear skies, but I wasn't about to correct the man. He was a mean sonofabitch."

"Arnie took the crate himself?"

"Yeah. We had to load it for him. Took three of us—he said he had a bad shoulder or something. Arnie left without even thanking us. That was the kind of guy he was. We left a few minutes after he did."

So he'd left the property and come back? "What was in it?"

"You sound like one of those TV detectives." Barry gave a quick chuckle. "But sorry, not a clue. It didn't have any markings or anything that gave away what it was."

"Do you know—"

"That's all I know, sorry." He sighed. "It wasn't like we were taking notes. I wish I could help you more. Levi's a good fellow."

"Thanks. You've been a big help."

Levi'd been getting ready for Paige's tournament at my house at nine, then at the hospital afterward. So the new info didn't help Levi's alibi. But it did add more questions in the Arnie column.

Questions that I'd run out of people to ask.

Levi could point me in the right direction. If he'd ever answer his phone.

I leaned back in my chair, massaged the back of my neck and tried to think like Levi. Why would I not answer my phone? Because I'd be afraid of the ass-whooping coming. Where would I go if I was hiding out from my best friend?

To one of my properties. Yep, if I was Levi running from me, that's where I'd go.

Plus, on a normal day he tended to go to a site and get so immersed he'd lose all track of time. "I bet that's where he is now." I could go look for him. I glanced at my watch. It was straight up seven o'clock. If I hurried I could check out a couple of his properties before it got too dark.

I checked in on Paige, who'd gone back to sleep. At my dad's door, I knocked—after I tried the knob. It was locked. I wouldn't have just barged in. I did that once in high school and caught my parents "wrestling." And that's what I'd swear to if anyone ever asked. Gaw, there were not enough therapists in the world to tackle that issue. I re-blocked the not-gonna-go-there images. "Dad, I need to run out for a sec. Can you keep an ear open for Paige?"

There was no answer. I expected it. He was acting just like I did when I was a teenager. I'd perfected the silent treatment, going two whole weeks without uttering a single sound in Casa Abercrombie. "Dad, I need to know if you're in there or not. I'm out of ginger ale and the pukey little puppy may need some more." I sighed. "If you don't answer, I may assume you've snuck out again." I leaned against the wall next to the door. "I guess I could always run out front and see if your screen is still in place, but I'd rather you speak to me."

From in the hallway, I could hear his long-suffering harrumph. What right does he have to get pissy?

I shoved away from the wall just as he opened the door. "Yes, I'm still here." He frowned but his face softened when he glanced down the hall toward Paige's room. "Is she doing okay?"

"A little green around the gills. She's not used to so much carnival food in one sitting."

He scratched at the thinning gray mop on his head. "Yeah. She seemed so down in the dumps about some boy at school."

"He's fourteen and won't give her the time of the day. She'll get over it."

"I just wanted to cheer her up."

"I know, Daddy." I patted his arm. He did mean well. "But skipping school and lying about it isn't going to help her." Though if my granddad had done that when I was Paige's age, I'd have had an awesome memory. My granddad's greatest thrill was to call me Barbara and say, "Pull my finger." I sure did love the old coot.

"Do you need anything from the store?" I waved my list.

"Nope. I got all I needed yesterday." He smiled.

"Cool." I smiled sweetly back. "Oh, and if Levi calls while I'm gone, tell him he's on my hit list. Because, no, I'm not going to let this go."

"DAMN. I SHOULD have brought a flashlight." The flashlight app on my phone barely illuminated more than a foot in front of me. I'd already been to two of Levi's properties to find them completely locked up tight and empty. This was my last stop. Tonight. If he didn't call me back, I was going to hunt his ass down if I had to go to every single plot of land he owned and make him explain why in the hell he'd introduced my dad to a freaking sports bookie. I wouldn't have even stopped here if I hadn't seen a light on.

Levi would have parked in the driveway in the back—which I wasn't about to try and find in the dark. Most people probably wouldn't be working so late, and he did usually keep pretty normal hours but there were times when he'd come to a house just to sit and listen. He says the house speaks to him and lets him know if he's on the right track with his renovations.

The man had some weird habits. Habits that led him to meet interesting people, which was why I didn't question him about his friend named Beetle.

I'd almost forgotten to be pissed about the surprise party. Between my massive hangover—which was his fault—and learning of my dad's gambling proclivities—again his fault—I'd pushed aside the fact that he'd done one of the few things I had begged him never to do. Throw me a surprise party. I wasn't against parties per se. I enjoyed them most times. And getting older sure as hell beat the alternative of not having any more birthdays ever. No, I had a bad taste for parties thanks to the debacle of my twentieth birthday. My then boyfriend, Neil, decided that right in the middle of my surprise party, thrown by my very best friend, JoAnn, was the best time to tell me that he was leaving me. For JoAnn. Who also happened to be pregnant. Yeah, that night hadn't gone well.

Come to think of it, I drank a little too much that night, too. And went over to Neil's house. I did not take selfies. No, I stood on his front porch and ranted and raved about what a lowlife scum he was and how he and JoAnn deserved each other. And how I hoped that their baby didn't have his stupid big ears.

His mother was none too happy to learn of her future grandbaby at two in the morning. Nor was she too pleased that her neighbors were all awakened, as well. I'd barely talked my way through an apology and promised never to darken her doorstep again if she would promise not to call the police.

Hmm. I guess my life of crime started way further back than when I came across Detective Shaw Muldoon.

I'd been humiliated. Several of my and JoAnn's friends took her side thanks to my outburst and I haven't been able to look at tequila since.

Once, not too long after Levi and I had become friends, I told him my sad bad-behaving tale and how I never ever wanted another surprise party. And up 'til this very year, he'd restrained himself. And once again, I'd made a total ass of myself. Still Levi's fault.

I had a full head of steam by the time I punched the code into the lockbox hanging from the front door. The man used his birthday. Anyone who wanted to break in only had to know he was born July second. Of seventy-two. Seven-two-seven-two. He used that code for just about everything. I told him he needed to come up with something different, but he was convinced no one knew when his birthday was.

The front room of the house was bare except a single sawhorse. This house was nearly complete from what I could tell. It still needed a final coat of paint and the customary wooden floors Levi liked to use and then he'd have it on the market.

One summer, when Colin and I were still married, I'd helped Levi out. I couldn't believe how much work went into refurbing a house. I swear I still got an ache in my thigh muscles just thinking of all the lifting we'd had to do to get the cabinets installed.

"Levi?" I made my way into the kitchen area, where

I'd seen the light. "You here?" So I can kick your ass, I added to myself. There was no one in the kitchen and the garage was empty save a large crate. It didn't look like any of the crates from his suppliers that I'd seen before.

It could be the new floors. The crate was large enough. I started to turn to go, but was curious what floors he'd planned for this house. It couldn't hurt to peek. I tiptoed—though, I don't know why I did that, I was alone in the house—over to the crate. The lid was popped up at one corner. If I lifted it slightly I could peer inside.

I held my cell/flashlight to the little opening. When I expected a shiny brown laminate, I saw a bright pink and lavender leather instead.

"What the hell…?"

I tugged at the corner of the lid until I could get more light into the opening. The pink and lavender sat atop a black-and-white leather with tortoiseshell handles.

"It's a frigging handbag?" A handbag from the same Bassani collection as the one sitting in the floorboard of my car. The one I thought Levi had gotten me for my birthday. I yanked the crate lid off completely. The crate came up to my hip and was just as long and wide as it was tall. And it wasn't one Bassani handbag but many. It was filled to the top with handbags. I even bent over the edge and dug down to the bottom to see if maybe there were only a few on top of whatever he might have had shipped, but the entire box was nothing but handbags.

Why would Levi tell me he didn't get me the bag if he had easily three dozen more? A better question is why would he need so many bags?

I dug out several of the handbags. They were gorgeous. And Levi had so much 'splaining to do. Yet again,

I tried his cell phone for it to go straight to voice mail. "Levi Weiss, if you don't call me back ASAP, I'm going to kick your butt from here to Milan, where Bassani makes her bags."

I wanted to slam the bags back into the crate to match the anger welling up in me, but I couldn't do it. I was still just girlie enough to treat the bags with the reverence they were due. But I did slam the top of the crate back on there—even got a stupid splinter for my efforts. Dammit. Then I snapped a couple of pics of the crate. I wanted to show them to Barry at the very least—since he'd seen the other crates. I quickly took a shot of the label plastered on the side. It was too dark to make out much of the address. I needed to get out of there. I was creeping myself out and wasn't about to hang out in the empty house all night waiting for Levi to show—even with a hoard of Bassani bags.

I did actually need to stop at the store for some more ginger ale. I'd barely left the house when I pulled my cell from my pocket. I had to yank my steering wheel to the right as I approached the intersection. "Learn to drive, jerk." A large truck nearly ran me into the curb as it made a wide turn onto the street. It had nothing to do with me trying to dial as I drove. Nope.

Another strike for Levi. Nearly getting my new-ish car flattened. He was racking up the ass-kicking points.

Levi would come crawling in sooner or later. Then I'd kill him for putting me through all this. I tried his cell one last time as I pulled away from the curb. "Levi, if you don't call me tonight, you are dead to me."

EIGHT

WHEN I GOT back from the store, Daddy still wasn't talking to me. Paige's tummy had, thankfully, settled down. Despite all the fun she professed to have, the way she moaned about missing science and her lab partner Caleb—ah, puppy love—I didn't think she would ever play hooky again. Who knew I'd have such a conscientious student? Once I got her back to bed, I made a quick dinner for me and Dad. He grumbled a few comments to my attempt at chitchat but that was pretty much it.

Gaw, when did the roles reverse?

Later, as I loaded the last dish in the dishwasher, the doorbell rang. It was close to ten. No one other than Levi would come over so late. I frowned as I hurried to the door. Levi wouldn't ring the bell, though. Of course, after all the messages I'd left him, he might be afraid to waltz right on in.

The man on my front porch, however, wasn't Levi. "Detective, twice in one day…" I smiled, but he didn't return the gesture.

"May I come in?"

"Sure." I continued to smile, but got nothing in return. His frosty demeanor worried me. He smelled slightly of smoke and had a dark smudge on the side of his nose. "You know the way to the living room. I'll be right there." I stood in the kitchen and took a deep restoring breath, afraid I was about to get hit with something unpleasant.

I found Muldoon sitting on the sofa.

"If you've come to tell me they're charging me after all, I'd much rather not hear it from you. Though I appreciate the thought."

"What? No. It's not about that." His voice was husky, almost raw.

"Oh. Okay." If it wasn't about Levi's case… Now I was confused.

"Sit, please." He patted the seat next to him.

"Are you getting sick? You sound kind of gravelly."

He shook his head. When I sat, he held my gaze for a long moment. "I guess you didn't happen to see the news tonight."

I glanced over at the darkened television. The Muldoon-flutters were running rampant. This time however, I was pretty sure it was for the wrong reason. "I never had a chance to turn on the TV." I reached for the remote but Muldoon grabbed my hand to stop me. "Did something happen?"

"There's been an accident." His thumb stroked across the back of my hand. "A fire."

I sucked in a deep breath and held it. "Where?"

"At a vacant house across town. It's under renovation."

"Which one?" I asked once I let out my breath.

"A property off Sagebrush."

"Levi's?" I scrunched up my face. "I was just there. The place is fine."

"When?"

"I don't know, two, two and a half hours ago." I glanced over at the clock. "Closer to two and a half. I was looking for Levi."

"Was he there?"

"No. No one was. I thought there was when I got there. Someone just left a light on." I pulled my hand from his grip. "Should I have turned off the light? Did it start the fire?"

"The fire department is still on the scene. They haven't gotten that far in the investigation yet."

"Investigation? How badly was it burned?"

He swallowed heavily. "Completely." Dark shadows settled into his eyes.

There was something there…a guarded look that crept through his expression before it morphed back to his usual steely cop-face. "You went inside," I said. It wasn't a question. It explained his hoarse voice. "You should've let the firemen do that, you know. You sound like you may have gotten a little smoke inhalation. Did you get checked out?" I swiped at a smudge of soot on his face.

"I'm fine." He said the words, but his expression begged to differ with his mouth pulled down at the corners and the way he fidgeted.

My gaze landed on the Bassani bag sitting in the chair across from us. "Well, shit."

Muldoon frowned at me. "Celeste."

"What? There was a crate of pretty pricey handbags in there. Thousands of dollars. Gaw, I hope he's insured for that." That sucked. I loved my purse, but I'd seen one I was thinking of asking if I could trade for it. That wasn't bad birthday etiquette, was it?

"I didn't see a crate in the house."

"Are you sure? It was in the garage. Could you check on that for me? Levi will have a fit."

Muldoon grimaced. Very strange reaction but something deep inside me didn't want to find out why. I could focus on the handbags though.

"Gaw. I'm going to have to find out if they're there. If Levi would just answer the damn phone." I waved my cell, the unease was growing, but I didn't know why. "If you thought he overreacted to losing his sunglasses at Christmas…" I lifted my eyebrows quickly. "Those houses are his babies. I think he named that one Charlotte." My hands shook slightly as I gripped the phone tighter. "Wait. Why were you in the house, anyway? You're a homicide detective."

"Celeste."

No. I was not going to let him finish whatever inane thing he was going to say. "I should try calling him again." I dialed Levi's cell for what seemed like the hundredth time. "He's been ignoring me. He did something stupid and he knows I'm going to kill him when I get my hands on him."

Yet again, the phone went straight to voice mail.

Muldoon cleared his throat. "I don't think he's going to answer."

"Why? You didn't haul him off to jail again, did you? I didn't even think of that."

"No. But, um…" He glanced away for a moment. "Inside the house, they found a body."

"Whose house?"

"Levi's."

Um, no. I shook my head and laughed a little too loud. "You're a jackass. That's not funny."

"I'd have been here sooner, but I had to—"

The peal of the doorbell stopped him mid-sentence. I didn't want to hear the rest of what he had to say so I jumped up from the sofa. "Excuse me." My numb legs were surprisingly steady as I walked to the door.

"Celeste, hi." Kellen leaned in and kissed my cheek. He smelled faintly of smoke. When he pulled back, he had a solemn look on his face. "I came over here to tell you…something. Can I come in?"

"Sure. Why not? The more the merrier." I waved him in and into the living room. "Muldoon's already here."

Kellen slowed his step. "So you know?"

"I know this cockamamy story that Muldoon's weaving."

"Celeste, I was there. I saw the house."

"Did you see this body?" I did air quotes when I said *body*.

"I didn't get that close, no. I was on the other side of the crime scene tape."

Crime scene tape. When did that become an everyday occurrence in my world?

"Shh, shh, shh. You're going to wake up Paige." Dad came hurrying into the room. "Whoa." He pulled up short. "What did I interrupt?"

Muldoon repeated his news to Dad while I stared out into space. Muldoon was mistaken. I hated that for the first time he was wrong on a case and it had to be because of Levi. It happens. Every great detective gets it wrong once in a while.

But Levi wasn't answering. The little nagging voice repeated over and over in my head and made it more difficult to breathe because of what Muldoon was trying to tell me. It wasn't right, though. Something about it was…off.

"Baby girl," Dad called to me. He had only to open his arms and I walked straightaway into his embrace. I should cry—hell, I even wanted to cry, but I was numb. I stood in my dad's hold for what seemed like an hour, but in truth it could have been as short as a couple of minutes. I took a deep breath and moved back.

I always figured when I lost someone close to me I'd feel it. In the pit of my stomach. My grandfather died when I was seventeen, and I'd felt it. When we'd gotten the call from my grandmother, I'd already known. Had already grieved without really understanding why— though I'd known my grandfather was gone. Levi and I were like brother and sister. Probably closer than some. If—when—*if* I were to lose him, I'd know. I'd have to know. But when I searched down in my gut I got… absolutely nothing.

"Are you okay?" Dad rubbed my shoulder.

I shook my head, afraid to try and speak. All three men were watching me. What did they expect? I'd swoon? Go through stages of hysterics? No, I was not okay. My brain was shutting down because it didn't compute. "He can't be gone." I hugged myself to ward off the chill that had wrapped itself around me.

"I know it's hard to believe—" Muldoon stepped toward me, but I backed away from his outstretched hand.

"You don't understand. Levi can't be gone. I don't feel it." I smacked my fist over my heart. "I don't feel anything."

Dad settled his arm over my shoulder. I shrugged it off with an apologetic grimace. I didn't want to be comforted. I couldn't explain it to any of them.

A noise came from the front of the house—like the door opening.

"Hey-ho. Looks like there's a party going on over here. What's with the celebration?"

Kellen's mouth dropped open and he swiveled on his feet toward the door. Muldoon flinched. It looked like he was about to draw his weapon; instead he stilled.

Levi walked into the living room all smiles and sunshine. "What's with all the sad faces?" He shifted the tote bag on his shoulder and dropped it to his feet. "Detective," he scowled. "You here to unjustly arrest me again this week? Because really, I could do without another incarceration right now. Today's been about the craziest I've had in a while."

I ran over to Levi and wrapped my arms around his neck. A hefty shudder racked through me and I sobbed out loud.

Levi patted my back. "Chill-lax. It's just takeout. Italian. Now, maybe if it was Greek…"

"You were dead," I whispered.

"What are you talking about? What is she talking about?" he asked over the top of my head. I didn't give anyone a chance to answer as I squeezed tighter.

"Muldoon said you were dead. I knew you couldn't be gone."

"Sweets, I'm right here. Look at me." He pushed me back to arm's length. "I'm fine. You see."

"You're okay? You're really okay?" I kept my hands on my friend, felt his biceps. "You're really okay," I said one final time as I reassured myself. "I told you. I told you he was not dead." I glanced over my shoulder at Muldoon. When I turned my gaze back to Levi, I tightened my grip until his eyes widened and he barked out a quick, "Ow."

"You have a lot of nerve, mister." I balled up my fist and punched him as hard as I could. "I've been calling you all damn day. Not once did you call me back."

"My phone died and I forgot my—"

"And you introduce my dad to a bookie. Don't think I've forgotten about that." I stood up on my tiptoes and got right in his face. "I don't know which thing I am madder at you for. Oh! And don't get me started on the humongous crate of Bassani bags I found at your property. Though they're pretty crispy now—so I can't be mad about that."

I lost all my steam. I'd properly chewed out Levi and then remembered someone hadn't been so lucky.

"I think I need a minute." I stumbled over to the sofa and plopped down, my breath coming in and out just as heavy as when Muldoon dropped the news of the house fire.

Levi worked his mouth like a fish out of water for all of thirty seconds before he finally asked, "Muldoon, care to explain?"

"Do you own a property off of Sagebrush?" Muldoon pulled out the little notebook I've seen him with almost every time we've been together.

"I did, well I still do. I was in the process of selling it up until about a week and a half ago." Levi came over in front of me and squatted until we were nose to nose. All his usual flamboyance was gone and the man who'd cried on my shoulder when he lost his mom was there. There was no snark or pretense. Just raw concern and emotion. "Why do you ask, Detective?"

"It burned down. One of the city clerks went in to see who it belonged to. Through tax records. Since it was unoccupied. You're listed."

"Yes. I sold it. But it fell through." Levi ran his hand down my cheek. "Breathe. Everything is going to be fine." His words were soft and soothing. "Deep breath in and then back out. You're okay. Why did you think I was dead?" he asked finally.

"They found a body in the rubble of the fire."

Levi's eyes rounded. "Nuh-uh."

Muldoon stepped into my periphery and held a little bitty notebook, his pen poised for the information. "Who were you selling it to?"

"Arnie Showalter."

"A CRATE OF Bassani handbags?" Levi poured wine into his glass, then held the bottle over mine but I waved him off. I'd had enough alcohol to last awhile.

I nodded and shifted my hand on Levi's. I wasn't ready to let go of my friend. "Right in the middle of the garage. There had to be thirty or more bags in there. You didn't order them?"

"I told you the other day, I wouldn't know the first thing about those. I haven't had any deliveries there in weeks. Not since Arnie and I worked out the sales con-tract. Arnie's check didn't clear and I never had a chance to talk to him about it, because you know…"

Right after Levi revealed who he'd been selling the house to, Muldoon and Kellen left. Muldoon had to let the investigators know that the body wasn't Levi's and Kellen was going to do whatever it was he did to uncover more information. Dad had gone back to his room, our truce a little wobbly but in place.

"What did the crate look like?"

I frowned at Levi. "Wooden. Rectangular. I don't know, crate-ish."

"Did it have a bill of lading on the side?"

"I took a picture of the label on the side." I found it in my phone, but it was just a white blob with a wooden background. All the pictures were blurry and indistinguishable. "The light from the kitchen wasn't that bright; the flash was too much for it, I guess."

"Light? There shouldn't be any power to the place. The wiring wasn't even close to done."

"Maybe Arnie got it going." I ran my finger over a scratch on the tabletop. "Did Arnie have access to the house yet? Could he have gotten in and started working or something? Already had deliveries coming in?"

"He shouldn't have." Levi picked at the wine bottle label.

I rolled my hand in a prompt. "But he could have?"

"I guess so."

"I told you not to use your birthday for the lockboxes." I leaned back in my chair and crossed my ankles.

"Nobody—"

"Knows your code. So you've said, but someone— several someones—got into one of your houses tonight."

"Including you."

My eyes widened and a spurt of anger balled up in my chest. "I didn't do it."

"I didn't say you did." Levi said the words slowly and in an even tone. He held up the wine bottle again and offered the remainder.

I moved my glass away. "Sorry. This has been a megamessed up day. And frankly between the two of us, we've had many messed-up days to compare it with."

He sighed. "I know." He started to dump the rest of the wine into his glass, but instead shoved the bottle to the other side of the table. "Wonder who was in the house when it burned." He shook himself. "Horrible way to die."

"I knew it wasn't you," I mumbled.

"We should drive over there and see what we can see."

"They won't let us anywhere near the house. Not with an investigation going on."

"You can get your boyfriend to sneak us in."

I sat up straighter. "One, he's not my boyfriend. And two, there's no way he'd compromise a scene. Have you learned nothing of the man?"

"We could dress up."

"As what? Firemen? That's the only way we'll get near the place." I rolled my eyes. "And I'm pretty sure that's illegal."

Levi lifted one shoulder in a shrug. "Just a thought." He extricated his hand from mine. "Sorry, sweets, but it's losing its feeling." He shook his hand.

"Do you think Arnie was running a side business? Starting a boutique? Yesterday before all this went down, I spoke with Marlon and Barry. Both of them remember seeing crates at your other properties. One the morning of…you know…" I let him fill in the blank for himself. "What if they all had handbags in them?"

"Arnie running a boutique? That man's idea of fashion was wearing suspenders and a belt." He made a gagging noise.

I thrummed my fingers on the tabletop, then wiggled my foot as a bone-weary exhaustion pulled me down. "It makes sense." I frowned. "In a weird sort of way." Grit rubbed the backs of my eyelids every time I blinked and I sank lower in my chair. "Why'd you sell him the property?"

"He made me an offer."

"You couldn't refuse."

Levi rolled his eyes. "It was a decent profit and I wasn't in love with that one."

I yawned. "I'm exhausted. People telling you your friend is dead takes a lot out of you."

"I don't ever want to find out."

We stood and I walked him to the front door. "Oh, hey, you remember when you made me promise to delete those pictures off my phone? No questions asked."

"Yeah, that worked out well."

"Do me a favor and delete the messages from me on your voicemail."

"Hey, you're so much less green than you were last night." I cupped Paige's chin and kissed the tip of her nose. "Green was not your color. You're much cuter looking just like you."

"Ugh, stop. You have to say that."

"No, I don't. And I don't lie."

Paige stepped back from me and glanced at the ceiling.

"What are you doing?"

"Waiting for the lightning to come zap you." A huge smile crossed her face.

"Cute and sassy." I tweaked her chin. "We don't want to keep your dad waiting."

"He could have come to pick me up."

"I was headed out anyway. I thought I'd save him a trip."

"You're such a pushover."

I pulled up short. "I beg your pardon."

Paige took a step back. "It's what Naomi says. Any time Daddy doesn't want to do something, she says to hand it off to you because you never say no."

There are so many reasons why I don't like this woman. Why does she feel the need to constantly give me more ammo? "They talk a lot in front of you and don't even know you're listening." It was a statement, not a question. Colin always underestimated our daughter's power of observation.

"Mmm-hmm." Paige nodded and pulled a book from her backpack. Almost as an aside she added, "She thinks you're a rube."

"Really now?" I fumed all the way to Colin's house. That skank had a lot of nerve calling me a pushover and a rube. Much less in front of my daughter. "At least I'm not some stupid hussy."

"What?" Paige looked up from the book in her lap.

"Nothing." I pulled into the driveway at Colin's town-home. "Ready?"

"Yep." She scooped up her backpack and tucked the book inside before she got out. She frowned when I got out of the car, too. "You don't have to walk me to the door."

I pasted on a sickly sweet smile. "I don't mind."

"Mom…"

"You called me Mom again. I like that so much better than when you call me Celeste."

"It's your name."

"True, but I much prefer Mom."

"Stop changing the subject." She skipped ahead of me a couple of steps. "Why are you walking me to the house?" She stopped a few feet before we reached the door, blocked me from getting any closer.

I adjusted the Bassani handbag on my shoulder. "I always walk you to the door. Sometimes." Okay, I never walked her to the door. More often than not, Colin picked her up and dropped her off. I reached around her and knocked.

"I have a key. I can just walk right on—"

"Celeste?" Colin opened the door before Paige could even dig her key from her backpack. "What are you...?"

"She's being weird again." Paige gave an exaggerated huff and pushed past Colin into the house. And stopped.

"Her tummy is doing better, but I'd lay off the sweets today. My dad filled her up with enough to last a month." I kind of peered around the pair of them, trying to see if she was here—call me a pushover. How many times had I helped her out of a bind?

Okay, once. Once, I tried to help her and it ended up getting me and Colin on the PPD's most-wanted list for about ten minutes.

I wanted to say something to him about watching what he said in front of Paige, but what kind of example would I make if I did it with her standing right there. "So, Sunday night?" Run, on off, Paige, I mentally said. Apparently my parental telepathy was on the fritz though because the sweet child just stood there staring at me over the top of her glasses. Like she knew I was going to yell at her dad. Hmm. Maybe the telepathy wasn't on the fritz after all.

Colin nodded and narrowed his eyes slightly. "Yep. The usual time."

"I heard the doorbell, who's... Oh. It's you." Naomi turned her uppity nose even higher up.

"Celeste was just dropping Paige off."

"Hmph. Well, thanks for dropping our—"

"Our?" Oh, no, she didn't.

Colin must have seen the murder-lust in my eyes because he stepped closer to me and headed me back toward the driveway. "Alrighty."

"I never would have expected you to carry a fake bag," Naomi yelled over Colin's shoulder.

I dug my feet in and stopped. "What?"

"Your Bassani, it's a counterfeit." Naomi sounded a wee bit too gleeful as she tossed that out there. "Where did you get it? It's a pretty good fake."

My mouth worked open and closed but not much more than squeaks came out. I didn't want to engage her any further, but I couldn't stop myself from asking, "How do you know?" Worse, it came out all whiny and pathetic.

"The edges don't match up." She pointed to the pattern on the side of the bag as she walked up to me and Colin. "The lining should be dark red, almost maroon, but it's more of a fuchsia. And—" she reached out and flicked the spot where the handle was attached to the body of the bag "—the hardware should be open screws in shiny gold, not flatheads in brass."

"And you can tell all that from groping my bag once at a dimly lit party the other night?"

"I looked it up." She seemed so smug and pleased. And I'd swear she wanted to add, "So there," on the end of it. Well, that's what I would have said. To Naomi.

"Yeah, well." Great, I'd turned into a fourteen-year-old with my comebacks. *You're stupid and ugly* hung on the tip of my tongue. Loosely.

"Look at the time." Colin clapped his hands together. "Didn't you say you had to be somewhere?" He looked pointedly to me.

I hadn't said squat to Colin about my plans but I did in fact have places to be, people to see. And once Naomi had dropped that bomb on me, I had some additional research to do. "Tell Paige bye for me." I turned quickly on my heel and headed straight back to my car without ever once looking back. Even from so far away, I could feel Naomi's condescending glare boring a hole in the middle of my back. She took so much pleasure in telling me she thought the bag was counterfeit.

I had my cell in my hand before I even got the car out of reverse.

"Muldoon? Hang on a sec." I shifted the car to Drive and set the phone in the cup holder. "Hey."

"Celeste? Is everything okay?"

"Yeah." I frowned at the phone then quickly shifted my gaze back to the road.

"Are you driving?"

"Maybe." He'd lectured me more than once on talking while driving. He seemed to think I was easily distractible. "It's the hands-free Bluetooth thingie."

I could almost hear him shaking his head.

"Listen, I have a question for you."

"Uh-oh."

"Be nice." I smiled and made a left going toward the playhouse. "The fire yesterday, did you ever find out if there was a crate of handbags there?"

"No."

"No, you didn't find out, or no, there wasn't anything there?"

"No, you're not looking into this, Celeste." He huffed out a sigh. "Do you remember last year at all?"

"Of course I do. What kind of question is that?" I switched lanes as I neared the playhouse. "You can't keep throwing that out any time you think I'm doing something."

"I can and I will. Especially if it keeps you safe."

"Safe from what? A house burning down?"

"The victim was killed before the fire." The way he

said it, I didn't think he wanted to tell me, but was using it as a warning.

"Hmm." I didn't really know what else to say to that. *That's too bad* seemed irrelevant since there was also a fire. Dead was dead no matter how you got there.

"I talked to the fire marshal. Marshal Woodard will want to speak to you since you were there not too long before the fire started."

"He doesn't think I set it, does he?" That would not be a pleasant experience. Been there, done that.

"She. And I don't know exactly what she thinks so don't screw around with this one."

Man, he doesn't trust me for spit. Could be why he'd backed out of our last date and was playing coyer than coy lately.

"I'll call her myself, set up the appointment and be completely—"

"—sane."

"Wow, rude. But sure, sane. If you'll tell me, crate or no crate."

There was silence on the other end of the line, all but his breathing. Otherwise, I might have thought he'd hung up.

"There was nothing large enough to be a crate, much less a full crate. Call the fire marshal and stay out of trouble."

"When do I get in trouble?"

NINE

"ARE YOU SURE you actually saw a crate?"

"Levi, I was bent over the edge of it digging all the way to the bottom. I touched every single one of those bags. And I was pissed at you with each new bag, so trust me, it was real." I was sitting in the playhouse parking lot. I'd called Levi as soon as I got off the phone with Muldoon.

"I think you're just hallucinating. It's like the time you saw Harrison Ford at the mall."

"I did see him. I don't know why you won't believe me." I'll swear to it until the day I meet him in person and can ask what he was doing out at the Peytonville Mall—well, I know what he was doing. He was buying froyo, with sprinkles. "Focus, man. Between when I was there and when the fire started, someone took out an entire crate of bags. And…" My phone beeped telling me I'd gotten a text. Muldoon, giving me the name and number of the PFD fire marshal. "Kate Woodard."

"Who's Kate? And what and?"

"The fire marshal. Never mind her. And…they might be fake."

"Fake?"

"Yeah. I haven't had a chance to look them up yet, but Naomi—" I snarled her name "—said she looked them up online and pointed out all the fake-ness things of mine. I hate to say it, but I think she's right."

"Why, because someone doesn't just leave a two-thousand-dollar bag lying around a house under construction?"

"No, because I would never get lucky enough to own a two-thousand-dollar handbag." I tugged at my ponytail. "I want to see what I can find out about this bag. Maybe it'll give us a clue of what's going on. And if we can find that warehouse…"

"What warehouse?"

"Arnie's warehouse. Didn't I tell you?" When would I have told him? Between him being in jail and me freaking out over his not-dead body, I'd completely forgotten about it. "Barry told me about it." I repeated what his lumber supplier had told me the other day when we'd spoken. "He said Arnie was apologetic and nice even. Which made it all stand out to him."

"Don't even go there. Physically or metaphorically."

It might not matter. It was going to be hard to find with little to no info to go on. Between the distorted picture I snapped of the label and no one else who'd heard of the warehouse… I did have a wee bit of information. I could just make out the number—4481—and that it was in fact a Peytonville address, but nothing else. "I'm just saying."

"Me, too."

"Sure, fine, whatever." We both knew I wasn't going to let it go. By agreeing with him, it gave him a window of delusion in which to relax. Briefly. "Come by the house tonight. You, me and Dad can start up a card game or something. I think he's getting bored."

"This is Celeste Eagan calling for Kate Woodard." I was sitting at my desk inside the playhouse. I'd already done several internet searches and damn if stupid Naomi wasn't right about the bag. When I'd gotten as far as I could online, I decided to take a break and do the dutiful thing and call the fire marshal. I had to keep at least one promise I'd made to Muldoon, because staying away from the handbag mystery wasn't going to happen.

"Mrs. Eagan. Oh, yes, Shaw said you'd be calling." Shaw?

She was on a first-name basis with the man? I'd dated him and I still called him Muldoon. And very rare were the special occasions I did say his first name—most of those times it seemed like my life was in jeopardy when that happened.

"Do I need to come in and speak to you or can you take my statement over the phone?"

"The phone is fine for now. If I have any follow-up questions we may need to meet in person." She paused and I could hear some papers rustling.

"Can you go over your timeframe going to the house and up until you left?" she asked.

I described getting to the house and opening the lockbox for the key.

"You often let yourself into someone else's property?"

"No." Yes. I did. I frowned. "My friend Levi is a special circumstance that… I don't need to explain to you. And I was looking for him. So yes, I let myself into the property."

"Even though he was in the process of selling it?"

"I didn't realize that. The lockbox still had his combination on it." What the hell… "I saw a light on there and thought it was him."

"What light? Where?"

"It was in the kitchen." I toyed with the stack of headshots on the corner of my desk. There was a young actress—Brailee Helprin—who wasn't quite ready yet for a leading role, but had major potential. If I brought her on, I'd have to mentor her. Was I ready for that?

"Which kitchen light?" Kate Woodard asked.

It took me a minute to remember what we were talking about. I was being pulled in so many directions, I couldn't keep everything straight anymore. "The one over the sink. There was no one in the house that I saw."

"And then you left?"

After shoving my head inside a crate of handbags? "Yes."

"What time was this?"

"I don't know, seven thirty, eight. I went straight to the grocery store afterward. The receipt might be time-stamped." I said it a little sarcastically. Did she really want my store receipt?

"I'll need a copy of that."

Apparently yes. She had all the info I had, now I needed some in return. "What time did the fire start?"

I'd swear there was laughter in her voice when she said, "I can't give out that kind of information."

"Even to me?"

"What's that supposed to mean?" Kate Woodard seemed truly stymied by my question.

"I was out there that night and if you need to know specifically where I was I need to know when the fire was so I can give you the right info. Right?" Was she going to buy that? Sure, I just wanted more information on the fire, but as the reasoning rolled off my tongue it made total sense.

"I'll just need a copy of your store receipt and we can work from there."

"Sure, sure. I'll make a copy and get it to Shaw—" two of us could play the drop-the-first-name bit "—later today." I was heavily implying that I knew where to find the detective on a Saturday. Which, knowing him, was at the police station—he never seemed to leave the place. "Sound good?"

There was a long pause then she finally said, "Okay."

"Super." I rolled my eyes. "Please let me know if you need anything else. Bye now." I stabbed the little red icon on my phone before she could say another word.

What did it say that I was getting old hat at being interviewed by authorities? Hell, I was a little ballsy even.

"Oh, yes, Shaw said you'd be calling." No, I was not above mocking the woman. Was it horrible that I hoped she had a hump on her back and smelled like a raccoon? Eh, I wiped her from my mind. I so didn't need to court karma to come bite me on the ass any more than it already had in the last six months.

I stood and stretched my back as I weighed what I knew.

Arnie Showalter turned up dead at one of Levi's properties.

A potentially counterfeit Bassani handbag was found at said property—which I never did tell Muldoon about—oops. But in my defense I didn't know that it was possibly counterfeit—though real or fake I guess I should have told him what I found. Especially now. I needed to remember to do that.

A fire and a second body was found at another of Levi's properties, which also had a collection of the Bassani bags—which one could assume were also counterfeits—and was connected to Arnie, too.

And the crates of unknown wares that were delivered to Levi's properties. More Bassani?

That was all I had. It was a lot of little pieces, but out of specific context I didn't know how any of it tied together—other than good old Arnie. And I knew for damn sure Levi didn't have anything to do with it. I huffed out a breath and flopped down onto the sofa against the back wall. My brain was weary. I needed caffeine. My body was also weary, I wanted nothing more than to snuggle into the cushions for a quick cat-nap. But a nap wouldn't uncover anything to help Levi and me out of our bind.

I scrolled through my call log until I found Guy Bueller's number. The man answered after the first ring.

"Mr. Bueller, Guy, it's Celeste."

"I was hoping you'd call. I may have gotten a lead."

"Wow, I did, too."

"What did you find out?" he all but demanded. A moment later he apologized. "It's exciting to gain some traction."

Traction? Whatever.

"Arnie had a warehouse. I'm not a hundred percent sure of all the details, but someone I spoke to said he mentioned it."

"Do you know where it is?" Bueller was a little breathless.

"I'm still trying to figure that out."

"Did you tell the police?"

"Not yet. I don't really have anything to tell them." I leaned my head against the back of the sofa. "You had news, too?"

"Oh, nothing as interesting as yours. I have someone buzzing in on my other line. I'll check back in with you soon?"

"Sure." I sat staring at my phone slightly bewildered. Was that weird or was fatigue making me overanalyze things? "Probably fatigue." I lowered my hand and cell to my lap and sank farther into the soft leather. "Just a few minutes."

No sooner had I closed my eyes than my cell phone went off. I debated just ignoring it altogether. Ten minutes of a snooze would revive me enough to start going over the headshots Annabelle wanted me to assess. It vibrated again. I was a glutton—what could I say? I peeled one eye open and glanced at the screen. Dad's number popped up.

"Hey, Dad."

"Baby girl, I kind of had an accident."

I PULLED INTO the closest slot to the bakery as I could—six spaces down. "Busy day," I mumbled as I turned the engine off. I didn't think I'd ever be back at the bakery/bookmaking establishment. But here I was thanks to my dad backing his car into another car, creating a little fender bender—quite literally. The dent in Dad's fender bent it enough that his car was undrivable.

"I wonder if I would have found out how you spent your day if you hadn't needed a ride," I said as I approached him and the tow truck driver.

"When did you get so judgy?"

"Judgy?"

"You were such an easygoing child. Open-minded."

"I'm not closed-minded. I just don't care for you hanging around a place like…this." I waved my hand toward the bakery.

"You have something against kolachkes?" Dad said it with such a straight face that I couldn't help the guffaw—yes, guffaw—that came out. I sounded like a damn goose honking, which made my dad laugh.

Tears were running down my face by the time I came up for air. "Dad, what am I going to do with you?"

"Give me a hug?" He held his arms open.

I nodded, getting all teary-eyed for a completely different reason. I hugged my dad until the tow truck driver cleared his throat.

"Got it loaded up, sir."

Dad turned to deal with his car.

"I'm going to run in there a sec." I motioned toward the bakery. Since I was there…

Paul was at the counter. "Afternoon, ma'am."

"What's good today, Paul?"

"Kolachkes fresh out of the oven." He waved to the case where the cookies sat.

I stopped at the cakes. My stomach growled. Between handbag hunting and talking to everyone and their brother about the fire, I'd lost track of time. I set my hand over my stomach and glanced up at Paul to see if he'd heard. Judging by the upturned eyebrow, I'd guess yes.

"Had a busy morning, missed lunch."

"We have a kielbasa sandwich."

"Yes, please." My stomach growled again in agreement.

"Mrs. Eagan."

My shoulders stiffened slightly, but I pasted on a smile as I turned. "Mr. Grady."

"Gabriel."

"If it's Gabriel, then you should call me Celeste."

"I wondered if you'd be out to collect your father."

"Yep. That's me, collector of stranded fathers."

"Ma'am." Paul set the sandwich on the countertop.

"Thank you." I scooped up my lunch and would have devoured it had I been alone, but I felt weird scarfing it down with Gabriel standing there watching me.

"Don't let me interrupt you." He stepped aside and motioned to the table.

I nodded. "Can I get the chocolate raspberry cake, too. To go. I'm not that hungry." I believe I blushed. I couldn't remember the last time I'd blushed. I slid into the little booth, then bit into the sandwich.

"Mind if I join you?"

Not wanting to talk with my mouth full, I waved at the empty seat across from me. Who was I to tell him no? It was his bakery. A bakery that was suspiciously empty considering how many cars were parked out front.

Since I had company, and it would be rude to eat and bolt, I asked Paul for a bottle of water when I swallowed the enormous bite I'd taken. I set my purse on the seat next to me. Gabriel was looking oddly at it, so I asked, "What's so interesting? You know Bassani?"

"Hmm?" His attention shifted back up to me. "There're a bunch of those floating around, huh?"

Interesting. "What do you mean?"

"I had several handbags offered to me to settle a patron's balance."

"Arnie Showalter?"

"You are more impressive than I anticipated."

Yikes. Was that good or bad?

"So he was a patron of yours? Tell me more."

FIFTEEN PAST SEVEN, Levi arrived at my house. He was not alone.

"Kellen, what are you doing here?"

"Levi said there might be a card game tonight. I asked if I could tag along."

"Absolutely. The more the merrier." I waved him into the dining room, where Dad had decorated the table with a green tablecloth. He'd set up the small folding table in the corner with snacks. "We were just going to play for fun but we could always make it more interesting."

"Like?" He tucked his arm over my shoulder and gave me a quick hug.

"Play for sources." I nudged him in the ribs. Several times last year, when he'd been reporting on all the trouble I'd gotten myself into, I'd asked who his sources were. Of course, he never once told me. Journalistic integrity and all that. But as I was too curious for my own good, I continued to badger him about who they might be.

"How about we stick to good old currency." He patted his wallet.

"Sure, if you just want money. I do have one question, though." I leaned against the table next to the chair he was about to sit in. "How did you and Levi run into each other today?" The two were not necessarily friends as far as I knew, so it was curious. "Hmm?"

Kellen opened his mouth to answer just as the doorbell rang.

I narrowed my gaze. "This is not over." I'd like to think I'd left him quaking in his loafers as I headed to the door, but the man was not the least bit intimidated by my inquisitive nature. "Muldoon. Hey. What are you doing here?"

"Can't a man just stop by to see a friend?"

"Not when he has his detective face on."

"No detective face. This is my card face."

"What?"

"Levi called me. Told me there was a game going on tonight." He lifted a six pack of beer in one hand and a bag of munchies in the other. "I think he was trying to make up for the fact he overlooked me for your birthday."

Heat crawled across my cheeks. He'd gotten plenty of me on my birthday. No invite necessary.

"Ahem. Are you going to let the man in or keep him standing on the porch?"

"Sorry, sorry." I moved back away from the door.

"Let's do this." Dad walked into the room wearing a blue see-through visor.

We all took our seats around the green felt tabletop. I lifted a cup of coffee to my mouth, peered at each man one at a time, then said, "Okay, boys, who wants to go first?" I handed Muldoon the deck of cards. "Shuffle this for me, will you, please." I batted my eyelashes at him.

He coughed in the process of drinking his beer. "Why do I feel like one of her minions?"

Levi and Kellen both laughed. Dad dropped his head with a quick shake.

"Bwahaha." I saluted him with my pink Queen of the Smartasses mug.

Kellen raised his hand. "I'll go." He leaned his elbows on the table and twined his fingers together. "I spoke with the fire marshal. They've had a string of fires set similarly across the metroplex. This was the first one in Peytonville, but the point of origin is similar as well as the time of day and time of the month. However, the one difference is the house size." He looked at Muldoon.

"The other dwellings were multi-story buildings. This was a one-story ranch house." Muldoon set his beer down and shuffled the cards. "The marshal—"

"Kate Woodard," I all but snarled under my breath. Levi kicked my shin and shushed me.

"—thinks someone is copycatting the Mid-cities Arsonist."

"To cover up the murder," Kellen finished.

Levi leaned back in his chair. "I can't believe y'all thought that was me."

Turned out, the charred dead body in the fire was a woman. If Muldoon had waited just a couple of hours, I might not have ever unnecessarily worried—even though I'd known it wasn't Levi. Her identity was still unknown, however.

"Was that all you had, Muldoon?" I divvied out the poker chips.

He hesitated. "Yes."

"Uh-huh. Levi's got nothing or he'd have spilled the moment he walked in the door." I stacked and unstacked the chips in front of me. "I learned something."

All the men paused in various states of readying their small corner of the poker table—except Dad. "Excuse me just a minute." Dad pushed his chair back but before he could stand, Levi clamped his hand down on Dad's arm.

"Gil, what did you do?"

Dad cleared his throat and settled back into his chair. "I didn't do anything."

"That's true." I nodded. "Ish."

Muldoon snorted as the cards fluttered from his fingers into one pile. "Ish?"

"Thanks." I snagged the deck of cards from Muldoon. "Toss in your blinds, gentlemen." Kellen and Muldoon tossed in the appropriate chip designation. "Really,

Levi?" I waved the cards at him. "The cards with naked dudes?"

Levi raised his hands in mock-innocence. "You asked me to bring the cards. That's what I had." He snapped his fingers in my face. "Stop changing the subject. What did Gil ish-do?"

"Somebody was just out around town minding their own business. Until someone backed into his car. At a certain bakery. And he needed a ride home." I narrowed my gaze at Levi. He might have gotten off the hook—when everyone else thought he was dead—but he was still on my shitlist. I dealt the first card to Dad sitting to my left. "Dad called the rental company about a new car, thought he was in the clear, but they were backed up so he had to call me to come get him. At the bakery. Did I mention he was at the bakery?"

"I bought a chocolate raspberry cake." Dad pointed to the folding table with all the food on it.

"After I showed up. Which I picked out. There're some cookies, too." I dealt the last card and glared at Dad. "While Dad and the very nice gentleman who was supposedly out picking up his wife's dry cleaning exchanged insurance information, I was entertained by the bakery's owner."

Muldoon and Kellen stiffened. Levi sank lower in his chair. As low as the padded seat would allow.

"Gabriel's a lovely man—he told me to call him Gabriel, by the way. Quite entertaining. He told me the story of his grandfather getting out of Poland just before the war started." I leaned forward and set my elbows on the table and looked over the cards in my hand. "How once he settled in Chicago, he started his own bakery.

And other venues." I waved. "I won't bore you with the details of that."

Muldoon's dark eyebrow arched upward.

"However, he did mention something, almost in passing, that I found interesting." I took a long swig of my coffee—doctored with raspberry and chocolate to accompany the cake.

"What did he tell you?" Muldoon's clipped tone was highlighted by the glower on his face.

"Bets, gentlemen." Everyone tossed in a chip. No one seemed to be into the game. I discarded the next card and dealt the flop. The three cards lying faceup on the table did little to help what I had in my hand.

"Celeste." Muldoon covered my hand as I started shuffling my chips again. "Finish. Please."

"Impatient much? Seems Arnie Showalter was a… patron of his. He—how'd he put it?" I tapped my chin. "Arnie had extended his line of credit until he owed enough flour to bake a kolachke the size of the Cowboys' stadium. I don't know the going rate for flour, but I'm guessing that's a lot."

Levi's cheeks reddened as another round of bets—if you could call everyone just tossing a chip without really paying attention bets—circled the table.

"I'm guessing by the look on your face you knew that." I tossed out the burn card and dealt the turn. At least it gave me a pair—of threes. "At first I was a little shocked. But then I had to wonder how you knew Gabriel, Levi. To introduce my dad to him. Then I started wondering who this friend of yours was who paid your super high bail. So I asked."

Levi blanched. Muldoon cleared his throat—I'm

guessing he already knew this, too. Dad and Kellen kept their gazes intently glued to their cards.

"Turns out it was Gabriel. That's a pretty darn good friend to put up so much bail. But seeing how you're not only a client of his, but he's a client of yours—four houses. You sold the man four houses?" I tsked. "You'd think a friend, a BFF, would tell a girl if they'd sold one person four different properties. Y'all've known each other for going on ten years, he tells me." Yeah, Levi's status on my shitlist was the top slot and maybe even two and three. And considering that Naomi was next in line, it said a lot that he outranked her. "Even more interesting—"

"More interesting?" Muldoon dropped his hand. "How long were you there?"

"Long enough." I rapped my knuckles on the tabletop. "In or out, guys?"

Muldoon folded. Kellen tossed in the minimum. Levi raised it and the rest of us called. I discarded the last burn card and flipped over the river card. This was one of the worst hands I'd had in all the years playing poker with my dad. Kellen folded. Levi put in the minimum, Dad folded. I should have folded, too, but I tossed in a couple of chips. "I raise you twenty."

Levi looked at his cards then back to me, then the cards. He thrummed his fingers on the tabletop and volleyed his gaze again. "Fold."

Was it a pity fold? I'd won a whopping two dollars. "We are still not even." I told him as I scooped up the chips. "Even more interesting," I began again, "he tells me someone tried to pay off Arnie's balance with a crate of counterfeit Bassani handbags."

Levi's gaze shot to mine. "Seriously?"

"Uh-huh. They told Gabriel they were genuine, but he did his research and knew they were fakes."

"Who's Bassani?" Muldoon toyed with the chips in front of him.

Damn. I'd totally forgotten to tell Muldoon about the handbag I'd found at Levi's property.

I tossed my three of hearts onto the three of clubs in the community cards. "Look, guys, you're all sucking at this. We need to get down to business or pack it up. I came here to play."

"You live here." Levi tossed his hand at me.

"So to speak." I gathered up the cards. "Are we going to play?"

"Don't you go changing the subject." Levi leaned back in his chair. "Someone forgot to mention Bassani to the detective here."

On a sigh, I said, "I did." I explained the circumstances of acquiring my new pretty—which he promptly said he'd need to take into custody. Even though I knew it was a fake and part of a double-murder investigation, I wanted to pretend it was real—and mine—for just a short time more, but I relented and retrieved my bag. "Be gentle with her."

Levi snorted and Muldoon looked over the bag. "This thing goes for two grand?"

"Not that one." I reached out to pet it but pulled my hand back. "I may have just solved your case for you."

"How do you figure?"

I lifted one shoulder in a shrug. "You have a lead now that you didn't have earlier." I didn't expect Muldoon to shout Eureka but maybe an atta-girl would have been nice. But the man was going to keep his thoughts on the bag to himself. Whatever.

"Can we play?" I passed the deck to the next dealer. Despite all my yammering on about the lack of attention from the men, my head was on the fire with the mysterious dead woman in the house. The fact that Levi sold it to Showalter only days before his untimely demise… I wasn't sure if one had anything to do with the other, but add in the handbags and it would be an astronomical coincidence if not.

"Who's not paying attention now?" Levi tapped a chip on the table. "Penny for your thoughts. Or a chip." He tossed a red chip at me.

"Sorry. It's nothing."

"Mmm-hmm." He leaned toward Kellen. "Gabriel or Arnie?"

Kellen stacked and restacked his chips. "Methinks both." He snagged his beer, took a sip and set it back down. "Probably trying to work out the connection between the two. And the fire. And the purses."

I sighed. I so liked being talked about like I wasn't there. "I fold. Deal me out the next hand. I'm going to refill the snacks. Anyone need anything from the kitchen?" I got a round of noes and took the half-full bowl of corn chips to the kitchen. For appearance's sake. I dug around in the fridge for something covered in chocolate. I could go grab a slab of the cake, but that would mean walking back out to the guys and I needed a little time to myself. I'd cleared out most of the sweet confections throughout the week. I love my dad, but he'd thrown my world off-kilter and only sugar or liquor helped—and I apparently couldn't hold my liquor very well lately, so that option was out. I found a jar of chocolate sauce in the fridge and spied a package of peanut butter cookies in the cabinet.

"Hmm." I dipped a cookie in the sauce and took a bite.

It wasn't horrible. I finished the cookie as the squeak of a shoe on floor sounded behind me. I shoved the package of cookies back into the cabinet. "I'll be right back out."

"Is everything okay?"

"Muldoon? Hey." I whirled around. He was standing far closer than I expected. I leaned my hip against the counter to gain a little personal space. "Hey."

"You have—" he motioned to his mouth "—something…"

Flames spread across my cheeks. "Busted." I swiped at my mouth, but he shook his head.

"Here." He reached out and dragged his thumb across the corner of my lip.

The flames multiplied and spread down through my chest and to the nether regions. "Thanks." I was a little pissed at how squeaky it came out.

"Sure." He mimicked my stance against the counter, stood hip to hip with me. Without even thinking about it, I leaned my head against his shoulder. I gave myself a moment to just inhale his glorious scent. It was one of the first things I'd ever noticed about him. Musky with a hint of cinnamon coffee—which was weird because I'd never once seen him drink coffee with cinnamon or any flavoring for that matter.

It seemed like it'd been forever since he and I had been so companionable. He was always working, always in cop-mode—which I totally respected. He had an amazing work ethic.

Case in point when he said, "I'm going to have to turn the bag over to Bush. He's going to have questions." Statements like that made him, him. And held quite a bit of his appeal. But it also kept him walled off from me.

"I know."

"You should have told him immediately about it."

"I didn't know it was pertinent. At the time I thought Levi got it for me."

"He'd buy you a two-grand bag?"

"I, uh…" Levi would if he thought it was something I would die without, but until I had the Bassani on my arm, I didn't know I'd fall for something so extravagant. "Maybe not."

"I don't understand how you…" He stopped and shook his head.

I shifted away from him. "It was a fluke."

He sighed. "That's what makes it…worse. It's out of your control."

"I could lock myself up in the house and never leave."

"Would you?" Muldoon smiled over at me. "That'd be great." A round of raucous laughter erupted from the other room. "Are you going to come back out there and play?"

What could have happened in the few minutes since I'd left the room? Then I heard the tail end of what Levi was saying. And I laughed. "Levi telling his jokes again?"

"Yeah." His cheeks reddened slightly. "He's just so…"

"Bawdy?"

"I was going to say full of it." Muldoon flashed a rare toothy grin. It disappeared as quickly as it came.

"Yep. To both." I matched his grin and turned him toward the door. "C'mon, let's go show these boys how to play poker."

TEN

I WOKE WITH a killer headache Sunday morning. On top of not sleeping well.

Muldoon had called Detective Bush about the Bassani bag. Despite being late on a Saturday evening, the detective had immediately driven over. Muldoon transferred custody of the bag—who knew that was a thing for a freaking purse—to Bush, who then promptly questioned me for over an hour.

I should have called Coz but I hadn't done anything wrong. Or at least I hadn't known it was wrong at the time. When Bush was approaching the second-hour mark I was ready to whip out my cell and get Coz to put a stop to it, but the man wrapped up his grilling and left with my Bassani.

To make it worse—if that was even possible—I had a hangover. Not from drinking. I stayed away from alcohol to keep from having a repeat of my birthday. A sugar hangover. Once we cut into that chocolate raspberry cake, I ate almost half the thing…by myself. It was magnificent. Were the bakery not a front for gambling and God knows what else, I'd recommend it to every chocolate-loving person I knew. And then invite myself over for coffee and cake. I mean, really, it would be the least they could do after I introduced them to such a delicacy. Right?

I tried to nestle back into the quilt but the lure of coffee was stronger than the warm-snuggly of my bed.

Instead of getting some more Zs, I donned my robe and headed to the kitchen. I was surprised Dad had gotten up before me; I'd bowed out of the game somewhere south of midnight, but the guys were going strong. There was no telling what time they'd called it quits.

I was scrubbing my fingers through my hair and yawning when I came into the bright kitchen. I pulled up short, my mouth still gaping open, at the sight of the man at the counter. "Muldoon? What are you...? Did you guys play through the night?"

Muldoon turned from the counter with a steaming cup of coffee in his hand and smiled sheepishly. Dark circles ringed under his eyes. "Yeah. I hope we didn't keep you awake."

"Didn't even know y'all were still here."

"Good." He took a tentative sip of coffee. "I just need some coffee so I can drag my ass home."

"Go sit while you drink it." I nudged him toward the kitchen chairs. "You look like you're gonna keel over." I pulled my robe a wee bit tighter, self-conscious about the fact that he kept dropping his gaze down to my bedclothes and back up again. It wasn't like he hadn't seen me in PJs before. One of the first times he interviewed me, in fact, he'd woken me at the ass-crack of dawn and got a gander of my pink polka-dot nightie. But he hadn't seen me in PJs since then. Okay, he had seen me naked once, but that was sort of by accident and we'd never spoken of it again, so I would continue to pretend that it never actually happened.

"Can I make you something to eat?" I pulled the frying pan from the cabinet and set it on the stove. "Bacon and eggs?"

"You don't have to—"

"I have to eat, too, so it's no trouble making a little bit more." I flashed him a quick smile. "Over easy? Sunny-side up?"

Muldoon took a sip of his coffee. His gaze never wavered from mine over the rim of the mug. I should be intimidated by the intense look on his face but truth be told, it got the warm and fuzzies stirring every time. When he finally set his cup down he said, "Sunny-side up. Please."

"Coming right up." I sucked at making eggs. Regardless of how I started out, they almost always ended up scrambled. I don't know why I offered. But with Muldoon sitting in my kitchen, I felt so domestic. And I hadn't felt like that in years. I flitted around the kitchen like I knew what I was doing. Maybe in his poker-induced stupor he wouldn't notice if I burned the edges of the eggs. "How much did you take them for?"

"What makes you think I won?"

I chuckled. "Had Dad or Levi been winning, y'all'd have called it a night hours ago. The only thing to keep pushing them until dawn is the chance to win their money back."

Muldoon's laughter rumbled from across the room. "Let's just say I'll be buying my mom a really nice birthday present."

I glanced back at him. "Your mom's birthday's coming up?" I'd only met the woman once. She was supersweet and the kind of mom who could bring up six kids and have them all turn out to be well-adjusted adults. I want to be her when I grow up.

"Next month. She pretends she doesn't want to make a big deal out of it, but she'd be devastated if we didn't fuss over her." He flashed a quick cheeky grin, then drained the rest of his coffee. "Would you like me to fix you a cup while I'm refilling?"

"Sure."

He opened the cabinet with the mugs and pulled down my World's Best Mom mug.

"Cream and sugar, please."

He added a couple of spoonfuls of sugar and a dollop of cream to my mug and set it beside me on the counter. "How's Paige feeling?"

"Better. She's at Colin's."

"I figured. She seems like the type of kid who could have taken all of us."

"Easily." Which was more than I could say for the damn eggs. I stuck a couple of pieces of bread into the toaster, then fought with the pan, trying to get the spatula under the egg, but it was sticking like a sonofabitch.

"I haven't played cards in a while." He scratched at his tousled hair. "Probably when I watched Darcy's boys last summer." Darcy was number three in the Muldoon clan. I'd met her at his family's restaurant when I met his mom. As many times as he'd interacted with Levi, Paige and even my ex—that's as weird as it sounds, yes—I didn't know his family that well. Hell, I'd only met his siblings once each and never at the same time. I shuddered. Imagine, all those Muldoons at once.

I plated the eggs and scrunched my nose up when I handed him the first plate. "Sorry. They're kind of more like runny-side up."

"Looks great. Do you have any ketchup?"

The toast popped up. I handed him both slices, then

grabbed the butter and the ketchup from the fridge. I curled up my lips and handed him the bottle. "All I can say is ew." I settled in across the table from him with my eggs and coffee. We ate in silence for a little while.

"Don't knock it 'til you try it."

"I'll pass, thanks." I toyed with the last bite of egg on the end of my fork. "Did my dad talk to you?"

"About?"

"Anything." I dropped my fork back to my plate. "He hasn't really given me details about why he's here. Or what's going on with him and my mom."

"And you think he'd talk to me?" Muldoon shoved half a slice of toast into his mouth.

"Maybe? Guys talk. I thought maybe he'd be more willing to talk to you or Levi than to tell me what's what."

Muldoon chewed for a long moment. When he swallowed he said, "We're not women. We don't just put our feelings out there to dissect." He swiped the other half of the toast across the plate and sopped up some of the egg yolk I hadn't managed to cook the hell out of. "You want me to ask him—"

"No." I got up and put my plate in the sink. "Thank you, but no. If he's not wanting to talk about it, I don't have any room to pry." When I turned around, I leaned my hip against the sink. Muldoon sat with his eyes wide and his toast stopped just before his mouth. "What?"

He shook his head. "I never thought I'd hear you say you shouldn't pry into something."

"Har-har." I crinkled my nose at him. "Finish your breakfast."

"Yes, ma'am." He ate every last bite, ketchup and all. Even when Colin and I were married, he never ate all of anything I made. Not that I even needed to be thinking of the detective that way. "Can I get you anything else?"

"No, this was perfect." He stood and put his plate in the sink with mine. It surprised me every time.

I snorted.

"What?"

"I didn't know guys knew how to clean up after themselves." I glanced at my reflection in the refrigerator. "Gaw, I can't believe… I look like hell." I started to move but Muldoon caught my sleeve.

"No, you don't." He ran his thumb over the soft chenille. "You and your affinity for pink."

"It's my thing." I shrugged.

"Thank you for breakfast." He leaned in close. When I thought he was going to give me a full-on lip smacker, he settled in for a chaste peck on the cheek. Even still, chills shot straight down to my fuzzy-slipper-covered toes. Even Fuzz and Sherbet—that's what I called my bunny slippers; yes, they have names—quivered with the thrill of it.

He leaned back and peered at me. "What do you say—" He stopped abruptly.

I wanted to scream. Always interrupted. Grr. A girl could not catch a break.

He grabbed at his hip to snap up his cell. I hadn't even noticed the darn thing going off.

"Muldoon?" Levi came into the kitchen. "There's a breaking news story. Hey, sweets, you're up."

I frowned and pushed away from the counter. "What breaking news?"

"The body has been identified," Levi and Muldoon said at the same time. Both men stood wide-eyed.

"Wh-who is it?"

"Mandy Crenshaw," Muldoon provided.

I frowned. "Who's she?"

Levi cleared his throat. "Arnie Showalter's girlfriend."

LEVI AND I went through his contacts most of Sunday morning and on into the afternoon. It was one thing for Arnie to die and Levi to be semi/sort of framed for it, but to have the dead man's girlfriend die as well...again on one of Levi's properties...

"Are you being targeted?"

Levi shrugged. "Why?" He dialed a number for one last contact.

"Maybe to do with the partnership you and Arnie were thinking about."

"I wasn't that close to even considering it. Hell, I'd all but said no. That's when he made the offer on the Sagebrush house."

"Who is your next biggest competitor?"

"No one. Everyone else around here is small-time." He held up his hand to stop my questions when the person answered on the other end of the phone.

"Jojo. It's Levi... Yeah, I heard."

I doodled on the notepad in front of me as I listened to his end of the conversation.

"I haven't spoken to Mandy in a while... Really." His eyebrows rose. "Yeah, yeah... Okay, thanks. Talk soon."

He hung up. There was a long moment where he stared off into nothing, then he zeroed his gaze on mine. "Good news or bad news?"

"Good news. We could use some good news."

Levi's mouth turned down. "There is no good news." He ran his hand over his face. "After Arnie's death,

Mandy went around talking to a bunch of subcontractors and vendors. And several clients."

"Just like I did."

"Exactly like you did. Quite a few of the same people." He took a slow breath in, then out again. "She would tell anyone who would listen that I was innocent in Arnie's murder. That she wanted to find out who really killed him."

"Huh." Muldoon thought it was me sticking my nose into his case. It hadn't been. Then. But, oh, how things change. I'd been asking anyone who would talk to me about events surrounding Arnie's death, telling people Levi wasn't responsible. Just like Mandy.

I'm not sure what it says about me that knowing that, I'm still ready and raring to jump in just as the previous snooper's body is identified. It was crazy—insanity didn't necessarily run in the family, but really that all depended on who you asked.

"There's more."

"More?"

"She was the one who tried to pay off Arnie's debt with the handbags." Levi glanced down at his phone, answered a text, then look back up at me. "Jojo overheard Arnie rip into her—didn't necessarily know what all they were yelling about. But in light of what we've learned…you know where we're going to have to go. To the bakery."

I leaned back in my chair and stretched a kink in my back. "We?"

"Yes, you and I. That constitutes we."

I scrubbed my hands through my hair. "Do you think Gabriel's involved?"

"You're really sticking with Gabriel now, are you?"

I shrugged. "It's his name. It's what he told me to call him. And considering how I got involved with this man, you really have no room to question me." I refrained from smacking him at the end of that.

"Do you think he is involved in the deaths?" I asked slower and made a point of keeping eye contact with the man.

He didn't answer. Not right away. "I doubt it."

"You doubt it. But you're not sure. Well, then sure, let's go ask him what he thinks about all this."

"He told you about the handbags."

I narrowed my eyes. "So what?"

"As far as Arnie's concerned, the man was into Gabriel for big bucks. He told you so himself." Levi drained the rest of his coffee. "Arnie being dead gives the man zero return. Broken legs, maybe. A handful of threats, sure. But no breath, no money."

"Okay, I get that." Yeah, sure that made sense. "But what about Mandy?"

Levi raised his hands. "Why would he kill her?"

"I don't know." Why does anyone kill? I wanted to ask him. Crazy, careless or stupid doesn't really need a motive. I set my elbows on the table and dropped my face to my hands. "It seems like we'd be walking into trouble." I was the voice of reason?

"It wouldn't be the first time." Levi laughed. "So... we go see Gabriel? He has resources that we don't. Plus, he knows at least two of the players involved—we don't know how far this goes, though, so it couldn't hurt having him on our side."

"Our side?" I blinked several times. "We can't be one hundred percent sure he's not the one who killed one or both of them." I waved away my comment and heaved a heavy sigh. "You've bet with Gabriel?"

"So?"

"So wouldn't that fall under a conflict of interest of sorts?"

Levi opened his mouth to comment, then closed it, then opened.

"Plus you deal with him through your business. And…" I kept talking when he tried to interrupt me. "And, he paid your bail—which I still don't understand why you kept it so hush-hush—what if your questioning him mucks that up? You could lose a good client. Or he could ask for a refund or something. That's probably a thing. Then you'd be back in jail. Maybe you should sit this one out." I patted his hand.

"And you're going to what? Just go in there and demand that Gabriel give you the answers you want?"

"Why not?"

"Hi, Paul." Yes, I was now on a first-name basis with a bookie's…he wasn't a secretary, was he? He was the counter man at the bakery, sure, but you had to get by him to get to the main man, so he was what, like a gatekeeper? I didn't know the bakery/booking establishment hierarchy. Maybe I was making a major faux pas.

I swallowed hard. I might have acted all "cool as you please" when I told the guys about meeting Gabriel again—they were none-too-happy, surprise surprise—but the man was a wee bit scary. And cool, at the same time. But mostly scary.

"Good afternoon, Mrs. Eagan. What can I get for you today?"

"I could use a cup of the dark roasted coffee." Paul

filled a cup and handed it to me. I scooched over to the sugars and creamers they kept out for patrons and doctored my java. I handed him a ten for the coffee. Before I lost my nerve I blurted out, "And I was hoping to see Gabriel. If he's in."

Paul stuttered his step as he walked to the register. He didn't acknowledge that I'd asked to see Gabriel when he came back with my change and set it in my outstretched hand. "Anything else?"

"No, thank you." I took my coffee to one of the booths.

I guess it was too much to think I could waltz into the building and ask to see the man in charge. As I took a sip, a shadow came over me a moment before Gabriel Grady sat on the other side of the booth from me.

"What can I do for you, Celeste?"

I nearly dropped the coffee. "Mr.… Gabriel. How are you?" Why I was surprised he'd shown up so quickly, I didn't know.

He smiled. "You didn't come here to inquire on my day. What do you need?"

"I, uh, I wanted to ask you a question." I cupped my hands around the coffee. "I was wondering what you— how you, um…"

Gabriel leaned back against the seat and draped his arm across the back. "You came here to see if I know anything about Mandy Crenshaw."

"How did you…?" I took another sip of coffee to give my brain a moment to think of something witty to say. And then another sip when nothing was forthcoming. "Right," I said when he tilted his head. "That's why I came here. Because you know things," I admitted even though my knees were knocking under the table. I hadn't been nervous when he'd told me all about his family's start in the bakery business, but coming to him, wanting information made me squirm.

"I knew Arnie. He was a…patron. As I mentioned before." Gabriel glanced over his shoulder when a man walked in. Paul ushered him back through the swinging kitchen doors. "I did meet Mandy once. But she was not a customer—other than for pastries."

"She was the one who tried to pay off Arnie's balance with the Bassanis."

Surprise danced across his face. He mumbled something under his breath that sounded suspiciously like, "So intriguing."

I sat still and waited.

"She did. But as I mentioned, I declined. And yes, I heard she was identified as the body they found in the burned house." He frowned. "Do you think I had something to do with her death?"

I tried for a no-way laugh but I'm afraid it came off more like a vibrated hiccup. "Of course not. Would I be here talking to you if I thought you'd killed her?" I wasn't actually sure of the answer to that, so I doubted he was. "I was hoping you might know something."

"Why?"

I frowned. "Why what?"

"Why do you care?"

Why did I? "My friend was arrested for the first murder."

"That doesn't answer why you're involved."

"I've been implicated."

"Have you now?"

"Please, like you don't know."

He chuckled. "You give me much too much credit."

I gave a single-shoulder shrug.

"Levi has a lawyer. He has a passable alibi."

"Passable but so far not enough to get out from under it. Which you know, too."

Gabriel Grady knew more things than I did.

"I'm interested?" Truth be told, when I had investigated my principal's death, something sparked inside me. I'd always been drawn to acting, but there was a thrill I'd never known when I'd searched and questioned the people involved in that case. And while I didn't exactly solve it by myself, I'd like to think I helped, a lot—if you can call being the next target/victim and drawing the killer to me *helping*. There was something satisfying about that—after getting past the death-defying parts.

A mountain of a man came up to Gabriel and whispered into his ear. I'd seen him both other times I'd been in the bakery. At first I'd thought he was just a customer, but I'd adjusted my opinion to him probably being a bodyguard type. And in Gabriel's line of work, he'd need one more often than not, I'd guess.

"Thank you, Stanley." Gabriel waved a dismissive hand to the man, who walked back to the corner booth to stand. And wait. And watch.

"That's not intimidating at all." I tipped my coffee to Stanley's perch.

"You do just say whatever is on your mind, don't you."

A quick smile quirked up the corner of my mouth before I could help it. "Much to my detriment. And often others' amusement."

He cocked an eyebrow as if in agreement. "Don't have anything better to do?" Before I could answer he held up his hand. "I don't know what I can tell you."

"Anything would help."

"That's not what I meant. I know things. But some could be incriminating."

I'm pretty sure my eyebrows slid up to my hairline. Why in the hell would a man like him make an admission like that? "I'm not a cop. Anything incriminating would be hearsay." I'm not a lawyer either so I had no idea if that was true or not. "No wire." I did a half-assed pat-down of myself. "You'll have to take my word on that." I gave him a half shrug. "And I'm not your priest so I can't absolve you of anything."

"Tell you what, have dinner with me and I will tell you what I know—within reason."

"I, uh, what?" My mental gears ground to a halt at the massive detour.

He smiled. "Dinner. People sitting down to eat a meal."

"You want me to have dinner with you?"

His smile faded. I worried that could be potentially bad if his smile faded any more.

"I didn't mean it like that." I needed to salvage this. Somehow. "I meant that you want to have dinner with me. I'm flattered." I was, kind of, in some far reaches of my feminine self. And it was just dinner. Food. Eating. I wasn't committed to anyone that would prohibit sharing a meal with a man. Hell, my last date with Muldoon was before the first thaw of the season. Muldoon had never once intimated there was anything serious between us even when we did go out. Never once in so many words. I shook off my mental dithering. It was just food. I ate with Levi and Kellen all the time. And I was dying to know whatever information he was teasing me with. "Okay, sure. I'd like that."

His smiled beamed again. "Are you free tonight?"

"YOU WHAT?" MY dad slammed his hands down on the kitchen table. "You need to call him and cancel."

"I can't cancel. I just made the plans."

"You damn well can and will."

"Daddy, it's just dinner. And information."

Dad snatched the phone off the counter. "Call and cancel."

"I appreciate that you're getting all protective here, but really, you have a lot of nerve trying to make me cancel dinner with a man you have no qualms spending time and money with."

"That's different."

"No, it's not." I took the phone from him and set it back in the cradle. "And the last time I checked, I was a grown woman."

"Then stop acting like a child," he said under his breath.

"If you'll excuse me, I want to go say hi to Paige." I hurried down the hall before Dad could waylay me with more reasons why I should cancel—all of which I would probably agree with. But I needed—I guess *wanted* is a better term, I didn't really need to talk to him for any reason—any information Gabriel might have. "How was your dad's house?" I asked when I stepped into Paige's room.

She slammed a book shut and slid it under the covers. Her cheeks reddened exactly the way mine did when I was caught doing something I shouldn't ought to be doing. "Same as always."

I pretended I didn't see the book and sat on the bed next to her. I leaned in and kissed her forehead. "Sorry if I embarrassed you yesterday."

"Don't worry about it. Naomi is such a hard—"

"Hey, now." I bit back a smile. I swear I didn't try to influence my daughter to feel one way or the other about her father's girlfriend, but she knew skank when she saw it, too.

"I think she likes being snooty just to be snooty."

I wanted to give my sweet child a big ole hug, but the parent in me was screaming to correct her. "Naomi is the way she is. Your dad likes her, so she can't be that bad. He liked me, too, remember. So he does have good taste." I tweaked the tip of her nose.

"If you say so." Paige looked down, then across the room. "Um, I have something to ask you."

I frowned. I couldn't imagine what could make her so anxious. "You know you can always ask me anything."

"If a girl wanted to ask a boy out, it's acceptable in this day and age?"

My eyelashes nearly locked up I was blinking so fast at my child. "Well…"

She ducked her head. "I knew I should have asked Naomi."

"Stab me directly in the heart next time. Right here." I pointed to a spot on my chest. "Make the death quicker and less painful." I tried for playful and light, but I didn't think my pinched mouth and tight voice would convince Paige.

Paige sighed. "She just has way more experience than you. You've dated two guys, Dad and Muldoon."

Yes, because I was a complete spinster before I ran over my ex-husband. I did date a little after her dad and I divorced. Men she didn't know and until or unless I thought it might go somewhere—which obviously it hadn't or she wouldn't think me so spinsterly—I didn't introduce them to my daughter. I might not have introduced her to Muldoon if she hadn't already met him. And I definitely wouldn't introduce her to Gabriel Grady. Not that we were dating. We were going to dinner. To eat. And converse. So not a date as far as I was concerned. But lest she think I was a total waste of womanhood, I informed her, "I'm going out to dinner tonight. You and Grandpop can order in something."

"Detective Muldoon?"

"No."

Paige frowned, her eyebrows pulled down and mimicked my own expression. "Who, then?"

"His name is Gabriel. Mr. Grady."

She turned to fully face me and sat cross-legged. "And you know him from…"

"I, uh, Grandpop introduced us. Sort of." I couldn't hold her gaze.

"Is he nice?"

"Do you think I would go to dinner with someone who isn't nice?" Sure it was a non-answer. If I'd met him in a bakery and knew nothing else of him, I would be able to say that without qualms. And so far he was nothing but nice. It was the potential of what might happen if he felt wronged.

"Can I help you get ready?"

"Sure, sweet pea. Come on." I held my hand out for her and we walked to my room together.

"Where's he taking you?"

I opened the closet door and flipped on the light. "It's called Dominique's. But I don't know what it's like."

"That's okay. We can find something semi-dressy that will work for just about everywhere. Except fast food maybe."

"I don't think you need to worry about that." Gabriel didn't strike me as a burger, fries and shake kind of man.

"We need something other than your usual pink. Something that will make your eyes pop."

"You're a little scary. Where'd you learn all this?"

"Uncle Levi. All those seasons of watching *Project Runway* and *America's Next Top Model* will not be wasted."

ELEVEN

Dad whistled when I walked into the kitchen. "Wow."

I had on a formfitting, knee-length emerald-green dress. Something I'd bought on a whim and never once had a chance—or the nerve—to wear. It was a little slinkier than I remembered, but I had to admit, I looked good. "Thanks, Daddy." I draped a shawl over my shoulders and tucked a small purse under my arm.

"I can't talk you out of this?" He grabbed the handle of the door leading to the garage.

"It's just dinner. I'm taking my own car. There's nothing to worry about." If I could convince my nerves of that, I'd be golden.

"Be careful. I love you." Dad leaned in and kissed my cheek, then opened the door for me. "Call if you need anything at all. I can be there in five minutes flat."

I chuckled. Dad didn't know his way around Peytonville. There was no way he'd find the small out-of-the-way restaurant Gabriel suggested. I was hoping I'd be able to find it without having to pull over and triple-check the GPS.

I stopped at Levi's on the way to get a nod of approval. When I knocked on his door, I wasn't expecting Kellen to answer. "Well, look at you. Big date tonight?"

I wrapped the shawl tighter around my shoulders to ward off a chill. "You could say that." I frowned at my friends. "Kellen, what are you doing here?"

Kellen cheeks reddened. "I, we're...dinner."

"Mmm-hmm." I glanced around and took in the state of dishevel of the living room. I pushed past him and walked into the house. "Where's Levi?"

"Did I hear my name?" Levi sashayed from the back of the house. "Hey, sweets."

I volleyed my gaze between the two men. "How could you?"

They both gulped and simultaneously said, "What?"

"You're cheating on me." I shoved my finger into Levi's flannel-covered chest. "You're wearing flannel?" I waved away my words. "You're cheating on me with... with...him." I snagged Kellen's sleeve and pulled him into the fray.

Kellen scoffed and his face turned ten shades of alarming red. "I am totally straight."

"Duh." I pawed through the papers on the table but didn't really see anything. "You two are working on Arnie's case. Without me."

"It's all I think about. All damn day long. My neck is on the line here." He glanced away when he added, "If I go down, you do, too."

"Don't be like that." I enveloped him in a big hug. "We *will* get this figured out." I subconsciously ran my hands down over my hips to straighten out the dress.

Levi looked me over from head to toe, thoroughly distracted by my clingy dress. "Why do you look like sex on a stick?"

"She has a date." Kellen plopped down on the arm of the sofa, keeping his gaze riveted on the both of us.

Levi whistled. "Va-va-voom. Who dressed you?"

"You don't think I could have pulled this off by myself?" I gave a little twirl to make the skirt flare out.

Did everyone normally think I looked like a bag lady?
"I bought this dress." All by myself, I wanted to add.

He arched an eyebrow.

I ducked my head. "Paige."

"Muldoon's going to—"

"Not Muldoon. I'm supposed to meet Gabriel Grady
in half an hour."

Both men's chins dropped.

"Gotta go, boys." I headed for the door while they
both remained mute. "I will expect a full update on what
you've uncovered. And I'll fill you in on my night out."

I SAT IN the restaurant parking lot for a full ten minutes,
trying to work up the nerve to go in. "You are doing this
for Levi," I said aloud a couple of times, then silently in
my head as I made my way to the entrance. I might have
sat longer had it not gotten stuffy. I didn't want to wilt
before I could show off my smoking hot dress. It was
one of those places that had month-long waiting lists,
and even then you had to be somebody to get in. I was
so not "somebody." And truth be told I didn't aspire to
be somebody. This place was out of my league and the
league above that and maybe even one more.

I would probably never come here of my own accord.
And I'd almost turned around at the sight of the swanky
new restaurant on the far outskirts of town.

When I walked in, the maître d' greeted me with a
wan smile. See, it wasn't a real date. A "real date" would
have picked me up at my house, escorted me in himself
and not had a man in a penguin suit give me a pitying
once-over—at least not where I could see it despite the
expensive surroundings. "I'm meeting Gabriel Grady."

The man in the penguin suit straightened, and a courteous smile spread across his face at the mention of my dining partner. "Oh, yes, ma'am, this way." The maître d' himself escorted me through the small groupings of tables to a door off to the side. He held the door open and motioned me through.

I walked into a small private dining area. The walls were covered in a silky burgundy fabric and candle-laden sconces. A lone table sat in the center of the room topped with a dark silky tablecloth, cream-colored china, fancy crystal and a candelabra. My first instinct was wow, the second was please don't let me knock over the tall candelabras and set the place on fire. Or knock my drink over or break any of the tableware. Or…crap, I was working myself up into a huge ball of nerves.

A throat cleared behind me. I jumped a little and turned to find Gabriel next to the door. He thanked the maître d' and shut the door. "You look lovely." He took my hand and kissed the back. "Just lovely."

A blush crept across my cheeks. I swore I wasn't going to get swept up in his well-mannered facade. But it was not going to be easy.

"I have to admit, for a minute I thought you might not show up." He settled his hand on the small of my back and guided me to the table. Then he pulled out the chair for me.

"Why's that?"

"Clearly you're aware of my reputation." He sat across the table from me. "We might not be here otherwise."

When my mouth did nothing more than work like an out-of-water fish, he chuckled. "You don't have to comment. I'm just glad you said yes. You'll see I'm not such a bad guy."

"I never…"

"Maybe not you, but I'm sure some of your friends, namely the detective, have advised you to stay away from me."

"How do you know about Muldoon?"

"I have people. Who know people."

I sort of regretted not telling Muldoon about this so-not-a-date meeting. Dad knew where I was but he didn't know the area at all. Levi and Kellen knew who I was meeting with but not where. I was calling myself all kinds of stupid. Of course Gabriel knew people. "That's not scary at all." I laughed a shaky sort of reply.

Gabriel joined in. His smile transformed his fierce face to something akin to playful, almost sexy—and gawd, how I so didn't want to go there.

"Most people don't say what they think. You, I can't imagine you keeping a thought to yourself."

I managed to keep that one to myself, thank goodness. I toyed with the silky napkin in my lap. "Mmm-hmm."

"It's a compliment. You're refreshing."

A waiter came in with a bottle of wine followed by another carrying salads.

"I took the liberty of ordering for both of us, if that's okay." He sniffed, swirled and sipped the wine when the waiter poured a small amount in his glass. "Perfect." Both our glasses were filled and small plates set before us. The two waiters left as quietly as they'd entered. "They make the most wonderful beef Wellington in the state."

I took a quick sip of the wine. I wasn't the biggest wine drinker. I tried not to grimace at the dry, tart flavor.

"You don't like it?" He sipped his own again. "It's a three-hundred-dollar bottle."

I just about choked on the next sip. My dress—shoes,

purse, hell, everything on my person—didn't cost three hundred dollars.

"It's an acquired taste."

"Hmm." It was a taste I would rather not acquire—not at three hundred a pop. We ate our salads with minimum small talk. When the main course arrived, Gabriel sent back the wine. A few minutes later another waiter appeared. With a flourish he handed Gabriel an amber drink—that looked suspiciously like beer—and me a dark purple martini. "What's this?"

"Blueberry martini." Gabriel sipped his drink. "Taste it."

I sipped the dark concoction. It had just enough sweet to balance the tang. Both hid the bite of the vodka. "Mmm. This is heavenly." And that was coming from someone who swore off alcohol after the birthday debacle. I hadn't thought I would be able to drink something like this for a long while, but it was so delectable that I could forget it was booze.

"I'm glad you like it." Gabriel held his glass out and I clinked the martini against it. "Can I ask you a question?" He cut into his entrée. When I nodded he continued, "How long have you been dating Detective Muldoon?"

My fork stopped an inch in front of my mouth. "Your little spies didn't give you that info?"

Gabriel tilted his head with an arched eyebrow.

"We just met last fall."

"Because of your case?" There was a hint of humor in his voice but nothing showed on his face.

"Yes, he was the detective in charge. And I was a person of interest." Muldoon and I had been almost instantly attracted to one another. Or at least I had been.

I can't say for sure when he started to like me. He still held himself back, but every once in a while his professional demeanor would slip and he'd get close to me. You could almost see the self-reprimand on his face when he pulled himself back in check.

"Are you two serious?"

"I'm not sure what you mean." I picked up my water glass.

"Well, it's obvious that you aren't sleeping together."

The glass slammed down to the table. "I beg your damn pardon?" I grabbed the napkin from my lap and started to stand.

"Forgive me. I didn't mean that to come across so crassly. I only meant to say that no man would let his significant other go out with another man."

"I am my own person." I eased back into my chair.

Gabriel smiled. "I am becoming more aware of that every time we meet," he said almost as an aside. "This is just a meal, remember." He dabbed at his mouth. "Relax, please." His smile was a little less genial. "I was only inquiring because it's bad form to poach another man's woman."

"I am not livestock."

"I am making a mess of this." He leaned across the table and settled his hand atop mine. It unnerved me a little, his touch, but I wasn't about to smack his hand away. "You and I can be friends, can't we?"

"I suppose."

"Then as friends, we're getting to know one another. I do apologize if I've upset you in any way. Please, let's enjoy the meal." He let go of my hand and settled back on his side of the table.

I should have just left, but I still hadn't learned anything. And at least now he knew—and I knew he knew—that I was sort of, almost dating Muldoon—a cop. Surely he wouldn't try anything. "Friends."

His smile shifted back to amiable companion. "Yes. You have other male friends. Like Levi." When I lifted my martini and took a sip, he continued, "It's funny that Levi has never mentioned you."

"I could say the same thing." I set my drink down and cut off a small piece of the beef Wellington. It was even better than the drink. "I hate that he was framed-ish."

"Ish?"

"Arnie was in Levi's house for some reason, killed there on the property." I pointed my empty fork at him. "And his body left to be found." I left off the part about Levi's hammer being the murder weapon. I wasn't sure if that info had been released yet. Let Gabriel's people be the ones to give him that detail. "There were way better places to hide someone if they didn't want him found." And when did a statement like that become part of my regular conversation? A worry for a later date.

I forked a bite of food. "Maybe the killer wanted Levi to find it himself. And fairly quickly. On his property, found by him, he'd be accused—like he was—and they'd be in the clear."

"You're giving someone a lot of credit. Criminals are not necessarily that forward-thinking, despite what you may see on TV." He took a long sip of his beer.

"All a guess on my part. So, is it my turn to pick your brain?" I took another bite of the beef Wellington. I wondered if I could order a second and take it home to share with Dad and Paige. I almost moaned, but I was far from *that* relaxed around my new friend.

Gabriel took a bite of his own meal and nodded.

"Do you have a theory on who might have killed Arnie Showalter?"

"What makes you think it wasn't me?" He chuckled when I dropped my fork to the plate. A loud clang echoed in the cozy room.

"Sorry." My hands grew clammy. "I guess I don't really know for sure. But I'd venture that the amount of money he owed you was a pretty good incentive to keep him alive. At least until he paid you back. And now that his girlfriend is dead…" I let that beat hang there for a moment. "You're probably just as anxious to find out who cost you some big bucks." I took a bite of green beans. When I swallowed, it all but stuck in my throat. "I'd also guess that if you did know, there'd be another body heaped onto the pile and you wouldn't need to talk to me. So you're actually feeling me out more than I'm getting info from you." All my nerves and curiosity deflated. "I don't know why I didn't realize it before."

Gabriel smiled. "Now that all that's out of the way, maybe you can enjoy the rest of your dinner."

"So much for friendship."

A feral grin turned up the corners of his mouth. "Let's not get all sanctimonious. Didn't you join me for dinner for the same reasons I invited you? To get information. We're using one another for the same thing. We might as well have a lovely dinner in the meantime."

Half of me knew he was right. I'd agreed hoping to get anything out of him, so yes, I was guilty as charged. The other half of me was mad—at myself—for getting played. "Fine." I'd like to say I stayed because he made sense, but honestly, I was a little scared of what he might do if I walked out the door. "I will say, it feels pretty one-sided though."

He chuckled. "That's what I like about you, Celeste. Most people are afraid to tell me how they feel. What they're really thinking. Not you. You just blurt it right out."

"More than one person has tried to remedy me of that habit."

"Thank goodness none were successful." Gabriel leaned his elbows on the table and steepled his fingers over the plate. "It's your turn to ask me questions."

I waved a forkful of green beans at him. "I don't even know what to ask."

"Do you think I'm the only one Arnie owed money to?"

My eyebrow arched almost of its own accord. "There's more than one bookie in Peytonville?"

"We like to think of ourselves as economic stimulants. When our customers are on a roll they add to the city's growth by their purchases."

"How very...entrepreneurial."

Gabriel smiled. "I try." He watched me while he took a bite of his beef Wellington. Once he swallowed, he said, "Since you aren't asking, let me tell you. Arnie owned no less than four bookies money."

I gasped. "Four?"

"Not all in Peytonville. There's one in Dallas—who is a mean sonofabitch. And one in Houston."

"How do you know all this? Surely there's not a union for your..." I waved my hand at him. "In your line of work."

He laughed. "Hardly. Arnie talked to me. We became friendly. As friendly as one can be when money is involved." He patted his mouth with his napkin and eased back in his chair a bit. "Arnie recently purchased a couple more houses. And then there was whatever he had going on with the handbags."

"Those are fakes."

"Yes."

"Was he trying to pass them off as real? And where'd the crate from the Sagebrush house go?" I downed the rest of my martini. Another showed up before I could set the glass back on the table—which was less disconcerting than the fact I'd never heard the waiter enter the room. "And his girlfriend dies."

"Yes." Gabriel waved the waiter away when he went to set down another beer. "I assume Levi had an alibi for the new development."

I grimaced. "At the time the fire started, yes, he was with clients. But the murder…" I shook my head. "The coroner hasn't been able to narrow that down so he's still right in the thick of it." When did Levi and I ever have to supply multiple alibis in just one week? Yeah, I could see how I might entertain a man like Gabriel. He broke laws and seemed to not get busted, while I was totally aboveboard on everything—except maybe eating food with expired best-by dates—and seemed to always be on the PPD radar.

Yep, I was a novelty.

I dragged a green bean around my plate. "Did it bother you he was spending money when he owed you so much?" I didn't know if I could take another bite so I pushed the plate away and sipped the new drink. It was pretty darn good, one of the best I'd ever had—not that I was a connoisseur or a lush—despite my birthday—or anything, but I'd had my fair share of shaken not stirred.

"We had an arrangement."

I sputtered around my drink. "Like a payment plan."

"Not exactly. But nothing you need to worry about."

"You brought it up. Okay, so Arnie was into several people for a lot of money. Again, if he's dead, said people aren't getting paid so where's their motive?" I tapped my lip. Who would kill him? For a split second I wondered if Gabriel was still playing me. "Do you suspect anyone? I mean someone who might be on your radar."

Gabriel stared at me for a long moment. "No. In fact, I don't. One thing you need to know, he wasn't a nice man. He cheated anyone he thought he could get away with cheating. I heard rumors he beat poor Mandy."

I gaped at him. "Why would she go looking for his killer then?"

"Maybe to thank them. I don't know. Women like her don't know what to do if they're not someone's punching bag." He pulled his cell phone from his pocket, scrolled though it for a moment and tucked it back away. "You don't strike me as a woman who would take any guff from anyone."

"I, uh… I'd like to think I wouldn't let a man treat me that way."

"Why'd you get divorced?"

I paused with the drink almost to my lips. The liquid splashed over the edge and dropped down the front of my dress. "Can't take me anywhere," I mumbled. After I dabbed at it with my napkin, I looked back at Gabriel. "And this is your business, why?"

He leaned back and held his hands aloft. "Trying to make conversation."

"By asking personal questions?" Was I poking a bear with a stick? "I'd have thought you'd have had me fully investigated by now."

He didn't bat an eye as he said, "I have, but some things you can't ferret out."

"I was only half kidding. You had me investigated?" He could probably get a hold of the last five years of my tax returns. Hell, for all I knew he could tell me what I had for breakfast. Sweat beaded in…places.

"It was a standard background check."

My mouth flapped open and closed. Like a dang carp. When I did finally squeak out a sound to say something, he held up his finger, withdrew a cell from his pocket and glanced at the screen. "Excuse me for just a minute." He rose and walked to the corner and whispered in hushed tones. When he came back to the table, he was pocketing his phone. "I'm really sorry, but I have an emergency I have to attend to. Please stay and have dessert. I ordered a chocolate mousse so light it will make you cry and a raspberry torte. I know how fond you are of the raspberry cake the bakery makes."

Heat crawled across my cheeks. There were times it sucked being addicted to chocolate…

Gabriel leaned down and kissed my cheek. "Thank you for an, uh, interesting evening. I hope we get a chance to do it again."

Not if every person I knew had anything to say about it. I watched his retreating back and considered hightailing it out as soon as I was sure he'd left, but the waiter came in with the desserts. No point in being rude and leaving the food uneaten.

I dipped a spoon into the mousse. When the fluffy chocolate landed on my tongue, I moaned so loud I looked around the room, sure someone would laugh—but I was alone, thankfully. I ate every last bite but did refrain from licking the bowl clean. I would have started right in on the raspberry torte but I was full to the point of bursting. The waiter magically appeared, with a container in hand, for the torte.

The young man wrapped up the dessert and handed me the check. I frowned. "Mr. Grady didn't take care of this?"

"No, ma'am."

I tried not to shake when I saw the total. I'd never once in my entire life paid that much for a meal. Hell, my grocery bill for a week wasn't even that high. I pulled out my credit card and handed it to him.

Walking back to the car, once the bill was settled, the heel of my shoe caught in a crack in the parking lot. As you can probably guess, my heel snapped right off. "Can't get much better than this." I dropped into the front seat to slip both my shoes off, sighed and started the car. My hands shook slightly as I backed out. I might not have been on many dates in my lifetime—not that this was a date—but I was pretty sure that it ranked up there in the top two of the worst ever—only beaten by a date in college where, after dinner, the man took me home to meet his wife and tried to explain the new age of swingers.

I shivered more forcefully. The air was a wee bit nippy. I glanced down to turn on the heater. When I glanced up there was a dog in the middle of the street. I swerved to keep from hitting it. I only breathed easy when there was no thud—I'm sorry, but I don't think I could have dealt with that on top of everything else. A moment later red-and-blue lights strobed behind me.

"Just freaking great." I pulled over to the side of the road. When the officer approached the car, I had my license in hand and ready.

The uniformed officer shined his light in my eyes. "Do you mind stepping out of the car?"

Actually I did. I was barefooted and cold. But I wasn't about to share my protestation with the man.

He glanced down at my un-shoed feet and frowned. "You were driving a little erratic there."

"I'm sorry. There was a dog in the road. I'd looked down for a second to adjust the heat in the car and when I glanced back up there he was. I was trying not to hit the poor pup."

He sniffed at me then flashed the light in my face again. I squinted at the light as he asked, "Have you been drinking?"

"Well, I..." Hell.

TWELVE

PEYTONVILLE LOCKUP. I was becoming all too familiar with the water-stained ceiling panel—the third one from the back—as I lay on the small cot shoved up against the wall. I picked at the itchy bandage in the crook of my elbow.

"I'd heard you were here but I didn't believe it."

I didn't believe it either. I didn't even bother to look at Muldoon. "I'm not drunk."

"You could have taken the Breathalyzer. And proven it. By refusing, you ensured the blood test." He pointed to the bandage covering the spot they drew blood from. "Down here. At the station."

"I didn't know." I tilted my head toward the cell door. "I've never been pulled over before."

Muldoon scoffed.

"I mean never pulled over for drinking and driving. Which I was not. Yes, I had a drink with dinner, but my driving was…compromised when I swerved to avoid hitting a dog. I suppose I could have run right over it and kept on going."

His eyebrow arched.

"I'm not drunk."

He flipped through some papers he was holding. "Your BAC came back at 0.04."

I frowned. "Is that good?"

"It's 0.04 below the legal limit."

I sat up. "See. I told you." My bare feet smacked the floor and stood up. "I had two—" I held up two fingers "—martinis. That was it. And half of one ended up down the front of my dress so that doesn't even count as having it."

He was still shuffling through some papers. "That could be enough to put you over the limit. It all depends on how much you drink and how quickly. Plus absorption rate. It can vary. Just think about the night of your birth…" He trailed off when he glanced up.

"You don't have to remind me of my birthday thankyouverymuch." I ran my hands down my hips—mostly to smooth out the dress where it bunched up—but partly to emphasize, well, the size of my generous hips that slowed my absorption rate. "Well, I can honestly say this is one time my womanly figure has helped out."

Muldoon continued to stare. His gaze traveled from the top of my coiffed hair, pulled up in droopy curls, to the shiny green dress—with the lovely blueberry stain down the front. If his gaze lingered and returned to the plunging neckline…it was all I could do not to preen just a wee little bit. So what if it was flattering. I'm a cheap flirt.

But enough gaping was enough.

"'Lo." I snapped my fingers. "Earth to Detective Speechless."

He swallowed hard. "Sorry. Um, where exactly were you going tonight?"

I glanced down at my toes. "Home."

"Where were you coming from?"

I named off the restaurant.

"Pretty swank." He swiveled at the waist and dropped

the papers onto the desk behind him. "I'm surprised Levi's not here pacing the floor."

"Why would he?"

"He wasn't in the car with you? Surely you didn't take two cars that far out of the way."

"I, uh… I wasn't having dinner with him." I swallowed hard.

"Oh?"

He would flip out if I mentioned Grady's name. I should tell him, but I couldn't get my mouth to work to say the name.

He leaned against the desk and his eyes narrowed. "Oh. You were on a date."

"Yes and no. Mostly no."

A pink tint crawled across his tanned cheeks. He held up his hands. "None of my business."

"It wasn't a date date." And it wasn't his business. "Just dinner."

"That's an awful expensive—and intimate—place for just dinner." He shook his head and shoved his hands on his hips.

"Am I free to go?" I stepped closer to the cell door and wrapped my fingers around the bars. "I'm not under arrest, right?"

"Yes. No." He ran his hands through his hair. "No, you're not under arrest. Yes, you're free to go." He pulled a key ring from the desk and unlocked the door. He frowned—yet again. "Where're your shoes?"

I sighed. "In the floorboard of the SUV. I broke a heel walking to the car after dinner. I took them off to make driving easier."

Muldoon walked me to the property clerk's room. The woman on the other side of the half door handed me a manila envelope with my name scrawled across the top. I looked at my meager belongings and moaned. No keys. "They towed my car. And my dessert. I didn't even get to taste it."

"The impound lot's closed. Won't be open 'til eight in the morning."

"Super." I leaned against the wall and let my head fall back onto the hard surface. "If it makes you feel better, I got stiffed with the check."

"No. It doesn't." Muldoon rubbed his warm hand down my arm. "Do you want a ride home?"

MULDOON WALKED ME to the front door. He hadn't spoken much on the short drive from the police station.

"Thanks. It seems like forever since you've walked me to my door."

He frowned. "Yeah, it's been a while."

"You were just keeping an eye on your suspect before." I laughed but it came out a little hollow.

"It wasn't always because you were a suspect." He shoved his hands in his pockets and rocked back on his heels. "I liked being around you."

Liked? As in past tense? I decided to leave that alone. For now. It was easier to go for friendly if a little flippant. "Even when you thought I was guilty?"

"I never thought that. I was afraid you were going to get into trouble."

In all the months we'd known each other, we'd never really broached the subject of how we met. I was afraid to bring it up fearing that he'd realize I was too much trouble and he'd cut his losses. I figured he didn't bring it up for the same exact reason. And until recently things had gone smoothly enough. But something had changed...

He leaned forward, bent a little until his face was right in mine. We were nose to nose. I could feel his warm breath against me. "Who were you with at dinner?" he whispered.

"Jealous much?" I teased, but only because it was easier to focus on that than how much I wanted to taste that little dimple at the corner of his mouth.

The corner of his mouth—and the little dimple—curved up. "Anything but. I don't like the idea of someone…getting fresh—"

"Getting fresh? My, you do have a way with words, Detective." I leaned a little closer still. "No need to worry there."

"I'll be the judge of that," he said and leaned back. "If you tell me who it was."

I shuddered. Despite being mid-May, it was a chilly night and my shawl was snuggled up next to my broken shoes and the torte I would never get to taste. Muldoon rubbed his hands up and down my bare arms. "Why didn't you tell me how cold you were?"

"I didn't really notice." Because I was so wrapped up in the does-he-or-doesn't-he-like-me game all the stupid teenagers play. I could have closed my eyes and stood there all night, but the porch light blazed to life and Muldoon jumped back so fast I nearly fell. He grabbed my elbows and steadied me.

"Celeste?" The door eased open and Dad stepped out. "Oh, hi, Detective." Dad gave me a perfunctory once-over. Then frowned and did it again slower, deliberately taking in my bare feet. "Didn't you leave here with more clothing on?" He glanced around me. "And with a car?"

I shifted self-consciously. Maybe I had somehow reverted back to my awkward teen years. And really, they hadn't been all that awkward so maybe that was why I was paying for it now. "Yes, to both. It's a long story. I'll tell you later." I waved him back through the door. "I'll be right in."

Dad nodded. "I told you not to go to dinner with Grady." The door shut quietly but it might as well have been slammed for the tension rolling off Muldoon.

"Your date was with Gabriel Grady?" He stepped back and balled his fists at his sides.

"I told you, it wasn't a date exactly. He invited me to dinner." I bit my lower lip. There was no way to say the rest without making Muldoon angrier.

"For..." He lowered his head. The angle made him look ready to charge at something—and sexy as all get-out.

I had to focus on what I'd been up to rather than what I'd like to get up to with Muldoon. "He was trying to see what I knew."

"About what?" His voice lowered to a steely whisper.

I crossed my arms, as much to ward off the late evening chill as to give myself something to do. "Stuff."

"Celeste."

"He was fishing for what I knew about Arnie's death." I leaned back against the wall—I couldn't really get any farther away unless I wanted to tunnel through the wall into my dining room. I hadn't dismissed the idea altogether yet.

Muldoon stared at me for a long moment. "I don't know if you're just crazy or if you have some strange death wish."

"I'd like to think neither." I scrunched up my forehead. What gave him the right to be so cold? "I was going to tell you." After dinner. Once I was home. And then I could give Muldoon anything I'd gleaned. In my head it was all altruistic, but I was kidding myself to think that it wouldn't turn out to be anything less than what it was—a battle between Muldoon and me.

He flexed his fingers at his sides then finally ran them through his hair, shoving the dark locks out in every direction. It made him look wilder if that was possible. "What did you tell him?"

I'd never seen Muldoon this pissed. Ever. And I'd done some pretty stupid things during the investigation of my murdered boss. "Nothing. I don't know anything." Not really. He had all the same info that I did. Didn't he?

"Uh-huh…"

My frowned deepened. "What, Muldoon? What's with the third degree?"

"Oh, I don't know. Maybe because you did go have dinner with him." He thrust his hands through his hair again. "You're telling me you agreed to go out with the man with no strings."

"I… I… There might not have been strings presented at the time I agreed."

"And you thought you were going to work him for info and he turned the tables on you. Started pumping you for anything you might have learned. And left you with the check." Muldoon sighed. "That alone should tell you about the man. He's not a gentleman. He's not a good guy. Sure, he's well educated, but that doesn't make him someone you should want to spend time with. He's dangerous. Right now you're not necessarily in danger because he's using you and you're probably a warped form of entertainment for him."

It stung slightly that Muldoon had read the situation

so clearly. And I hadn't. I thrust my nose up in the air, not about to confirm anything he said.

"Good night, Celeste." With that he turned and left.

"Thanks for the ride home, Detective." I walked into the house and only refrained from slamming the door because I didn't want to give him the satisfaction.

"Did I muck something up?" Dad sat in the club chair with a book in his lap.

"No, I managed to do that all by my lonesome." I leaned my hip against the back of the sofa and snagged the wool afghan to wrap around my shoulders. My teeth chattered and every inch of me shook. Some from the cold, some not.

"Care to explain how or why you came home with significantly less than you left with?"

I tilted my head to the side. "Care to explain to me why you up and left my mother?"

He didn't even glance up from his book when he said, "Nope."

Neither of us said much of anything else for a while. I was headed for the kitchen to get a cup of coffee—decaf, I would like to sleep at some point—just as someone knocked at the front door. It was just past ten, but still a little late for visitors.

"Maybe your detective came back to make amends." Dad set his book aside and stood.

"He has nothing to amend himself for." I flipped on the porch light and looked through the little curtained window beside it. I didn't recognize the tan-uniformed man. Levi had installed a chain on the door—which I rarely remembered to use—and I slid the little metal nub into place before I opened the door. "Yes?"

"Ms. Celeste Eagan? I have a delivery for you." He waved a clipboard at me.

"Isn't it a little late for deliveries?"

The young man shrugged. "Mr. Grady paid me extra to get it here tonight."

"Gabriel." I all but growled the word and the young delivery man stepped back. I shut the door and unfastened the chain. "What is it?"

The young man pointed over his shoulder. Out by the curb sat my Outlander. "How'd he…?"

"I don't get paid to know, just to deliver. Will you sign here to acknowledge receipt?" He handed me the clipboard and my keys.

I scrawled my name across the dotted line. "Let me get you a tip." I started to turn back into the house.

"No, thank you, ma'am. That's been covered, as well." The young man flashed a quick smile. Gabriel must have tipped well.

"Mr. Grady also asked me to give you this." He handed me a white box and an envelope. "Good night, ma'am." He tipped his hat and walked away.

"Your car?" Dad peered around me.

"It was impounded."

"Your detective got it out?"

"No. He said I couldn't get it until tomorrow." Muldoon couldn't get it out sooner. But Gabriel could? My fear of the man ratcheted up a couple more notches. "Gabriel Grady had the car delivered."

"How'd he manage that?"

"I have no clue. And frankly I don't know that I want to know." I shoved the box and envelope at Dad. "Will you hold this for me so I can run and put the car in the garage?"

I walked slowly out to the car and just stared at it for a long moment. I have to admit, I was a little wary. Having your car blow up once…jaded a person. I dropped to all fours and looked for any kind of incendiary device, not that I necessarily knew what to look for, but the lack of blinking lights gave me a little ease. I also walked the perimeter of the car and looked for any scratch or scuff marks. Nothing worse than a stray ding in the car, especially when it's out from under your watchful eye. It looked as it had the day I drove it off the car lot. If anything it might have sparkled a little more under the street lamp.

Had Gabriel made them wash it?

I shook my head. Again, I wasn't sure I wanted to know his process for anything. I stood back and pushed the ignition button on my key fob. It's a sad statement that I flinched when the engine roared to life. But no boom, so I let myself into the car. Why I was surprised to find a single white rose and a note that simply read *Much apologies*, I couldn't say.

"He's one smooth character." I held the rose up to my nose and breathed in the soft subtle scent. I shook off whatever warm and fuzzy feelings the flower and having my car delivered did to me. The man had stiffed me with the check and I got my car towed through the strange chain of events that followed. He found out and rectified the car at least. His resources grew tenfold-scary.

I pulled it in the garage and parked it.

When I reentered the house, Dad was sitting at the bar in the kitchen still holding the white box. "Wonder what it is." He lifted the box and shook it slightly.

"Oh, damn." I ran back out to the garage and looked for the dessert box from the restaurant. It was on the passenger floorboard next to my shoes and shawl so I snapped them all up and returned to the kitchen. "I forgot about this." I held up dessert and set the rest aside. "This was the leftover torte from dinner."

"You had leftover dessert?" Dad winked at me.

"It was my second and I was too full to eat it." I took two forks out of the drawer and held them aloft. "Want to join me?"

"Sure." Dad patted the barstool next to him. "What do you suppose is in this one?"

"Hmm." I handed Dad a fork, sat next to him and opened the chocolate raspberry torte. I set the box between us.

"Well considering the source, it could be anything from another torte to a bomb."

"Wow, Dad, do we know how to pick 'em or what?" I forked a large bite of the torte and held it in front of my mouth. Waiting. Anticipating. "If I have to go, death by dessert bomb isn't horrible."

Dad scoffed.

It was more heavenly than I'd anticipated. Thick rich chocolate crust, with a smooth raspberry filling. "Gawd, this is divine."

"Not too bad."

"Please. This is way better than not bad."

Dad set down his fork. "May I?" He jiggled the other box.

I closed up the torte box to save for later. "Knock yourself out. Just let me move across the room in case it goes boom." I slid off the stool. Dad might think I was kidding. I was. But only a little. I was way more wary than I cared to be.

"Hey, don't forget this." Dad waved the envelope that came with the deliveries.

"Thanks." I slid the flap open and pulled out the white folded paper. Several twenties slid out and to the floor. "What the…"

I read the note.

Celeste, please forgive the mishap at dinner. The maître d' and waiter have both been fired for the error at the restaurant. I never had any intention of leaving you to pay. Please accept this repayment and I hope that you will agree to join me again. Soon. Definitely my treat. Always, Gabriel.

I scooped up the cash at my feet. There was at least sixty dollars too much and I'd tipped well. I was torn between feeling cheap and thrilled that he hadn't truly left me to pay the bill. I didn't even know how to digest the fact that two people lost their jobs over the mix-up.

While I still held the cash contemplating it all, Dad picked up the letter and read it. "He got the waiter and maître d' fired?"

All I could do was nod.

"He's a scary man."

"An understatement if there ever was." I dropped the wad of cash to the counter. "Does that mean you'll stop seeing him?"

"Absolutely."

Why I didn't completely believe my dad, I'm not sure. Maybe it was his lack of eye contact when he agreed. Or even the speed in which he said it. But that was neither here nor there unless or until he went back on his word.

A little too curious for my own good, I motioned to

his hands. "So? What's in the box?" So what if I took a step or two back.

Dad peered inside. "It's a purse." He looked up at me, then back in the box and frowned. "Just like the one you got on your—"

"What? Why would he give me that?" I raised my hand to my throat. He sent me a Bassani bag. A real one. "This is too expensive. Holy…"

"How much are we talking?"

"Two grand."

Dad's eyes widened and he stepped back from the box. "And you thought someone just left one of those lying around Levi's construction house."

"No, I thought he bought it for me and was being really, really weird about it until I found out it was fake. Then I thought maybe he was being really, really weird about buying me a fake one. And…well…it's a Bassani."

I pulled the bag up out of the box. The rich blue offset the red and green strips that crisscrossed over the front. How could I ever have mistaken those knockoffs for the real thing? This leather was buttery soft. And the smell. There was something so comforting about the deep musky scent. Was it bad that it sort of reminded me of Muldoon? "I can't keep this." I wanted to. If I thought I was in love with the faux purse, it was just puppy love compared to the soul mate love of this bag. I hugged it to my chest and stroked it.

"A little on the dramatic side." He clicked his tongue. "It's just a purse."

"Just a purse." I stared at the man. "Dad, two people have died over fake ones of these."

"Hmm." Dad gave the handbag another once-over,

then shook his head. "No offense, it's just as fugly as the other one."

"You have no sense of fashion whatsoever."

He shrugged. "You going to give it back?"

"Yes." Maybe. Gaw, I didn't know. I should. Every instinct in me said I should give it back. What did it mean to Gabriel if I kept it? What did it mean if I gave it back? Why didn't I listen to Muldoon in the first place?

"I'm going to bed, Dad. I'm tired." I leaned forward and kissed his cheek. "Good night."

"Sleep tight."

I would as soon as I made a quick phone call.

"WHAT DO YOU mean he had you tailed?"

"What don't you understand, Muldoon?" My voice rose with each word.

"Back up a second. Why do you think he had you tailed?"

I paced my bedroom and ran my hand through my hair. "He told me he did a standard background check on me. I don't even want to know what that means. And— did you know he got my car out of the impound lot and had it delivered here? Tonight. Like ten minutes ago." I paced back and forth. "How did he even know I'd been pulled over much less had my car impounded if he wasn't tailing me? That scares the shit out of me, Muldoon."

"Didn't I—"

"Don't you dare say I told you so." I shifted the phone to the crook of my neck and glared at the purse sitting on my dresser.

"Are you still there?"

"Sorry, yes. Gabriel had my car delivered. To the

house. Along with a box. Inside the box was a purse. Exactly like my fake Bassani. But real."

"And…"

"Dude. You know how much those bags cost. You probably looked them up the second I told you about them. Am I right?" He gave a quick grunt of affirmation. "Did I mention it's identical to the fake one I had?"

"I believe you did." His words were tight and clipped.

"He only saw me with that thing for maybe fifteen minutes."

"Celeste." He sighed. "This is getting out of hand. Would you like to file a restraining order against him? Has he made any threats toward you?"

"Threaten me? Are you kidding, the man is amused by me. He finds me refreshing." I edged back on the bed and leaned against the headboard. "I know you think I brought this on myself."

"I didn't say that."

"You don't have to say it, it was written all over your face earlier. I swear to you I didn't set out to challenge this man and make him find any interest in me."

"And that's why."

I was stretching and missed something in what Muldoon said. "Why what?"

"You are guileless. There are no pretenses with you. Well, when you're not dressing up in strange costumes and assuming a different persona." He chuckled.

"You're never going to let me live that down, are you?" When I was trying to ferret out the serial killer who'd murdered my boss, I'd used my theater training to go "undercover." I'd run into Muldoon and he hadn't recognized me. Had I not been pulled over for running a red light the second time—and, not matching my ID, been swiftly taken to jail—the detective might never have figured it out. Muldoon had had to come and bail me out. He'd almost left when presented with the drooping septuagenarian. "You didn't know it was me, so my character could have been cunning. That gives me an idea."

"If you're thinking of approaching Grady dressed up as someone else, cross that off your to-do list. Now, before he takes you as a special gift for his entertainment."

Go in drag. "That thought hadn't even crossed my mind. I was thinking of an exercise for the troupe, but now that you mention it…"

"Celeste, promise me you won't do anything stupid."

"You know you can trust me."

THIRTEEN

"TRUST ME TO do something completely stupid." I walked down the sidewalk at the strip mall. At the theater Monday, I'd had the newest troupe members practice latex applications. Most looked like what you might expect from amateurs—Annabelle had a fully-fledged makeup artist for important issues during productions, but it never hurt to train the troupe. It was passable from afar, but a little tacky around the edges up close.

Two members, however, had done an outstanding job. So of course on Tuesday, I'd had them stay late for another attempt. On me. My quirky Rubenesque features were enhanced and exaggerated. Added with a heavy wool skirt and ruffly artist shirt, I looked…ridiculous. But fairly unrecognizable.

As a test, I went to my former employer, Peytonville Prep, and walked around the school. I stopped at Colin's office. Not one iota of acknowledgment. Not even from Naomi, who was seated in the middle of his desk giggling like some damn teenager—not that I cared. Wonder what she'd have done if I'd just flat out body-slammed her. I had enough padding to keep me well protected. Maybe for another time. I had places to be.

All of which led me to be walking into Gradkowski's just before sundown Tuesday evening. The storefront was empty save for one person.

Paul was at his usual perch at the end of the counter. "Evening, ma'am. What can I get for you?"

I feigned interest in the paczki. I'd tried one, but it was a little heavy for my taste, but my character… She'd love them. "I'd like three prune and three lemon paczki," I said in a near-perfect Jersey shore accent despite the fake teeth and mounting nerves. I cleared my throat and elongated my vowels. "Aw, make it four each."

I'd dated a guy in college from Hillside, New Jersey. His family had laughed when I'd tried to imitate them. Laughed because it was darn close. "Please," I added.

Paul nodded. "I'll get that right for you, ma'am." He didn't act like we'd ever met. Nor did he seem the least bit put off by my round figure. He grabbed a pastry box and pulled my order right from the case. Not once had I—Celeste—ever had food from the case. Paul had always gone in the back and grabbed fresh ones for me.

If my knees weren't shaking so hard, I might have cried weight or age or hell I didn't know, plain old discrimination.

Paul handed me the box and quoted me a price. I carried cash, smart enough not to use my charge card with Celeste Eagan printed on it. "Here ya go, Paul."

He did a quick double take, then took the cash. "You been here before?"

I mentally groaned. Think fast, girl. "I, um…" Oh, thank God. "Is that not your name? It's printed right there on your pocket." I waved at his shirt. "Sorry, I just assumed."

Before he could answer, Gabriel walked from the back. "How are you this evening?"

"Just fine, thankyouverymuch." For a split second, as the heat rolled across my cheeks, I'd have sworn he'd bust me for the fierce blush, but thankfully I remembered the latex was thick enough I could have freckles in the shape of the Big Dipper on my cheek and he wouldn't be able to tell.

"A Jersey girl." He flirted. A little. Having only known him a short while, I could recognize a half-watt flirt from the one he bestowed on regular old me. "What parts?"

"Hillside."

"Really? I have family over in Kenilworth." Gabriel leaned his elbows on the counter. He was more laid-back than I'd ever seen him. "You were practically neighbors."

"Imagine that." Crap. Why didn't I know he had family in freaking New Jersey? He left that off in his History of Gabriel talk we'd had.

"How long you been in Texas?"

"Sixteen years," I answered automatically with the truth. And cringed.

"Wow, and your accent's still so strong?"

"You know Jersey girls. You can take the girl outta Jersey—"

"But can't take Jersey outta the girl." He smiled but it didn't quite reach his eyes. "I haven't seen you here before."

A little rumble of fear tittered down my spine. He was scrutinizing me far too closely. Luckily, I had thought out something since he'd quizzed me the first time I'd come in. "A friend of mine mentioned the bakery. I was over on this side of town and thought I'd pop in and get dessert for the family."

"Really? Who would that be?"

"Mandy Crenshaw." I waited for any kind of reaction

that might prove he'd actually killed Arnie and Mandy. Damn, he was good. He didn't so much as bat an eyelash.

"Can't say that I know her." He straightened from the counter. "I hope you enjoy your dessert. Ms.... Sorry, I didn't catch your name."

I didn't give one. And we both damn well knew that. "Georgia," I said with a big bright smile that belied the growing unease in my chest. I picked up the box and jolted from a loud commotion behind me. My heart hammered as I turned. I wasn't sure what I expected, but the tactical officers with their large guns pointed at me—well, it wasn't just me, they had all three of us in their sights—was about the last thing I'd have expected.

"No one move."

Not a problem. Every fiber of my being froze.

"Can I help you, gentlemen?" Gabriel asked as calm as you please.

I had my back to him, but even still I could imagine a creepy, half-cocked smile turning up the corner of his mouth.

More officers moved into the small seating area of the bakery. One relieved me of my box. "Hey, I paid for that."

The man narrowed his eyes at me but didn't speak. He then took me by the arm and led me to the corner. He ordered me to sit. And I did. From my new vantage point I could see the entire room, both doors and a little out the front window. There were at least a dozen police vehicles in the small parking lot. And spectators galore were gaping from every free space of cement just outside the perimeter—where in the hell did they all come from? It was a pretty much vacant strip mall.

To make matters worse—because being in the middle of a raid while dressed as someone else wasn't bad enough—Muldoon walked in.

"I should have known you were behind this, Detective." Gabriel shoved his hands in his pockets. He and Paul stood in the same places as they had when the men walked in. "Did your little girlfriend come running to you?"

I frowned. No, not exactly.

"Be quiet, Grady. Go check the back." Muldoon motioned two men toward the door to the kitchen.

Gabriel moved to block their way.

"We have a search warrant for the premises." Muldoon tossed a couple of papers at Gabriel, then turned and scanned the area. "Who's that?"

He pointed to me. Sweat beaded just about everywhere. I suppose on the bright side I could go back to the playhouse and tell the guys how well the spirit gum held up. They'd been curious how it would do under the hot stage lights. Of course that was assuming I made it home anytime soon. I predicted a neat little jail cell in my future, if for no other reason than Muldoon was going to be so pissed...

"Don't you know?" Gabriel glanced up from the papers.

What was that supposed to mean?

The two men stared one another down for what seemed like an eternity, then Muldoon gave orders to a few different men. They moved about the room then toward the kitchen, as well.

It was a while before they herded everyone out of the shop into the parking lot. There were several tower lights to brighten up the parking lot. They segregated the girls—being me—to one area on the edge of the ruckus and the boys to another, where several officers stood watching them. A female officer joined the officer already assigned to me. The pair guarding me shifted and I saw a familiar face walk into the fray of men dressed in all black tactical gear. "Excuse me?"

My female guard stiffened and—had I not been watching, I'd have missed it—settled her finger closer to the trigger. "What?"

"May I speak to him?" I pointed to the newest arrival. "Please? I know Finn. Officer Muldoon."

The woman eyed me for a long moment, then said, "Do not move." She walked over and whispered to Finn.

Finn looked at me and frowned. He whispered back to the guard and they switched places. "I'm sorry, but I don't know…" He shook his head. His manner was genial, but his stance still action-ready, with his stiff shoulders and finger ready to plug a hole in me if I so much as said boo to him.

"Is this a joint…whatever." I waved my hand at all the Dallas SWAT members in position all over the parking lot but stopped when Finn stiffened. "Did the Peytonville PD ask Dallas to come in and help?"

"Yes, ma'am." His frown increased. "Is there a point to all this? You asked to speak to me specifically."

I swallowed. And whispered, "I met you last fall." I glanced over at the other Muldoon. He'd come out the front door and was coordinating the people around him. I couldn't be sure with all the commotion if he could hear me, but still I lowered my voice slightly. "My name is Celeste Eagan."

Finn Muldoon—Detective Shaw Muldoon's baby brother and a member of Dallas SWAT—eyed me skeptically. "I'm sorry, ma'am. I can't hear you." He leaned his body forward, but didn't step closer.

Again, I glanced toward my Muldoon. He was busy speaking with someone. Gabriel and Paul stood off with the men they'd pulled from the kitchen area of the bakery including Stanley, Gabriel's humongous bodyguard. If there were any other people in the building, they'd either gotten out the back or hadn't been found yet.

I opened my mouth to speak as Gabriel looked in my direction. He frowned. "I just came in to get dessert," I said loud enough for him to hear me across the lot. "I need to be going. I have kids waiting at home for me."

"I'm sorry, ma'am, you're going to have to wait until the scene is released. What did you say your name was again? I can't recall where we might have met."

"I met you last year." For about two seconds at a crime scene. I was certain he'd heard of me. Certain enough that I'd give up coffee for two weeks if he didn't know my name. "I'm..." I clamped my lips together when the older Muldoon walked over.

"Excuse us just a minute, ma'am." My Muldoon didn't give me a second look as he walked a bit away with his brother.

I couldn't hear what they were saying. Not that I was trying—that much—to eavesdrop. It was a little creepy how much they looked alike—they could be twins if they weren't ten years apart and one was a supersized version of the other. While Finn was beefy and brawny, Shaw was sinewy and tight. I could make a bundle if I made a Muldoon calendar featuring the pair.

Before I could start drooling over June and July, a sleek black Mercedes pulled into the edge of the lot. A silver-haired man in what had to be an expensive-as-hell suit stepped out.

"Christ. When did he call his lawyer?" Muldoon—Shaw—slammed his hands on his hips.

"They probably have a silent bat signal like a bank alarm." Finn shifted his gun on his shoulder.

You might have expected a man with such a sleek car and killer suit to be suave and debonair, but alas no, the man started screeching, in a nasally, whiny voice about his client's rights being violated the minute he got nose to nose with the closest officer. "Who's in charge here?"

The lawyer flipped open a briefcase and pulled out a camera. With the flash strobing, he took picture after picture of the crowd around the lot as well as onlookers.

Muldoon hurried over to him and shoved his hand in front of the camera. "I'd appreciate it if you'd stop taking pictures."

"Why, Detective? What have you got to hide?"

Even from the twenty feet or so that separated us, I could hear Muldoon growl. His brother Finn edged closer to the two men. The entire crowd was focused on the ruckus between the two. Not a single soul was paying me any attention. I edged a few steps away. Then a few more.

I was halfway across the parking lot when Gabriel's lawyer took a swing at Muldoon. All hell broke loose then. I turned my back and kept walking, like I had every right to be leaving. Every second I was waiting for a hand to clamp down on me—or worse, a bullet between my shoulder blades, however overly dramatic that might have seemed at the time.

I'd parked my car three blocks over when I'd gotten there. I'd been afraid that Gabriel might see it and know that I was snooping. I was ever so thankful when I finally reached my SUV cloaked in early evening dusk. There was not a single solitary soul around. I sat behind the wheel of the car for a good ten minutes, waiting to see if anyone came looking for me. I didn't want to add evasion charges to whatever else they could pin on me for being at the scene.

I'd love to have taken off the stupid latex mask right then and there, but despite how easy it looked in movies to whip the sucker off…without the spirit gum remover I didn't even want to try, lest I lose several layers of my own skin, as well.

Once I was sure I was in the clear, I drove back to the Peytonville Playhouse. I didn't want Dad or Paige to see me like this. They might not guess what I'd been up to, but even so I didn't want to have to explain.

It took half an hour to go from dowdy gal back to Celeste Eagan—I changed out of the extra padding and frumpy-dumpy clothes and into a pair of jeans and an I Heart Texas T-shirt—and another thirty minutes for the nerves to get back to regular harried rather than just-about-busted-in-a-raid-dressed-as-someone-else, off the chart harried. I'd left my hair pinned up. It was way too much trouble to pull out the umpteen bobby pins that'd kept my auburn locks up under the ash-blond wig.

Once I cleared up the mess in my office, I gathered up my belongings ready to head home and prop my feet up, maybe have a tall glass of something eighty proof—for this I'd forgo my ban on hard liquor. I was backing out of my parking space when a flashing red-and-blue light pulled up behind me. With a quick blast of the siren the car stopped, blocking me in my slot.

I'd never seen Muldoon in a squad car before. I didn't

like the thrill much less the trepidation that shot through me simultaneously. I shifted the SUV back into Park and got out just as he got out of the black-and-white. His brows pulled down in a fierce V. His full lips were hidden in the tight-pursed frown.

"Hi. What's up?" That harried level bumped up about forty-two-thousand degrees in a flash.

Muldoon gave me a once-over, then a twice-over. It was only then that I noticed his brother get out of the other side of the vehicle. He was still all in black, but minus his tactical gear.

"Is everything okay?" I took a step forward. Closer, I could see the shiner he'd gotten from the lawyer. "Oh, my goodness. What happened to your face?"

"He was born that way." Finn chuckled and leaned his forearm on the roof of the car.

Being that I was an actress and dramatic on a good day, I played it up. "Did you hit him, Officer Muldoon?"

"It's Finn. And no, I didn't have the pleasure." He was eyeing me with an odd expression.

If I had to wager a guess, once they cleared out the area and found themselves short one person, they tried to figure out the hows and whys. Add to that the fact that said woman said she knew Finn Muldoon... I'm surprised it took them so long to come and check me out.

I glared at the younger Muldoon and hurried over to the elder. I grabbed his chin in my hands and turned his face this way and that and tsked at the sight.

"I went by your house." Muldoon lowered my hand away from his face. He didn't however let go.

"To show me your shiner?"

"Something like that." Muldoon looked back at his brother. The two shared an almost imperceptible shrug and headshake. Had I not been all too aware of both men I might have missed it. My Muldoon then glanced around the empty lot. There was not one other car here. Not even Annabelle. She was out on a date.

"I had some work to catch up on." As if me being alone at the Peytonville Playhouse was a normal thing. Which it was not. The place freaked me out at night—I didn't know how Annabelle lived in her little apartment on the back side of the building—but Muldoon, however, didn't know that. "What does the other guy look like?" I motioned to his eye.

He shook his head. "Do you mind if I stop by later this evening? After I finish up a couple of things at the station."

Uh-oh. "Sure."

He started to leave, but paused and reached up into my hairline. I thought he was going to cup my head and reel me in for a kiss. Instead, he pinched my neck.

"Ow. Hey."

He held out a piece of the latex. "Missed a spot."

WHY DID I always pace when I knew an appearance by Muldoon was imminent?

"You're wearing a hole in the carpet." Dad looked up from the laptop on the coffee table. "In my day—"

"Dad, I love you but right now I don't think I can handle ancient yarns."

"I'm not ancient."

I jumped a foot off the ground when the bell rang. "Would you go into the kitchen to give us a few minutes?"

"Us who?" Dad asked as I opened the front door. He stood and tucked his hands into his pockets. "Good evening, Detective," he said when Muldoon walked in. Dad went into the kitchen as I'd asked, but his expression guaranteed questions would follow later when it was just him and me.

Muldoon held a white pastry box. "For you."

"What is it?"

"Paczki." He held the box out to me. "Really? Georgia from Jersey." When I didn't take the box, he walked in and set them on the coffee table next to the laptop. "It sounds like you're developing a few more characters in your repertoire."

"Uh…uh…" I'd been rendered speechless. It had never really happened before. Even when I'd had to wing it I'd always come up with something somewhat intelligible. I picked up the box and looked inside. Sure enough, four lemon and four prune pastries lined the box. Any hopes that Muldoon was fishing for something flew out the window.

I hesitated for a minute but found his heavy gaze.

Muldoon's bruised eye was darker than before. It made his brooding a little scarier and way sexier. "Tell you what, don't deny it. We both know that was you. If I don't press the issue, you won't have to lie. It's funny…" He paced over to the fireplace and looked at the photos. "After the last time you were all dolled up in makeup and whatnot, I swore I'd be able to tell it was you. There's something about you…" He shook his head and slumped his shoulders. "I should have you arrested, but I have no proof. Finn didn't recognize you."

I sat on the edge of the sofa still holding the box of paczki. The inexplicable urge to cry was so strong it almost hurt.

Muldoon turned around. "If you thought Grady was

scary before, can you imagine what he might do if he thinks you're capable of spying on him dressed up as any ol' person?"

Holy shit. All the heat drained from my face and my ears rang.

"Hey, hey now." Muldoon's scowl disappeared. He hurried over and settled his hands on my shoulders. "He has no clue it was you. His lawyer was accusing us of planting an undercover officer in his bakery. Said it was entrapment. You're not even on his radar of possibilities." He rubbed his hands up and down my arms. "There's no way he'd know. If I wasn't wise to your antics already…"

I stood and moved away from him. I couldn't look him in the eye.

"I'm sorry if I scared you." He cleared his throat. "Actually, no I'm not. You can't just go barreling into situations you are not trained to handle. You drive me crazy," he whispered from his spot across the room. I wasn't sure if I was even supposed to hear it until he added, "Not always in a bad way."

"I'm sorry."

The rumble of his chuckle was closer than I expected and I jumped when he said, "I don't think you are. On either front." Muldoon sighed.

"Oh, um….ahem."

Muldoon and I both swiveled around.

Paige stood with her hands balled on her hips.

I stepped toward my daughter. "Did you need something?"

Paige only stood and stared at us as if we were breaking some rule. Her dad had a new significant other who practically lived with him. All I had was a man standing in my living room telling me I drove him nuts. And I was getting the mini-me stare-down.

"Did you need something?" I said again, slower, as much to let my heart even out as to get my sweet precious interrupting child to the point.

"It's my bedtime." Paige tapped her toe impatiently and lifted her chin.

"Okeydokey." I set the box of paczki I was still holding back on the coffee table. "I, uh, I'll be right back." I settled my hand on my daughter's shoulder. "Let's go in the kitchen and tell Grandpop goodnight."

Paige let me lead her into the kitchen. Dad was eating the torte from the night before. Despite my constant yearning for chocolate, I don't think I could eat a single bite of it and not think of whatever retaliation methods Gabriel might employ on someone he thinks has wronged him.

Paige kissed Dad on the cheek. We were in her bedroom before she said anything. "Are y'all going steady?"

"What? Steady?"

"I know it's the twenty-first century, but I kind of like the idea of you having a steady."

Those *Brady Bunch* reruns were infiltrating her impressionable brain.

"You deserve someone like Detective Muldoon. He's a good guy."

"Have I told you how much I love you lately?"

She rolled her eyes again. "All the time. Stop avoiding the subject. Are you going steady?"

I ruffled her hair. "Not yet."

FOURTEEN

"Dᴉᴅ ʏᴏᴜ ɢᴇᴛ her to bed okay?" Muldoon was sitting on the arm of the sofa.

I nodded. "Can I ask you question?"

He stood. "Always."

"Why aren't we dating?" I fidgeted with the hem of my sleeve, didn't exactly look him in the eye. "We were kind of heading there. Though in light of all the crap that's happened with Gabriel, I could see why you'd change your mind." I hazarded a peek at him. "I wouldn't blame you if you walked away and never looked back."

He held my gaze but didn't comment.

I looked away and walked to the other end of the sofa to sit. "I'd be devastated but I'd understand." Again I messed with the hem of my sleeve. I clamped my mouth shut. Could I embarrass myself much more?

The sofa depressed next to me as Muldoon sat.

I flashed him a quick glance. "Sorry."

"For?"

"Diarrhea of the mouth. You know how I get sometimes."

"It's a conflict right now. With Levi." Muldoon set his hand on my knee. He stroked the side of my knee with his thumb, then pulled his hand back. "And you. You're still in it up to your neck."

"I didn't do it on purpose."

He gave a rough laugh. "You never do," he mumbled.

He shifted to take my hand in his. "I've also been having trouble with Colby."

"Your son?"

Muldoon had a sixteen-year-old son. He lived in Dallas with his mom, Muldoon's ex-wife. I'd never met the boy. The way Muldoon spoke about him, he was your typical sullen teenager and more often than not begged out of his weekends with his dad. I hadn't pressed the issue because it wasn't my place and because I didn't want to add to Muldoon's problems.

It was hard enough to deal with being a single parent when your child cooperated.

"He's been staying with me."

"Really?" That surprised me. Muldoon hadn't said anything.

"He and his mother had a fight and she packed him up and sent him to me." He leaned back on the sofa, my hand still entwined with his. "He's been giving me fits about spending time…" He trailed off.

"Spending time with me."

"Not you per se." Muldoon sighed. "I haven't dated much since my divorce."

"Which was how many years ago?" I know he told me at one point but it was when we'd first met, and I hadn't kept a dossier on the man. That would just be creepy.

"Seven years."

My chin hit my chest. I knew he said he hadn't dated much before me, but that's practically never.

"I believe you've been divorced for more than three years yourself. I don't see men beating down your door and you accepting."

Maybe I was waiting for one man in particular. Thankyouverymuch. I sniffed. "That's different."

"How?" Muldoon shook his head as the corner of his mouth tilted up.

"I'm a single mom."

"I'm a single dad."

"My daughter lives with me."

"And goes to her dad's after school and every other weekend. You have time, but you don't put yourself out there."

"And you work yourself to exhaustion so you don't have to put yourself out there." I pulled my hand free of his. "So we're both skittish. Sue us."

Muldoon shook his head, but didn't comment.

"Why doesn't he go to Peytonville Prep? Between you and your sibs' legacies at the school, I bet he could forgo half the admittance process." All six of the Muldoons graduated top of their class. Between them, they'd been in nearly every extracurricular activity possible; I think the Chess Club was the only one not inhabited by a Muldoon.

"There's no way in hell I'd subject my son to that."

"Wow, tell me how you really feel." I rubbed my chest just above my heart. Sure, I was no longer employed there, but ten years in their employ did leave a warm spot for the school itself.

"Sorry. Colby wouldn't fit in there any more than I did. My brother and sisters may have had a decent time there, but I—"

"You were valedictorian," I interrupted trying to remind him it wasn't all bad.

"I remember. That was about the only good thing that came out of it." Muldoon ran his hand over his face. "I did meet my ex-wife there, too."

"Is that good or bad?"

He chuckled. "Depends on the day."

I bit my lower lip and willed myself to stay quiet. But I am a weak-willed woman. "What went wrong? In your marriage?"

"Infidelity." All the playfulness fled his face and his cop mask slammed down leaving his face devoid of human emotion.

"You cheated on her?"

"No."

The anger in his voice straightened my spine. "O-kay. Obviously the conversation is treading into a raw place." I stood and straightened out the legs of my pants that'd bunched up all around my thighs. "I apologize for overstepping." Again. I wanted to throw that out there, but clearly whatever wall the man had built up was just reinforced with armor and made moot anything else I might say. Coupled with the mind games going on with his son, he wasn't in a good place at the moment.

"Well, it's getting late…" I didn't want him to leave mad, but I had no idea how to console someone who'd been hurt so bad. If I knew what to say, I would throw the words out there over and over until he heard me and believed me. And last time I checked, they didn't make Hallmark cards that read: "Good thing you're rid of her then, isn't it?" Yeah that's a big fat not-gonna-happen.

Muldoon stood and we walked to the door. "Thank you for going after Grady for me."

"Stay away from him." Muldoon looked like he was going to say more but didn't. He turned to go without so much as a peck on the cheek.

"'Night," I called after him then shut the door. I didn't wait to see if he turned back or not.

I leaned up against the closed door for a long moment.

Not only had he not answered my question about dating, but after the way he pulled ever further back, I wasn't even sure if we were still friends.

"Everything okay?" Dad glanced up from the magazine he was reading at the kitchen counter when I walked in.

"Not really." I waved off whatever questions might be coming next. "I'll be fine."

"I know you will. You're a strong woman."

"Thanks, Daddy." I gave him a quick hug. "I don't remember things ever being this complicated with Colin."

"And look how that turned out. Nothing that comes easy is ever worth much." Dad's philosophy shared, he bid me goodnight.

I sat at the kitchen bar and let the quietness of the house wash over me. So his kid had moved in with him. Big deal. That was the lot in being a single parent. You dealt with it. And dating…it shouldn't be something you wait to do. So says the woman who waited nearly three years to get off the bench and into the game, that stupid little nagging voice said in my ear.

A yawn escaped and I stretched. All the excitement I'd gone through the past couple of days was catching up. I settled my head down on my arms for just a second, then I'd go turn out all the lights and go to bed.

I bolted upright when the table vibrated. "Wha…" I swiped at the drool covering my chin.

Paige stood beside my chair peering at me over the top of her glasses. "I swear, Celeste, you have become the most unconventional person. First you're dressing up like strange people, then I'm catching you nose to nose with Muldoon. Now apparently we've taken to sleeping in the kitchen."

"Kitchen? What time is it?"

"Ten 'til seven."

"In the morning?" I tried to stand up quickly, but my back and neck ached like crazy and pinched in protest at the sudden movement. "I just set my head down for a moment."

Paige tsked.

"Fix yourself something to eat, please." I headed toward the hallway. "And the name's Mom. Or Mother. Please stop calling me Celeste."

"CELESTE, CELESTE, CELESTE."

I looked up from my sandwich as Gabriel pulled out a chair across from me. "How did you get in here?" The Peytonville Playhouse wasn't exactly locked down during non-performance hours, but we also didn't let random people roam about as they please. And fewer still found their way to the kitchenette/break room at the far end of the building.

"Unhappy to see me?"

I pasted on what I hoped looked like a congenial smile. "No. Just surprised." I swiped at my mouth with a napkin. "Hungry? I could share my sandwich. Or there's something in a green container in the fridge." I motioned to the Kenmore in the corner. "If you value your intestines, though, you won't touch the stuff."

"No, thanks." Dressed in his pressed navy slacks and starched tan shirt, he sat in a paint-spattered chair. He looked like a bankroller in a world of artsy-fartsy players. "I came by to see how you're doing."

"Me?" God, I hoped my cheeks didn't flame as red as they felt. "I'm good. Why?"

"I haven't seen you since the restaurant." He eyed me.

Was he fishing for something? Did he suspect Georgia was a figment of my troupe's handwork with latex? "You did get everything I sent you, yes?"

I dropped my hands to my lap so he couldn't see how badly they shook. "Yes, I did. And I'm sorry. I meant to send you a thank-you note. The bag is lovely but too much. I can't accept it."

"Nonsense. It was the least I could do. I could see how much you adored the replica when you came into the bakery. I have a friend who knows someone."

I'd put money on the designer herself. He seemed like the type of man who had friends in every walk of life.

The back door burst open and the troupe that was scheduled for a workshop came in chatting and carrying on. It was enough to tear his eyes off me for a moment. A moment long enough to rein in my composure, startled by the fact that he'd just shown up. I would wing it. Yet again. "I was hoping I could invite you out to dinner," I blurted out.

For the first time, a little tension eased away from his eyes and mouth. A slight smile curved his lips. "What did you have in mind?"

Think, Celeste, think. I needed to come up with something that didn't seem like I was making it up as I went along—which I was—as well as someplace I wasn't likely to run into anyone—which, truth be told, could be any number of places since my acquaintances had waned significantly over the last few years. "Have you ever been to…" I coughed. Yes, as a ploy tactic it was weak, but a girl had to do what a girl had to… One of the troupe walked by. His dad owned several restaurants across the metroplex. "Excuse me. Sorry. Have you ever been to Sergeants?"

ME AND MY big mouth. Not only was Sergeants uber-crowded on a Wednesday night, I recognized no less than three tablesful of folks. Gabriel had his hand at the small of my back as we wended through the tables to a quiet corner in the back. Once the hostess left, we sat in silence for a long moment. Gabriel picked up his menu. "What do you recommend?"

"Honestly, I've never been here before." It was one thing to fake the plan, it was another to try and pretend I have a clue what's what at a restaurant I've never been to before. "But I have been wanting to come here for some time." True enough.

A smile tilted the corner of his mouth. "Well, then I'm glad I could be the one to accompany you."

We both perused the menu. Sergeants had everything from pasta to Asian dishes to burgers and steaks. Very eclectic. When the waiter came around we both ordered drinks. I stuck to water. Being even the slightest bit ine-briated with this man had proven to be less than ideal.

"I don't know if you heard, but we had a little bit of trouble at the bakery."

Acting training, do your stuff. "Really? What hap-pened?"

"Your beau paid me a visit with several of his friends." He twisted his flatware in circles.

As casually as possible, I sighed and said, "I don't have a beau."

Gabriel's eyebrows rose. "Hmm."

He didn't believe me—about not having a beau—I could tell, but for once I wasn't making anything up. I wasn't entirely sure where I stood with Muldoon. We hadn't spoken since he'd walked out of the house. "Was there an issue at your bakery?"

"Not really. There was nothing for them to find. Though—" he chuckled "—my lawyer got a good knock in."

My mind flashed to the bruise around Muldoon's eye. "Hmm." I didn't want to delve into this conversation any further than need be.

"Speaking of lawyers…" He paused when the waiter returned with our drinks. He swirled then sniffed the small amount of wine poured into his glass. Once he tasted, and approved, he waited until the young man poured a full glass and moved away before he continued. "I heard from a source that Arnie has been moving those faux handbags around town for a few months. Gets regular shipments."

All those crates.

I slid my finger around the top edge of my water. "So this wasn't a onetime thing. It's a racket."

"Racket?"

I ignored the almost mocking way he repeated what I said. "Why did one of the bag shipments show up at Levi's?"

Gabriel checked his watch. "More than one since the property that burned down was his property. What? You're frowning."

"When I was at the Sagebrush property, a truck came barreling around the corner as I was leaving."

"And?"

"And it was large enough to have hauled that crate away."

"Did you get the plate numbers from it?"

"No. I didn't think anything of it once I made sure it wasn't going to run me off the road." I paused, thinking. "It did have a logo on the side."

"What was it?" Gabriel leaned forward. He seemed truly interested.

I lifted my head and stared off into nothingness. "It was green and yellow." I closed my eyes and tried to remember. "Maybe a leprechaun or something." When I opened my eyes and looked back at my dinner companion, he had a faraway look in his eyes. I took a long slow drink of my water. And waited. When he hadn't commented yet, I set my glass back down.

The waiter brought our food over. I honestly tried not to flinch, but the little snort I heard from the other side of the table told me I must have. I did wait until the waiter was far out of earshot before I poked at a pale white cube on my plate. "I, uh, I don't know what this is."

"What did you order again?"

"Some spicy Asian medley thingie."

Gabriel laughed and cut into his steak. "That's tofu. You don't like tofu?"

"Do I look like I've ever eaten tofu?" I twisted the fork between my fingers and examined it. "Maybe if they fried it and doused it with barbecue sauce or something." I picked all the white cubes from the rest of the vegetables.

"Here." Gabriel set half his juicy filet onto my plate.

"You don't have to do that." Some of my fear eked away.

"I could go in the kitchen and get you something else. I doubt the chef would mind." And with his self-assured smile and not a doubt in my mind he could and would do it, all the trepidation rushed back into place.

"Don't be silly. I can't take your dinner. It's my fault for not reading the menu correctly." Darnitall. I wanted a smooth, easy evening because frankly the more I was around the man the more he scared the bejeezus out of me. But no, I have to rush through the menu, order something that looked—and probably was—healthy, and here some man in the back would be refreshing his résumé if I twitched my pinky finger. Okay, so maybe that was an exaggeration, but I wasn't willing to take that chance.

"Take the steak or…" He set his napkin on the table and scooted out his chair a fraction.

"Looks great. Can't wait to taste it."

"Good. Let's eat." He sliced off a bite of steak and popped it into his mouth. Once he swallowed, he pointed at my plate with his knife. "Eat."

I did not jump. No matter what the stupid waiter— who dropped a tray of water glasses right behind me— said. And unless there were cameras in the restaurant, no one can prove otherwise.

Gabriel was so disgusted he tossed a handful of bills on the table, grabbed my elbow and dragged me out of there lickety-split. We were in the parking lot standing between our cars when he finally let go. "Do you mind telling me what that was all about?"

"I—I don't know what you mean."

"If I blink too fast you're practically coming out of your skin. What's going on? Are you truly afraid of me?" He stood with his hands loose at his sides but tension rolled off of him.

I bit my lip for a moment and tried to formulate an appropriate response. Unfortunately, "Kind of" was what eked out.

He tossed his head back and laughed. Loud. Not the reaction I might have expected. I stood patiently and let him get control of himself. "Only you," he said with a shake of his head. He opened the passenger door of his car—a sleek as all get-out Beemer convertible. "Get in."

"I have my vehicle." I pushed the key fob in my hand and unlocked my door.

Gabriel took the keys from my hand, opened the door, tossed them inside and locked it before he shut the door again.

I lunged and tried to stop it before it closed, but I wasn't quick enough. "Hey."

"I'll have someone come get your car. Get in."

"If this is you trying not to be scary, can I say you're failing miserably?" Did I dare not comply?

He sighed and pulled out his cell phone, then punched a number into his phone. "Here."

I don't know who I was expecting but when Muldoon answered, a wave of relief and a little apprehension that Gabriel had the number memorized engulfed me. It notched the fear up another rung. "Hello?" Muldoon asked again.

I closed my eyes. Just what I needed now. "Hey, it's Celeste."

"Did you get a new number?"

"I'm borrowing a, uh, friend's phone."

"Tell him we're going to eat over in Fort Worth at Ol' South," Gabriel whispered. "Your detective will know where you're at and you can relax."

I felt like a wee bit of a heel. "I was just, uh, checking in."

"What's going on? Are you in trouble?" His voice was clipped and tight.

"Not exactly, no."

"Where are you? Better yet who are you with?"

I glanced at Gabriel and to the open door of the Beemer and back. "Out to dinner. With a friend."

I couldn't swear to it, but I'd say that at that moment Muldoon's teeth ground off a good millimeter of enamel. "The friend being Grady."

"Yep." I shifted and leaned my hip up against the Beemer. As soon as my butt hit the cool metal, I straightened and made sure I didn't leave a dent or anything. "Sorry," I mouthed.

Gabriel smiled with a quick shake of his head.

"Why are you calling? To rub it in or something?"

"What the hell kind of question is that?" And bam that set my spine straight and tense. "Sorry to have bothered you." I smashed button after button but could still hear Muldoon's tiny voice through the phone. "Here, I can't turn it off."

Gabriel retrieved his phone and ended the call. "I'm glad I'm not the only who gets you all worked up."

I slid into the smooth leather seat. "Where did you say we were going?"

FIFTEEN

"Oh, my gawd." I licked the syrup from my lips.

"So is it fair to say you like it?"

"Don't take this the wrong way when I say, duh." A never-ending coffeepot and to-die-for pancakes... I think I just found my next dress size.

"Better than tofu surprise?" A sly smile quirked up the corner of his mouth.

"Absolutely. I can't believe I've never heard of this place." I pushed my empty plate as far away as I could so I wouldn't be tempted to run my finger across it to get every last dribble of syrup.

Gabriel leaned back in his chair and settled his arm across the one next to him. "There used to be a bowling alley attached to it."

"I love bowling. I suck at it, but..." Chalk my new-found love of everything up to a sugar high. Gabriel wasn't complaining or running for the hills so I wasn't too worried. But it was not pretty to see a grown woman gush over...everything.

"Maybe you haven't had the right teacher yet."

I snorted and nearly lost half a cup of coffee out my nose. "Scary and smooth."

Gabriel chuckled.

"Thank you for bringing me here."

"I'm not such a bad guy after all." He picked up his napkin from his lap, tossed it onto the table and scooched his chair back. "I can't believe you're not bursting at the seams with Arnie questions."

I smacked my forehead. "I completely forgot."

"Good company and good food will do that to you."

"I guess. So where did we leave off? The logo on the truck that tried to flatten me. You know what it's for." Not a question. I could tell by the look on his face that he knew exactly what company that was.

"It's for a novelty store. The Blarney Shop. They sell candles and trinkets, mostly with an Irish theme."

I tapped my lips with my finger as my brain catalogued this new information, then frowned at Gabriel. "Do you think whoever whacked Arnie—"

"*Whacked?* You've been watching too much TV."

"An impossibility. There's no such thing as too much TV, coffee or chocolate. Anyway. If he's shipping in these bags, he has to be selling them somewhere. But it's illegal to sell knockoffs. So they wouldn't just be sitting around the store."

Gabriel chuckled.

"What?"

"The way your mind works. The process of going over information…" He shook his head.

"Assuming Arnie's killer's caught, what do you have planned for that person?"

"What makes you think I have anything planned?"

"Well, for starters, you're working awfully hard to help me look into who could be the culprit. I suppose you could be doing that for the sheer entertainment, which is what I hope, but…"

"Does the alternative fall into the scary category?"

I know I lack the little censor button that keeps most thoughts stored up in the brain somewhere. So it shouldn't have been a surprise when the candid "Most definitely" popped out of my mouth. With Gabriel, I no longer even had the decency to blush when I answered frankly.

He leaned his elbows onto the table and steepled his fingers in front of him. "Can I be honest with you?"

"As I told you once before, I'm not your lawyer or your priest so I guess that's up to you."

He smiled. "I guess my motives will be determined, or maybe redirected is a better term, once I know who is behind the deed. And then maybe even why."

I held a bottle of blueberry syrup and dropped a dollop onto the tip of my finger. "I'm not going to try and dissect that, if that's okay with you."

"Fine."

"Okay, back to Arnie. Why would someone whack a person they're in business with? What do they gain?"

"Total control of the business and profits."

"But they draw attention on them."

"True. But so far no one seems to be the least bit aware of the smuggling ring."

"Your contact was."

"They aren't likely to turn anyone over to the police."

"Who do you associate with?" The blueberry tasted, I repeated the step with strawberry, butter pecan and boysenberry. Did not care for the boysenberry. "Arnie could have had it coming from just about any direction. You said the man would swindle just about anyone he could. Who else has motive? Just about anyone who's had the misfortune of coming in contact with the man. I don't know that I ever came within spitting distance of him, but he was a piece of work from what I heard."

"That he was." Gabriel stood. "Let's head to the car

and walk off some of these carbs." He pulled out my chair as I stood. Were it not for the breaking-kneecaps aspect to this man, he might be an idyllic date.

We walked out to the cool Fort Worth evening breeze. I fought every instinct to jump when he settled his hand at the small of my back. Gentlemanly all the way. For a moment, my mind warped to him and a deadbeat customer. Did he apologize before he forcibly removed one fingernail at a time? Did he disinfect the knife? Have a bandage ready? Maybe send flowers the next day with a reminder to pay up. I snorted—mostly out of nerves.

"Did you say something?" When I shook my head he continued, "Did you ever wonder what Arnie was doing at your friend's property?"

"Sure." I figured he was spying or something. Not that that really made any sense.

"And curiouser still that he recently tried to buy a property from the same friend."

"I'm not even going to ask how you know all this, but yes, strange."

Gabriel just stopped and looked at me.

"How long does it take to get a crate that size shipped to a location?" I asked.

"Anything can be done as quickly as you want it with the right motivation."

That was true. Look how he'd managed to get my SUV out of a police impound lot after hours on a Sunday. Something that even Muldoon didn't seem capable of doing.

"But to answer where I think you're going with this, if those bags came from another country, which is most likely, then weeks."

"Before Arnie signed the contract on the property he

was trying to buy." We actually walked away from the parking lot and toward a strip mall next to the restaurant. I saw a shadow peel away from the building and balked.

Gabriel settled his hand on my arm. "That's Stanley."

Stanley? As we moved closer, I got a good look at the man. Yep, it was the giant from the bakery. The one who always stood in the corner. "Gotcha." I gave the man a little finger wave, which he ignored completely. "You know, Levi was telling me he'd had some of his shipments go missing. He always suspected it was Arnie."

"Why?"

"He was trying to convince Levi into partnering with him and some other man. He hung around his properties, made a nuisance of himself."

"Hmm." Gabriel rubbed his chin.

I slowed my step. "What hmm?"

"If he's using Levi's addresses for his bills of lading, it keeps his hands clean if anything gets intercepted."

"You sound impressed."

"From Arnie, yes. It's a risky venture. So many ways you could bungle a delivery and lose the money you've tied into it."

"You haven't once suggested Levi was in on it."

"He wasn't."

I knew that but... "How are you so sure?"

"Levi is an honest man."

I was a little shocked he'd say that. My friend was the best person around, but I wouldn't have expected Gabriel to think so, too.

"Would another bookie—"

"Financial facilitator."

"Whatever. Would another one be less hesitant to rid himself of a pain like Arnie?" Was it too much to hope that was the case? It meant someone with a clear motive and not connected to anyone else we knew did the deed.

"It's hard to say what might make one facilitator cut his losses over what another one might do. Me, I'd get my money. First."

"Yikes."

"I am a businessman."

We turned back toward the parking lot. Stanley was still shadowing us, but at a distance. "What would your next move be?"

"Hire a detective."

"Why haven't you done that?"

He chuckled. "I don't need to. I have you."

"Yeah, right," I said, but I didn't think he was kidding. "I don't know. Unless someone steps forward waving their hands swearing they did it, I doubt we'll know." I headed toward his car. "Thank you for dinner. It was truly wonderful."

Gabriel opened the door to the Beemer but didn't move to let me in. "It was all my pleasure. Where to now? Would you like to go have a drink somewhere?"

Despite being more relaxed, I was still not one hundred percent comfortable with him. "I'm practically in a sugar coma now," I used as an excuse. "I have work in the morning."

"Ah, yes, the dutiful employee."

"You say that like it's a bad thing."

"No, I think it's admirable that you take your job and your talents so seriously. What is it you do again?"

"I'm the principal actress and manage the theater itself."

"That's right. Costumes and makeup and plays and all."

Sweat broke out at my temples despite the cool air. "Yes."

"It must be an interesting job."

"It is." I tried to gauge his reaction to what I was saying, but other than a polite smile, he was very good at hiding any and all emotion.

"You had a stellar show this past December."

"I, uh…"

"*A Christmas Carol.* You are talented. From what I've heard."

He knew. Maybe he didn't have definitive proof, but somehow he knew that was me at the bakery the other day. And he was toying with me. I did not like to be toyed with, whether he scared the crap out of me or not. I snagged my cell from my purse and pretended to open an email. "Dangitall, my daughter isn't feeling well. Could you take me home now?"

Gabriel eyed me for a long moment. "Okay." He held the door open for me and I slid into the car. We drove back to my house in silence and as promised my car was parked right out front—again, I did not want to explore the powers this man wielded.

"Thanks for another interesting evening." I released my seat belt. I didn't expect him to walk me to the door—manners or no—so I grabbed his hand when he reached for the keys to turn off the car. "No worries, I'm good. I'll stop by the bakery and see you soon." Maybe. But I didn't know what else to say. How did you end a night with a man who scared the bejeezus out of you, but who you also didn't want to tip off or piss off?

He didn't say anything, but a muscle ticked in his jaw. Just great.

"Good night." I hurried out of the car and up the walk.

The door swung open before I could even settle my hand on the knob. A small but very formidable body blocked my entrance into the house. "Mom?" Why aren't you in Kansas, I wanted to ask.

It shouldn't be a shock to come home and find a slew of different people than when I left. The past few months should have steeled me to surprise visitors, but my mother was no ordinary visitor. Normally when she came to Texas, I fretted and worried for the entire month prior. And then it took another week to decompress afterward. Her standing in my doorway, scrutinizing another of my not-really-a-date dates... I inherited Gabriel's tic and it gravitated up my cheek to my left eye.

My mother peered around me. "He can't be bothered to walk you up to the door?"

"It was just a friend dropping me off. Not a date."

She harrumphed. Like a master, I might add.

I pushed past her into the house and drew her back inside with me. "What are you doing here?"

"I've come to collect your father."

"DADDY, YOU'RE WEARING a hole in the carpet. Sit down please." He'd been pacing for the better part of an hour. Ever since my mother took Paige to the store for "something decent to eat" my dad had not sat still.

"She always does this, you know. Barges right in and tells me what to do and to think. Why do you think I left? I needed to get away from her and breathe."

"I know, Daddy, I'm sorry."

"Don't you apologize for her." He scrubbed his hands through his thinning hair. "I'm sorry. I shouldn't vent to you about your mother. That's inappropriate of me."

"You need someone to talk to. Someone who understands how she can tie you up inside." I didn't even try to hide the bitter tone to my voice. I loved my mother, I truly did, but I loved her a hell of a lot better several hundred miles away. She loved me, too, but it was through micro-managing that she showed her love. An involved mother was a caring mother.

Blech. It was also a nosy, needling, harp-on-you-for-any-and-everything mother and it could make you gasp for air the few times you got away long enough to fill your lungs.

"We'll leave. First thing tomorrow morning. There's no point in both of us having to suffer." He smiled.

"I hate this." I stood and gave my dad a huge hug. "Maybe once you guys get back to Topeka you can see a counselor or something."

"Maybe." He gave me a last, quick squeeze and headed back to the spare bedroom.

I so didn't want to get in the middle of my parents' relationship, but it was hard to see my dad so...deflated. My mother could be overbearing on a good day. I never understood why. Then again, she and I never really talked. We spoke at each other, but not to each other.

It was nearly ten when my mother finally returned with Paige. "Go brush your teeth and get into bed. I'll be there in just a minute to tuck you in." When my daughter was out of earshot I whipped around and glared at my mother. "Are you kidding me, keeping her out so late on a school night?"

My mother stood all prim and proper, her spine straight and little-to-no emotion on her face. "It's not that late."

"It is when you're eleven. I called you several times but you didn't answer your cell."

"I never really got the hang of it. I never remember to look at it." She walked past me and set her purse on the coffee table before she sat on the edge of the sofa.

"That's all you're going to say about it?" I wedged myself between her and the table and sat precariously on it. "Mother, I don't know what is going on with you, but this is not like you. What is it? Talk to me."

"I'm dying."

All the air backed up in my lungs, and spots danced before my eyes. "I beg your damn pardon." The whisper was barely perceptible.

"Don't take that tone with me," she immediately chastised but didn't look me in the eye, didn't change her expression or demeanor. "I'm not getting any younger."

"Okay, but specifically what's wrong with you? What do you have?"

"I don't have anything. But Celeste, I'm turning sixty-five next month. My mother was dead before she turned sixty."

"She was hit by a train." I released my mother's hands. "Are you sick?"

She scoffed at the question. "No."

I clamped my hand over my eyes and counted to twenty—slowly. "Mother, your acknowledgment of your mortality does not constitute dying."

"I knew you wouldn't understand. Neither does your father." She stood and all but knocked me backward onto the coffee table.

"You're right, I don't get it. You're worried because you have a birthday coming up, but instead of celebrating life you drive away a man who loves you for all your faults. You have a daughter who loves you and has never done anything other than try to please you and all you can do is criticize her. You have a granddaughter who adores you and you plant the same seeds of inadequacy in her. We try the best we can, get by the best we know how. But we're not perfect. And we're never going to live up to the standards you've set."

"And once again, it's all my fault that you're a divorced woman living alone."

My chin hit my chest and I'm pretty sure my eyes did a little cartoon bug-out. "Where did that come from?" I ran my hand through my hair. "Mother, Mom, I do love you. I am glad you're turning sixty-five because the alternative is unthinkable to me. I'm sorry that Daddy and I don't understand what you're going through." I moved to hug her, but she backed away.

"I'll see you in the morning." She walked down the hallway and into the guest bedroom.

I just let my head slump. Tears stung the backs of my eyes, but I would not cry no matter how scary the thought that I might, one day, grow as bitter and scared as my mother. I obviously didn't know what to say to her. And unfortunately it might always be that way.

It did make me wonder though. I'd never gotten any kind of validation from my mother. My father, sure, he couldn't be any more supportive. Did her lack of... interest in anything I did make me the nosy buttinsky that has gotten into all kinds of trouble? Was I looking for the fulfillment elsewhere? In solving issues that had nothing to do with me, but that made me feel like I'd accomplished something? Did I look for trouble for that reason? I slapped my hand to my forehead. Really? My mother was right. I was blaming her.

Yeah, that was going to get me nowhere. Except maybe the loony bin. Though if I kept digging into the mess with Arnie, maybe it was where I should be. But was that going stop me? Probably not.

I scoffed about the same time as my cell vibrated at my hip pocket. I clicked the talk button and had the phone to my ear without even checking the caller ID. It was after ten. Only one person would call.

"Yes, I'm home, Muldoon. In one piece." I tucked my other hand on my hip.

"Good to know." His heavy sigh all but rattled the phone. "You have waded knee-deep into some scary waters. I hope you know what you're doing."

"Don't I always?"

SIXTEEN

"You're doing it all wrong, Celeste." Annabelle took the stack of headshots from my hand. The Peytonville Playhouse held quarterly auditions for new troupe members and we'd just had a batch of new applicants. Instead of separating them out by gender, I'd put them in piles of—I squinted and looked—by hair color apparently.

"Is it a man?" she asked as she stacked all the photos together then tucked her shoulder-length tresses behind her ears. "Of course it is." She waved her hand. "We women don't get that far-off look for anything other than a man. Give me all the details."

I looked at her and just blinked. How could I give her details when I didn't even know what was going on. I was involved—yet maybe not involved—with a smoking hot detective. I had a gangster bookie who scared as much as intrigued me—but mostly scared—sniffing around. I was supposedly helping a friend catch whoever had tried to frame him for murder, and other than gaining five pounds from all the damn pastries I'd been eating, I hadn't made any progress whatsoever. Details? I'd give her details… "Naw, I'm just tired. My mother came down to collect my father."

Annabelle made a face. "Was there drama?"

"Surprisingly, no." Which shocked me more than the woman standing at my door. "At least not yet. They couldn't get a flight until tomorrow. Ask me then if there's drama." The phone rang and cut off any further conversation. "Peytonville's finest playhouse, how may I—"

"Be at 2071 Flagstone at ten tonight if you want the information you've been looking for," a woman said.

I pulled the phone away from my ear and stared at it. When I placed it back at my ear I asked, "Say again?"

The caller repeated the address, which I had the sense to write down the second time around. "Who is this?"

"Ten o'clock," she said and hung up.

Right, like I'm gonna waltz my ass to some house late at night with a vague call like that.

I gave a mental headshake as I returned the handset to the base. Who was I kidding, that was exactly the type of call to get me to show up somewhere. With my computer already on, I pulled up a search engine and plugged in the address. It was a residential area a few blocks from Levi's flip-house, better known as the first crime scene.

Why would someone call me? The only person who knew I was looking into matters was Gabriel. And Muldoon. And Levi and Kellen. Bueller and probably Detective Bush. Hell, even Daddy knew I'd made a few, somewhat discreet inquiries. The list wasn't as short as I'd like. Still…who would call with the vaguest of vague demands? I know what the others would say: Drop it.

Not that there was much to drop. I hadn't learned anything really helpful up to this point so what could I gain by going? More confusion? Someone who didn't want me poking into things waiting with a hammer for my own precious noggin? A shiver ran up my spine.

"Yeah, no," I said aloud. I wasn't going to fall for that.

I ripped off the sheet, wadded it up in my fist and tossed the balled-up paper into the trashcan next to my desk. Let whoever wanted to play me find some other sucker.

"HELLO." LEVI LET himself into the house. The man was a little disheveled—his shirt was wrinkled and he lacked any spark. Something very far from his normally kempt self. "This has been a crapola week." He ran his hands through his hair, mussing it up further. "My lawyer called today."

"Coz? Why?" Before I could set a package of rolls onto the table, Levi grabbed the bag from me and pulled one out.

"Seems they want to question me more about Mandy's death." He finished the roll in a couple of bites.

"It's just procedure. Everything will be fine." I said the words but I didn't know that my head *or* heart believed them.

Levi sighed and rolled his shoulders. "Seems like forever since I've seen you." He opened his arms and I walked into the hug.

I needed one of my friend's hugs. A sniffle caught in the back of my throat. I could not go more than a few days without seeing Levi. I would not be able to function. No, I mentally reprimanded myself. We would figure this out, one way or another. He would not go to jail. And I needed to keep him preoccupied with other things so he wouldn't dwell on it until we made the breakthrough we needed.

Still in his embrace, I whispered in his ear, "I don't suppose you've seen my parents." I *was* curious and it was the perfect excuse to change the subject.

The sudden tightening of his grip, followed by a quick, "Um," told me he might very well know where they'd gotten themselves off to.

I tried to pull away but he wouldn't let go. "Levi." I gave him my sternest mom-voice. "What did you do?"

"*Do* is an overly strong word." He squeezed a little tighter still. "I might have suggested, heavily suggested, that the two of them go someplace romantic. Just the two of them."

"And that would be where?"

"Vegas."

A shrill harpy moment built in my toes and headed upward. "Paige, I need you to run off to your room and start your homework. 'Kay?"

Paige snickered. Maybe a little maniacally. "You're in trouble, Uncle Levi."

As soon as I was sure Paige was in her room I pushed Levi to arm's length. "You told my parents to go to Vegas? My dad, who was gambling here—"

"It's legal there."

"—and my mother, who has issues with the local church raffle because it invites unsavory people. To a church raffle. And you sent them to Vegas."

"I didn't send them. I merely suggested they need some time together where no one knew them so they could reconnect. And as it turns out your mother has a huge thing for Frank Sinatra impersonators." He shrugged like it was the most natural recommendation.

"You'll forgive me if I don't thank you."

Levi's eyes widened. "You wanted your mom gone, right? I got her and your father to have some together-time in another state."

I sighed. He did do that. And who knows, maybe in a relaxed environment the two could reconnect and... blah. I couldn't even fool myself that that was a good idea. "You will owe me big-time, when, if, when this goes horribly wrong."

"Have a little faith."

I scoffed.

He waved away the conversation as if a swish of his hand could right the world. The mood I was in, I decided to let him live. For now. "I have a little news of my own." I checked on the chicken breasts in the oven. "You staying for dinner? I made plenty."

"I could eat. Are you going to tell me or make me beg?" Levi's eyes shone with curiosity.

"Begging might be fun."

Levi started whining like a dog and tucked his hands up under his chin. "Pretty please tell me, sweets. Pretty please."

I couldn't hold out any longer. "I was telling Gabriel about a truck I saw the night of the fire."

"Gabriel? And you? You two are having full-out conversations now?"

I frowned. "He knows Arnie. He knew about the handbags and he says that Arnie has been selling them for a while."

Levi's response—or maybe I should call it lack thereof—was lukewarm at best.

"You know something. You...you've been holding out on me." I paced away from the oven and stood nose-to-chin with Levi. When he didn't do me the honor of bending to meet my gaze, I snagged a hold of his shirt and pulled until we were nose-to-nose. "Levi Alpheus Weiss, you'd better start talking or I'll..." I racked my brain for something that would make him squirm, something that would also make him spill what he knew. Aha. A wicked grin curled my mouth. "Or I'll sneak into your house and rearrange all of your CDs—better yet, I will replace them all with Hungarian polka." I released his shirt to let him straighten back up.

His face was a mixture of fear and incredulity with a hint of mirth for what couldn't possibly actually happen. Though he knew I would. I'd done it once before and it had taken him hours to right his extensive collection.

Levi swallowed heavily. "I suspected it was something like that. Arnie selling something off. I just didn't know what." He looked away, wouldn't hold my gaze.

I could always tell when he was holding out on me. That thought made me pause. He'd known this the whole time and never mentioned it to me. Granted the man was no choirboy; he enjoyed gossip more than any person I'd ever met. He'd never been one to withhold information from me. I was annoyed at this turn of events. "Oh, don't stop there."

"I might have been a little friendly with Arnie's girlfriend."

My chin hit my chest. No way. "Are you serious?"

"Yes," he mumbled.

"Why am I just now hearing about this? And when you say *friendly* what are we talking about? You had coffee once a year or the two of you painted each other's nails?"

"Somewhere in between." Levi walked over to the fridge and pulled out a bag of salad mix, then grabbed some bowls.

"And…"

He pulled out one of the chairs and sat at the table. "We met at one party or another. There's always some function that Arnie and I would both get invited to. It became a running joke between Mandy and me. Arnie'd been acting weird lately, secretive. She thought he was stepping out on her." Levi sighed. "She asked me to do something about it."

I took the time to fill up some water glasses and set them on the table. "And…"

Levi divvied out the salad into the bowls. "I tried to get Arnie to open up to me. We spent some time together." He shuddered. "He hit me up for the possible partnership. That was when the shipments started getting messed up." He toyed with a piece of lettuce that fell onto the table. "I think he lifted my keys and made copies. Mandy was acting a little weird the last week or so. I met her for coffee and she acted as if someone was following her. That's why…"

"That's why, what? Don't stop there. What were you doing for Mandy?"

Levi held my gaze but didn't speak.

"I'm sorry you lost your friend, but look, you're not breaking a confidence with her being gone. And maybe what you know will help us figure out who hurt her." I took his hand in mine. It shook slightly which unnerved me a teensy bit. "Okay, so explain what has you shaking. Something more is going on."

"Your chicken is burning."

"Ugh." I ran over to the oven. "We're not done talking." I yanked open the oven and pulled out the pan with an oven mitt. The chicken only smoked slightly. "It's salvageable. Paige," I hollered for the kiddo. "We'll finish talking after we eat."

Paige kept up a steady banter throughout the entire meal. If she noticed she was the only one talking, it didn't slow her down.

My brain was on overload by the time I put her to bed. I snagged a bottle of wine—for Levi—and a couple of glasses—I could drink my water out of a fancy glass. Levi was on the sofa with his head in his hands. Seeing him like that, I didn't think the wine would be enough. I dug around in my desk and snagged my backup box of Godivas.

"Here, you get this started." I handed him the wine. "And I'll get this going." I broke the seal on the chocolates.

We got situated, wine in one hand, chocolates in the other. "Okay. Spill."

Levi took a long sip, popped a truffle in his mouth, then leaned back. "One night Mandy came to me. She was scared. Someone had been following her."

"Why would someone be following her? Did she have something to be worried about?" My brain was heading at warp-speed to all the things Gabriel had told me.

Levi raised his hands in uncertainty. "She never went into much detail. I think she figured the less I knew the better. She did have me follow Arnie once."

My eyes widened. "You what?"

"I know it's so not like me." He narrowed his eyes. "More like you."

"Ha-ha. What did you find out?"

"Nothing. He just met with Guy Bueller. I figured since I turned him down, he was going after someone he could control a little more."

"That doesn't get you off the hook," I said as an off-hand comment then stuck a truffle in my mouth. I let the white chocolate-filled morsel swirl around. I took a quick sip and washed it down. "I need to go to the store."

Levi rolled his eyes dramatically. "Now is not the time to go shopping."

"The store Gabriel told me about. With the dancing leprechaun logo."

"Sweets." He sat forward on the sofa. "You don't need to get any more mixed up in this."

"I already am. I have been since the day Muldoon—" I scrunched my nose at the man's name "—tossed you into jail. And Bush threatened to charge me as an acccssory. I have had your back since day one. I'm not about to weenie out just because some lawman tells me to." I could just see Muldoon's face frowning at my insistence on pursuing yet another of his cases. But Levi needed me. And I needed him. I could not function with my best friend behind bars.

I wouldn't be butting into his cases if things hadn't gone all wonky the day Arnie died.

Something niggled the back of my brain but I couldn't pull it forward. Something about that day. Everything was in chaos that day. We'd missed the tourney and… and…

"What is it? You have that look on your face like when you're reworking script pages."

"I do not get a look when I'm…pages. Paper." Why'd that make the niggle wiggle faster? I bolted from the other end of the sofa and hurried down the hall to my bedroom. I dug around in the back of my closet for the jeans I was wearing the day of the tourney. In the pocket I recovered the note.

"What is that?"

I nearly bolted off the floor at the sound of Levi's voice in my ear. He wasn't more than a foot behind me staring at the scrap of paper in my hand. "This was on my car the morning you got arrested. I'd totally forgotten about it 'til now."

"What's it say?"

I couldn't remember. I hated to admit it, but my hands shook slightly as I unfolded it. "'You need to back off.'"

A shiver raced down my spine and straight to my toes, which curled in my fuzzy socks.

"This was on your windshield?" He leaned over my shoulder.

"Tucked under the wiper. I figured it was you reminding me what to bring." I turned and looked up at Levi. His mouth was pulled down into a deep frown.

He rubbed his hand across his forehead. "Before anyone found Arnie's body, so we could assume it has nothing to do with that."

"We could. We could also assume aliens flew down and left it."

His brow scrunched. "What?"

"Nothing." That was Annabelle's reasoning. If the obvious answer wasn't obvious, then the possibilities were too numerous to play the what-if game so she always invoked the alien scenario to end speculations. "There's no telling who it's from. Nothing in particular was going on that morning. As far as I remember the most pressing issue was seeing Colin and the skank at the match. The rest of the day snowballed once I got to the arena."

"For you and me both."

I waved at him until he backed up and out of my closet. We walked in silence back into the living room and recovered our forgotten glasses. We both tucked away another Godiva and sat quietly.

My mind whirled in every direction imaginable. "Not knowing what this has to do with, we're going to have to forget it altogether." I tossed the paper on the coffee table. "Let's get back to Arnie. All our trouble started with Arnie's death. Maybe if we can get that behind us everything else will settle down and we can get back to normal."

"Chaotic is your normal."

"Sadly true." I sighed and kicked my feet up onto the coffee table. "So do I go over to the shop alone, or do you want to go with me?"

Levi eyed me over the top of his wineglass. Contemplative. Thinking. Never a good thing.

"What's got you all clammed up all of a sudden?"

"I'm just wondering how much guiltier it's going to make me look snooping around the shop."

"First—" I held up my index finger. "It's a store and you have every right to shop wherever you want." My middle finger joined the count. "Second, if any of this pans out it won't matter. And, third—"

"Third, you'll go with or without me."

My ring finger was poised to join the other two in making my points, but since he made it for me, I relaxed my hand and dropped it to my side. "No worries. I can get Gabriel to go with me." I scrunched up my nose. "It *will* make him think I'm less afraid of him if I go to him for help." I stood and scooped up the box of Godivas. And counted: three, two and…

"I'll go." Levi let out a long-suffering sigh.

I looked at the clock on the mantel. "It's too late to do anything tonight. What say you come over right after I get out of work tomorrow? We can go over to the store before dinner."

"I say if I don't agree, you'll do something we both regret."

I patted him on the head. "I knew you'd see things my way."

"Yeah, right," he mumbled. "You're going to get me in trouble with Muldoon and he's gonna lock me up just for fun."

SEVENTEEN

Levi and I parked in front of The Blarney Shop.

"I've never noticed this place before." The little store sat between a trendy clothing chain and a children's shoe retailer.

"You're sure this is the right place?" Levi reached for the door.

The leprechaun logo was on both windows facing the street. "Yep." A bell jingled alerting everyone to our entrance. A woman behind the counter, who was ringing a woman up, lifted her head and did a quick double take before she smiled. "Evening. We'll be with you in just a moment."

"Thanks. We're just going to look around." I gave her a quick wave. I leaned closer to Levi. "Those are charming." I pointed to a set of cream ceramic candleholders adorned with shamrocks. "That would look good on your dining room table."

Levi picked up the pair, examining them. "Forty bucks apiece. They're not bad."

I perused the aisles of knickknacks and doodads, finding several things I would love to have—which was a shame—because I had to keep reminding myself it wasn't a shopping jaunt. More of a fishing expedition.

A customer caught my eye. She had a Bassani bag on her arm. From ten feet away, and not looking too closely, it could pass for the real deal. But once I knew what to look for… I could see where the pattern didn't match. And even from that distance you could tell the hardware lacked the sheen of the higher-quality merchandise.

My own—real—Bassani was still sitting in the middle of my kitchen table. I still hadn't decided what I would do with it. Would Gabriel take it as an affront if I returned it? Would he read too much into it if I kept it? It was a quandary I never thought I'd be in. One that had zero bearing on dropping right into the middle of something again that I should have stayed away from. But in for a penny… I nudged Levi when he joined me in the aisle. I whispered, "Look.

"I love your bag," I cooed. "Wherever did you get it?"

The woman's smile faltered a little. "Oh, I don't remember. Sorry." She moved away from me quickly and picked up a scented candle.

The woman at the register finished with the customer and approached us. "Was there something I could help y'all with today?"

I frowned. "Have we met?"

"I don't know. Have you ever been here before?"

"No." I racked my brain trying to place the voice. I know I'd heard it somewhere before. The woman was not someone you'd forget if you met her in person. She was a tall, leggy blonde with bazooms out to there that even the green apron with the dancing leprechaun couldn't disguise.

It would probably come to me one night as I was trying to fall off into sleep—wasn't that how it always worked. I shook off my mental wandering… "I was hoping to talk to the owner."

The woman arched a sculpted blond eyebrow. "That's me. Rebecka Nylin."

Rebecka Nylin stood with a price gun in one hand and a box cutter in the other—not ominous at all. Nope.

I eyed the box cutter. "Yes, hi." I swallowed a little heavier than I'd like to admit. I motioned to the woman who'd moved away from us. "I was just admiring her handbag. They are all the rage right now."

"Uh-huh," she said slowly.

"I've seen several of them around. I just wish I knew where to find them."

"Just about any department store, I'd guess." Her genial manner slipped in small degrees.

"Well, sure," I said. "If you want to pay their inflated prices. And definitely not somewhere to go if you want to, say, sell them yourself."

She narrowed her eyes at me. "I don't know what you're talking about."

"My friend Levi—" I snagged his sleeve and pulled him toward me "—was friends with Arnie Showalter."

A small tic twitched the corner of her mouth. "Good for him. If you need any help with the merchandise—in this store—please let me know." She turned slowly and walked back up to the counter as the phone started ringing. She pasted on a smile and answered.

"Well, that sucked."

"Why didn't you just come right out and ask her if she was selling them." Levi huffed and jerked his sleeve from my grasp.

"I was trying to be sleuthy."

"One, that's not even a thing. Two, you suck at it." He reached for the candlesticks.

"What are you doing?"

"Might as well not waste the trip completely. They're gorge."

I rolled my eyes. "Hurry up." I rounded a corner and almost ran into a stack of small crates, even had to put my hand out to steady myself. My palm landed on the packing label. The address in big bold print—4481 Industrial Parkway, Peytonville, TX—stood out. That was the number on the crate at Levi's house that burned down. I tried to be as nonchalant as I could as I slid my cell phone from my pocket and snapped off a couple of pics. As I checked it to make sure it was readable, I heard a strange noise behind me. It was almost a grunt. I turned to check and saw the stockroom door slam close.

Weird. And a little creepy.

Levi and I needed to leave. Whether Rebecka Nylin was selling the bags or not, she was definitely tied in with the warehouse.

Heading back toward the front door to wait for Levi, I passed an employee and bumped her arm. She dropped the items she was shelving. "I'm so sorry. Totally my fault. I wasn't paying attention." I was reaching out to help pick up the merchandise when I froze. "Bethany?"

The woman's head shot up, her eyes wide. She glanced around and shushed me, then pointed to a nametag pinned to her green apron that read *Jan*.

"Can I help you find something, ma'am?"

"I, uh, no." I scanned the area around us, suddenly paranoid, but I wasn't sure about what. "Just looking." Bethany—Jan—was a rookie with the PPD. I'd met her earlier this year. "What are you...?"

She tilted her head to the side in an *Are you serious?* look, then shifted her gaze to the register where Levi was paying.

"Y'all are investigating her."

"Yes, ma'am," she said loud enough to be heard across

the room. "They come in Citrus Zing, Peppermint Bark and Summer Breeze." She lifted a scented candle and held it to my nose. "This one's my favorite." She lowered her voice. "You need to leave."

I nodded. "Thanks. Not today. You ready, Levi?" I asked as he joined us.

"Ooh, yummy candles." He started to reach for the Peppermint Bark.

"No. We're late. Gotta go." I dragged him back out of the store.

"Explain yourself." He at least had the sense to wait until we were ensconced back in my SUV.

"I will. After I get an explanation first."

A DOG WENT crazy when I knocked on the front door. I'd dropped Levi off at my house and driven straight over to Muldoon's. Since when did he have a dog? I swallowed heavily. I was not a fan of dogs of any size, but the ones that could eat me in one bite especially terrified me thanks to a childhood trauma. My cousin Lucy had a gigantic dog. It had to have weighed ninety pounds. When I was five, the stupid thing knocked me down and sat atop me pinning me to the ground for a good ten minutes before anyone even noticed. When you're five it's quite traumatic.

I haven't cared for dogs since.

The barks and woofs told me that was not a small dog. Flashbacks to Ralph—who names a dog Ralph?—danced before my eyes. Maybe this wasn't such a good idea. I backed away slowly, not opposed to running for the SUV if need be. But before I could get down to the bottom step the door eased open.

"Celeste? What are you doing here?" Muldoon, barefoot in jeans and a PPD sweatshirt, held the collar of a massive beast. "Everything okay?"

I froze when the behemoth dog bared his teeth. His very large, sharp teeth.

"He won't hurt you." Muldoon tugged on the dog.

So you say. I just stared at the man for a moment. Had he ever been straight with me on anything? "No. Nothing is okay." I backtracked to his other question. "Every chance you get you lie to me."

He frowned. "Have you been drinking?"

"No. Why would you even ask that?"

"I don't know. You're standing on my front porch, after dark, accusing me of lying. You have your moments but this is a little out there even for you." The dog surged at the end of his arm.

I squeaked and pressed myself against the railing along the steps. Sweat popped out at my temples. "I sh-should go."

"No. Come inside. Please. Let me just put Waldo out back."

I stared a moment but nodded and followed him into the house—many, many steps behind him and the dog. I hadn't been to his house in a while—if you didn't count my birthday night, and seeing how I couldn't remember it anyway... We'd both been so crazy busy recently. It felt different being there, almost weird. I didn't like it one bit. I sat on the end of the sofa.

"So what have I lied about?" Muldoon came into the room, thrust his hands on his hips in his intimidating cop-stance.

"I saw Bethany today. Or should I say Jan. You warned me not to get involved, but it wasn't because you were worried about me. You didn't want me to find out y'all were already onto The Blarney Shop."

Muldoon's shoulders sagged slightly but he didn't betray any emotion.

"Nothing to say?" I shifted and set my elbows on my knees then looked down. "Who am I to ask anyway, right? I have no business looking into the crime that happened on my best friend's property, where he's thought to be guilty. And I'm his accomplice." I clasped my hands together. "As a matter of fact, a woman who did look into it got herself killed." I looked up.

Muldoon hadn't moved a stitch.

"I guess I really don't know why I even came over here. You didn't tell me something. Whatever. I'm not dead. A good thing as far as I'm concerned. And while I haven't been drinking, I am considering going home and crawling into something with considerable kick. Sorry to have disturbed you."

I stood and was rounding the sofa when a hand landed on my shoulder.

"Celeste…"

I was a little afraid to move. I'd yet again been swallowed by crimes that didn't involve me directly but somehow managed to suck me in.

I opened my mouth to speak, finally, when a towheaded teen rounded the corner. "Dad, I can't find my…" He pulled up short. "Oh, you have company."

"What did you need?"

Something niggled the back of my brain. Again with the niggle. Before I could pull it forward, Waldo barked from the back.

I squinted at the teen and rubbed the tip of my nose. The teen was familiar but I just couldn't place him. Then it all came back in a flash of recognition. "Is this some kind of joke?" I looked from Muldoon to the teen and back.

"What the hell?" The teen backed away a bit.

"Colby," Muldoon warned.

I jumped. "This is your son?" I glanced at Muldoon then back to the teen. Waldo barked from the back. "It was you. You were out in front of my house. With your big-ass dog. The morning Paige got hurt. You left me that note."

"What note?" Both Muldoons spoke at once.

I'd carried it around in my pocket, trying to figure out what it had to do with anything that was going on— not that I really thought it was part and parcel of Levi's mess, but the timing was just too coincidental. I pulled it free and handed it to the elder Muldoon.

"Colby, would you like to explain this?"

The teen blushed. "Not particularly."

"What do you think I need to back off from?" I used my sternest mom-voice but frankly I was a little discombobulated by the fact that mini-Muldoon had not only found his way to my home, but felt the need to leave me a note warning me off. "How did you even know where to find me for that matter?"

"Internet."

"Naturally." I swiped my hand through my hair. That bottle of amaretto I'd stashed in the back of the pantry was looking better and better. I turned back to Shaw. As many times as I had gotten in a bind and in turn put him in a bind, I had never seen the level of anger—or disappointment—on his face. I didn't think there was anything I could say to help or hinder the situation so it was time to cut my losses. And go. "I'm sorry to have bothered you. On so many levels. Good night."

"I'll walk you out."

I held up a hand. "I know the way." I turned to go. Colby Muldoon just watched as I walked by. When I reached the door I was almost free of the crazy new mess I'd gotten into. Until Shaw reached around me and opened the door. "I told you—"

"I know." His warm breath feathered over my ear. "I'd like to walk you out anyway."

I shrugged. We walked in silence out to my curb where the SUV sat. I pointed the key fob, about to unlock it, when Shaw took a hold of my elbow. I could have easily pulled away and gotten in, but something about his gentle manner made it near impossible to just leave.

"I'm sorry if Colby scared you."

"He didn't. Not really."

He nudged my elbow until I turned to face him. He didn't say anything. Just stared. And I squirmed under his scrutiny. Until he leaned forward, gave me a gentle peck. On the forehead. "Good night."

"How'd it go?"

I flopped onto the sofa, covered my eyes with my forearm. "Not good."

"Why? Where'd you go?"

"Over to Muldoon's. Jan, the sales girl that was helping me..." I peeked at Levi from under my arm. "She's a cop. For the PPD."

"Shut up."

"She's there undercover." A frown pulled down my mouth. "I sorta confirmed it. I went to Muldoon's house to get him to 'fess up."

"For doing his job?" He tsked. "You have balls the size of—"

"I know, right?" I snorted. "A lot of good it does me though." My cell phone went off. I glanced at the screen. It was Bueller. Ugh. I didn't have it in me to deal with him. I hit the ignore button and dropped the phone to my lap.

"Something else happened, though, too," Levi asked leadingly.

"I met his son."

"Whose?"

I swear I'd told Levi about the elusive son. "Muldoon's son. I think he's been stalking me."

"Are you feeling okay?"

I peeked at him again. "If you ask if I've been drinking I swear I will deck you."

"Wouldn't dream of it."

"Muldoon's teenage son usually lives with Muldoon's ex-wife. But he's been staying with his dad. Didn't I tell you?" I scrunched my nose. "With everything going on, I'm not surprised I forgot. I think he left the note on my car, by the way. He never outright admitted it, but he did admit he knows where I live."

"What would be the point of him stalking you?"

"He doesn't want his dad dating?" I shrugged. "Mission accomplished, I guess."

"I beg your pardon." He leaned forward. "Did you and Muldoon break up?"

"Honestly, I don't even know if we were ever really together, so *break up* may be irrelevant. We had a fight." I rubbed my hand over my face just as my cell went off again. And yep, it was Guy Bueller. He was a persistent bastard. Ignore. "Other than me getting all up in his face, we haven't even talked. And then we fought again. Sort of."

He set his hand on my leg, patted me like a parent would with a child. "I'm sure it's not as bad as all that. People fight, couples fight. You and I have had a few doozies ourselves. We got past it."

I didn't want his comfort or encouragement. I just wanted to keep wallowing. "Do you ever get those days when you think you're in a bad dream and you're just waiting to wake up so you can breathe a sigh of relief?"

"Hello." He waved at me. "Arrested for murder. Haven't been cleared yet."

"Yeah. Sorry." I sighed. "That's what my last two weeks feels like, too. Well, minus the threat of life in prison. I'll probably only get twenty years."

Levi set his arm around my shoulder. "We're a pair, aren't we?"

"Promise me you'll…" A knock sounded at the front door. I didn't even uncover my face, just sank lower into the sofa. "See what I mean." Gaw, please don't let it be Bueller. I didn't think he knew where I lived but the way my week was going…

"I'll get it." He stood.

A moment later, the sofa sagged next to me. "Well?" I asked.

"You look a little defeated. Want to talk about it?"

My chest seized for a moment. "Gabriel." I lifted my hand from my eyes. "It's a little late for a social call. Where's Levi?"

Gabriel's eyebrow arch upward. "Not happy to see me?"

"It's late." *You scare the crap out of me.* I thought it

prudent not to add that part aloud. "I've had a bad day. Levi?"

"Is getting me a glass of water." Gabriel settled his arm across the back of the sofa. "You are so jumpy."

Yeah, duh, shouted in my head.

"What did you think of Ms. Nylin?"

I shouldn't have been surprised by the question. Luckily, I was saved from stuttering through some incoherent answer when Levi returned with his water and a cocktail glass for moi. How'd he know I was ready to start drinking again? "You found the amaretto. You are a godsend."

He smiled as he sat in the club chair across from us. "I've been told."

Gabriel held the bottle of water but didn't open it. He eyed me for a long time. "Care to share?"

Not really. But I was ten minutes past the point of playing coy in this entire situation. "I went to the store, intimated that I was interested in selling some of the phony Bassani bags." I sat up and sipped the drink. "She acted like she didn't know what I was talking about. But there was a lady right there in the shop with one of the bags. I let it go. I couldn't exactly *make* her tell me."

"Anything else?"

I was not about to tell him about Bethany. I might bumble into things, but busting an undercover investigation was not something I wanted to lay claim to. Nor did I want to mention the warehouse address—damn, in all my haste I forgot to tell Muldoon about it. I'd call him when Gabriel left.

For a moment I toyed with the possibility that Gabriel'd had my house bugged. If so, he'd have already heard what Levi and I were talking about, and then when/if I called Muldoon. But if that was the case there'd be no point in coming to me late at night asking. Unless it was a test of some sort. Were there consequences for failing the test? And what would the purpose of the test be? I was a playhouse director and mom, for goodness' sake. This man was only paying any attention to me because he was slightly bored and out a whole bunch of money and hoped I could point him in the direction of the person who slaughtered his client—and cash cow. Five minutes after everything came to light he'd do whatever—I really didn't want to speculate on it much—to the person and be on to a new diversion. Hopefully. But if not…

I think I knew what Alice was feeling when she fell down the rabbit hole. I took a sip and then another. "Nope. Nothing else." Another sip and the glass was empty. I shook the glass at Levi. He reluctantly left with it.

"I feel like there's something you're not telling me." Gabriel leaned in.

"Now, why would I do that?" A warm rush scooted down my spine and around into my belly. I'd like to chalk it up to the alcohol.

Gabriel scrutinized me. He had a way of looking at you and you'd almost swear he was reading your thoughts. "I'm not."

What? "Not what?"

"Not trying to trip you up or get you to reveal something more."

"There is no more. Rebecka Nylin didn't bat an eyelash—and she had some killer eyelashes—when I mentioned I was interested in the Bassani." I frowned. "She seemed familiar… I can't put my finger on why. And she did seem a little annoyed."

Levi returned with another full glass for me and this time one for himself. "You tend to have that effect on people from time to time."

"Cute." I sat up fully when I got my second libation in hand. "Would you just come right out and admit that you were doing something illegal? I wouldn't."

Gabriel chuckled. "You are most fascinating." He cracked open the water bottle and took a sip. "To answer your question, no, I would not admit to anything. But most people don't just come right out and ask questions like that, so…" He gave a one-shoulder shrug.

"What if she did kill Arnie and Mandy?" With the glass pressed to my lip, I continued, "Where does that leave you?"

"That is the quandary, isn't it?"

"That's not really an answer." I snorted. "I guess I shouldn't have expected one."

"Yet, you asked anyway." He shook his head. "Guileless."

"Yep." I raised my glass to Levi and we clinked. "Just like I'm guessing you knew I would. Mission accomplished." I was getting rather ballsy—and apparently I was becoming a lush—when the liquor kicked in. "I get you want to be reimbursed, but at this point, I don't know what else to tell you. Unless you want to start selling fake bags." I scrunched my nose, gauged his reaction. He just stared at me in that piercing way he had. "Naw. I can't see you doing that. It's too fussy."

"Fussy." He barked out a laugh and stood. "I'll let you two get back to whatever it is you do." He winked. "If you learn anything new…"

"You'll be the first one I call." I raised my glass in a wave as Levi stood to escort him to the door.

When Levi came back, he had the amaretto bottle in hand. "That wasn't weird at all." He topped off his glass and motioned to me with the bottle.

"He's your friend." I drained the rest of mine and then covered it with my hand.

"Acquaintance. Business associate. Not friend. Where does that leave us?"

Where indeed? "Not a clue." I settled my glass onto the coffee table none too gently and flinched but thankfully it didn't break. "We should go follow Gabriel."

Levi choked on his drink. When he stopped sputtering, he said, "You're not serious?"

"Why not? He's been keeping tabs on me this whole time. Could be interesting to see where he goes, what he does." I rooted around under the table for my shoes. "I kind of think he's a vampire. All mysterious and spooky."

"You've seen him in the daytime," Levi pointed out as if this was a natural turn in everyday conversation.

"This is the teens. Vampires have some high-tech sunscreen nowadays. Makes them impervious to UV rays and whatnot."

Levi chuckled. "You've given this some thought."

"A little." I slipped my shoes back on. "Following him may not have anything to do with anything, but turnabout's fair play."

"Or it may piss him off and send him—or his goons—after us. He may find you entertaining, but that will only last for so long."

I waved off his worry. "If he catches us…" My head spun just a wee bit and I sat heavily on the arm of the sofa. "I'll just smile at him and bat my eyelashes then say something witty." I frowned. "Though I never know when I'm going to say something he finds witty. I just talk and it seems to roll out on its own. You ready?"

Levi shook his head. "I'm thinking not, but thanks for the offer." He set the bottle and glass beside mine. "I'm heading home." He snapped up his car keys.

"You can't drive." I snagged the keys back from him.

"Neither can you." Levi grabbed my keys from the table and raised a single eyebrow.

I harrumphed. Okay, it came out as half a harrumph and half a hiccup. "We're at an impasse."

It was Levi's turn to harrumph. "That we are."

Paige came into the living room, dropping her book bag in her wake. "I just got home. Are we going somewhere?"

"Nope. Nowhere." I tucked Levi's keys into my pocket. He did the same with mine. "You finish your homework at your dad's?"

Paige rolled her eyes. "Hours ago." What she left unsaid was, "Duh." That's my girl.

"Go brush your teeth. And I'll be in in a sec to tuck you in."

As soon as she left, Levi returned to his flouncy posture. "So I'll go make a pot of coffee?"

"You're the best." I pinched his cheek. "And no more liquor for a while."

"You've said that before."

"It makes me stupid."

Levi rounded his eyes and put his hands up in mock-confusion. "I would never have guessed."

I used Paige's patented eye-roll. "I'll be back shortly."

I got the sprite all tucked away into bed and met Levi back in the living room. "I don't know where that leaves us. Finished would be my best guess." I snapped my fingers. "Wait." I tugged my cell from my pocket. "I just need to forward…this…" I pulled up the photo from The Blarney Shop and sent it to Muldoon with the caption This was the same address as on the crate I saw at the house—before the fire.

"It's weird," I said as I closed my phone and set it off to the side. "Why you?"

"Why me what?"

"Why would Arnie mess with you? He's on your property. Do your competitors often come around?"

"Not really." Levi frowned. "Other than Arnie, I can't think of one ever coming to my sites."

My cell phone went off. It was Bueller calling again. I turned the phone to Levi. "Was Arnie courting Bueller since you turned him down?"

"Bueller doesn't have anything specifically for Arnie to court. I don't think he's bought a single property."

"Then why was he at all helpful?"

"Was he helpful?"

Once I thought of it… "Not really."

"Maybe you should lose his number."

"If only he'd lose mine."

EIGHTEEN

"FINISH UP, SWEET PEA, we need to get going." I scurried around the kitchen and gathered up all the set designs I'd been working on last night. I'd used just about every surface to look over the layouts. Luckily, I'd narrowed it down to a manageable pile for Annabelle and me to go through when I got to the playhouse. "Five minutes, or you don't get to use the makeup today."

Paige looked up from her breakfast for a second, then started shoveling the remainder in her mouth.

I chuckled. Saturdays, I brought Paige to the theater with me when it wasn't Colin's weekend. She enjoyed getting to nose around all the nooks and crannies in the playhouse and I had a secret hope that she would get the acting bug, too, be a mini-me through and through.

Five minutes later I was opening the garage door only to find a familiar sedan parked in the driveway. "Shaw. Hi," I said when the door was all the way up. "What are you doing here? Is Levi okay?"

"As far as I know. Haven't been to the precinct yet this morning, so…"

"Ha-ha." I jingled the keys in my hand. "What's up?"

He glanced down to his feet then back up at me. "I want to apologize about last night. Colby had no business speaking to you that way."

"Don't worry about it. Teenagers have many moments

like that. It's got to be hard on him, splitting time between two households."

"Your daughter doesn't seem to be acting out."

I smiled. "Paige is…different. She sat Colin and me down before we could tell her we were having issues." It had been surreal having our seven-year-old tell us the tension was getting too thick, and it was affecting her schoolwork—she was risking falling below straight As. She also told us we needed us to get our heads on straight. It might have taken a couple of weeks for us to get to the place we needed to be, but Colin and I did get it all worked out—meaning, he moved out and we started the divorce proceedings.

"Anyway, I'm sorry about Colby."

"Sure." I gnawed on my lip for a second. "What about The Blarney Shop?"

"What about it?"

"Did I screw it up?"

"Not yet."

I frowned. "Yet?"

"Well, there's no telling what you'll do next." He heaved out an exasperated sigh. "One of these days you're going to go nosing into something and there will be no one there to help you."

"If you'd just told me…"

"Are you kidding me?" He lowered his voice as he glanced at Paige, who had just walked into the garage. "It's no business of yours. It's a police matter. Do you honestly think I'd share that kind of information with you?" He ran his hands through his hair. "Actually, you probably do. Celeste, stay out of PPD cases. For both our sakes."

He turned and walked back to his car and without another word drove off.

Paige cocked her head to the side and volleyed her gaze between me and Muldoon's departing car. "Where'd Detective Muldoon go?"

"Work. Which is where we need to be going. Let's get moving."

"HEY, PAIGE." ANNABELLE came out from behind one of the makeup stations. "I left all the books you requested at the last station."

Paige beamed up at the woman. "Thanks."

Annabelle bumped my shoulder with hers. "If she ever shows the least bit of interest in acting, we're all set."

I laughed. "I wish. How was the trip to Oklahoma?" Annabelle had driven all the way to Tulsa on Friday to pick up some props.

"Great. I got most of what we'll need for the production. We'll just have to make a few extra set pieces." She yawned and stretched. "I didn't get in until three this morning."

"Go back to bed."

"Naw. I had half a pot of coffee on the way back and am wide awake now. I'll crash sometime just before dinner probably."

I set my bag down, pulled out the set designs. "These all look pretty good. There's a few tweaks we need to look over." I pointed to the top sheet where I'd made some alterations.

"Thanks, doll." She took the pages and looked through the rest. "Mmm-hmm. Mmm-hmm. I'm not sure about this one." She pointed out a rather ambitious layout for one of the last scenes of our next production. We discussed it for a few minutes. When there was a lull in the conversation, Annabelle leaned back in her chair and stretched her back. "So what happened with your parents?"

"They're in Vegas."

"Wha… Seriously?"

"Levi."

"Say no more." She shook her head. "Oh, hey, how would you and Muldoon like to have dinner with me and Ronnie?"

I slashed my hand in the air to hush Annabelle up then glanced around to see how close Paige was. She was still at the farthest station down, nose-deep in the stack of books. I leaned in close to her. "We may be on a time-out."

"I don't know which thing to address first. The time-out or that fact that you're not sure."

"We had an…um…issue."

"And that means what?"

"Oh, hell, I don't even know." I ran my hands through my hair. "I think I overreacted to something, but I'm not even sure what part I overreacted to. Then I made him mad, which was my fault."

"Have you talked to him about it?"

"That requires quiet and privacy." I heaved a sigh. "I haven't had five minutes alone with him in weeks. He came over this morning but with Paige sitting right there… I think I made it worse. I don't know when we would be able to talk about anything."

"You need to make the time."

"I know." I looked down at the scripts in front of me, but I didn't see them. I was seeing less of what was right in front of me. I was all turned around with the world thanks to Levi's arrest and then running into Gabriel Grady. I think I'd taken most of my fear and trepidation out on Muldoon. And I'd done it again and again. Getting all wrapped up in what I shouldn't. Muldoon had every right to be mad at me. I owed him an apology.

"What are you doing now?"

"Hmm?" I looked up at Annabelle. "Working." I tapped the script in front of me.

"On something that can wait."

"We have a deadline."

"In like a week. These—" she took the scripts from me "—will still be here this afternoon."

"But Paige…"

"I've got her. Go. See your man. Work it out. He's worth it."

My man. I smiled before I could help myself. "Be back in a few. Paige, honey, I need to run out for a moment. You stay with Annabelle, okay?"

Paige gave me a thumbs-up as I crossed over to the door. I think I broke at least three traffic laws getting over to the PPD building. Had I gotten pulled over I'd have been hand-delivered to Muldoon.

I walked into the station and my mouth fell open. There had to be thirty people crowding the small waiting area. "What the…" Everyone was talking at once. Shouting about being brought in wasting their time. There were several deputies with notepads taking down whatever information they were gleaning. Everyone looked annoyed, police and those being questioned. I scanned the crowd for a familiar face until I finally lit on one I knew. "Jenny."

There was so much noise, I didn't think she could hear above the din. I cupped my hand to my mouth. "Jenny!"

The desk sergeant looked up from the file in front of her, gave me a quick nod and motioned her head toward the far corner of the room where an information board stood. It took her several moments to weave through the irate crowd. She rolled her dark brown eyes and feigned straightening one of the posters on the wall behind me.

"What's going on?" I leaned my shoulder against the wall.

"The Weston Eatery was serving Saturday brunch and a fight broke out. These are all the witnesses." She cleared her throat. "They're none too happy to be here."

"That must have been some fight."

"You could say that. It was a doozie. There was…" Jenny's eyes widened a moment. "You should probably go. Now." She turned and waded back into the crowd.

"Go?"

"This is getting ridiculous, Chief."

I recognized the nasally voice immediately. It was Gabriel's smarmy little lawyer.

"You have a detective out of control. Now, I've talked my client down this time, but if there's another…"

"I assure you, there won't be another issue."

"Still, I want all these people's information." The lawyer waved his gold-watch-clad wrist toward the lobby. "In case my client changes his mind."

"We're getting it, as you can see."

It was all I could do to stay facing the information wall. I didn't want to see the weaselly little man. Or him to see me, though I didn't think he'd know me by sight. I was in costume the last time I was even in his vicinity.

"No woman is worth all this," he said as he walked off.

My shoulders stiffened. What did he just say?

"Asshole," I heard the chief mumble as he walked back into the hallway that led to the offices.

Once both men were gone, I pushed my way through the crowd and up to Jenny. "Um, Jenny, the fight. Who was in the fight?"

I held my breath. Ohplease, ohplease, ohplease, don't let her say what I think she's going to say.

"Gabriel Grady. And Muldoon."

Oh, geez.

Maybe one of them insulted the other's sense of fashion. It didn't necessarily have to have anything to do with me. I mean that would be pretty conceited if I thought that, right?

"And Muldoon is…?"

"Back in the break room." Jenny pushed the button to buzz me back.

I avoided the chief's office and the patrol briefing room and turned the corner into the break room just in time to see Muldoon change out a bloody bandage on his cheek. I gasped as spots formed in nanoseconds.

"Oh, shi…"

"Celeste, can you hear me? Celeste?"

It was Muldoon. He was calling me. But he sounded weird. And my head hurt. Which was weirder still. I shifted as I tried to figure out what was what. "Am I on the floor?" The words came out in almost a croak. I tried to clear my throat but it was awful dry.

"You fainted."

I pried my eyes open and squinted against the light. The first thing that came into view was a white bandage on Muldoon's cheek. Right. I'd walked into the PPD break room and seen fresh blood on my man's cheek.

I'd like to say that I'm the nurturing type. And I can be, as long as there's no blood involved.

"Not again." It was so embarrassing. I wish I could get over this phobia, but it didn't look like that was going to happen anytime soon.

"Your face?" I reached up and touched the bandage.

"It grows on you." A smile split his face.

I chuckled, then moaned as aches popped up all over from my fall to the floor. "Why does this keep happening?" I asked more of the universe than anyone in particular.

"You okay?" He gripped my elbow and helped me sit up.

"Peachy." But I was actually still a little woozy and swayed toward Muldoon.

"Stay put for a moment." He jumped up from the floor and dropped a few coins into the vending machine, then turned and handed me a lemon-lime soda. "Drink this." He squatted in front of me, ran his hand over my head. "No bumps. Look at me." He checked out my eyes. "You look okay, but it wasn't pretty. You went down like a sack of potatoes." There was a little too much glee in his eyes.

"Super. Graceful as ever," I scoffed. I sipped the soda and my equilibrium came back to me in degrees. "Thanks." When I was steadier, I pushed up from the floor and sat in one of the hard plastic chairs at the closest table. My knees were a little wobbly, but I was considerably better. I looked pointedly to his cheek as he pulled up a chair and sat knee to knee with me. "Looks like you had some excitement after you left this morning."

The crooked little smile that graced the corner of his sumptuous mouth fell away. "I ran into your other boyfriend."

I slumped in the seat. "He's not—"

"I know." He huffed out a breath and ran his hand through his hair. "I ran into Grady and lost my temper."

"Why?"

Muldoon looked around the empty break room. "I guess you and I need to sit down and talk."

The soda can grew heavy in my hand. "Yeah, I guess we do."

Totally unexpectedly, Muldoon chuckled. "Don't look like I just ran over your dog."

"I don't have a dog."

"Babe…" He cupped my cheek.

It'd been a while since he'd called me *babe*. My heart melted just a little bit. He leaned forward and gave me a quick peck, then settled his forehead to mine. "When did things go sideways?"

"I've no idea." I closed my eyes and breathed in his scent. I've yet to figure out why or how the man smells like cinnamon, coffee and musk—all the time. "Are we going to be okay?"

"Absolutely," he said as he leaned back, but he kept his hand on my cheek.

"Are you just saying that?"

His thumb stroked my cheek. "No. We'll be okay."

"And your son?"

"Knows he crossed a line." He paused. "And Grady?"

"I've no interest in Grady."

"Does he know that?"

My eyes popped back open. "As far as I know I haven't done anything to make him think otherwise."

"I know you haven't." His gaze held mine. "I know you can take of yourself. I know it as much as I know you somehow manage to get yourself smack in the middle of trouble. With very little effort." He smiled at me.

"I'm sure he can't resist your charms. I know I can't." He leaned in and kissed me.

"Detective?" A uniformed officer peeked his head into the break room.

Muldoon sighed. "I've got to go. Can you stay out of trouble for a little while?"

"No promises."

He laughed. "Yeah, I didn't really expect any." He eyed me for a long moment. "You really okay?" He shrugged toward the spot where I'd landed on the floor.

"Yep." I nodded. Slowly. My head was working on a world-class migraine, but I didn't want him to worry. "You go. Before the chief comes looking for you." I gave him the best smile I could muster. I really didn't want him to leave at the moment. But he had a job he needed to do.

He kissed the top of my head and hurried back out the door.

I sat there for fifteen minutes, got my equilibrium back before I headed out of the building. I waved at Jenny but didn't want to stop to gab, not with the group of café patrons still surrounding the information desk. I almost expected Gabriel's lawyer to jump out at me when I got out the door, but I had an uneventful march through the lot. I hoped to God that the man didn't know who I was by sight. He obviously knew who I was by name, since I'd become a bane of his litigious hide.

I was about to unlock my door when a shadow fell over me. I was expecting Muldoon. Though why I'd think he'd follow me out was just plain silly. The man lived and breathed the job. When he said he was getting back to work, he was getting back to work, with little to no deviation.

I wasn't expecting to see the man reaching for me.

"Guy, hey." I leaned against my SUV to get out from his immediate range. "I meant to call you back. It's been crazy lately." I laughed. It was more from nerves than anything. "Were you looking for me?" It wasn't so much a question as confusion as to why Guy Bueller was approaching me in the PPD parking lot.

He snagged my sleeve. "You need to come with me."

"Yeah, no. Thanks, just the same. I have somewhere I need to be." I tried to slide down the side of my vehicle to get away from the man, but he was quick and pinned me in place.

He growled slightly and leaned in closer. "Now." He pulled out a gun and shoved it in my ribs.

"Really? In the police department parking lot?" I scoffed before I could help myself. I opened my mouth to scream. I mean really, was he going to shoot me practically in front of a ton of armed witnesses? But as I wound up to let out an ear-piercer, he shifted and I saw into his car. Sitting in the backseat was Levi. And Rebecka Nylin. She held a similar gun on my friend.

My hands shook so hard at that moment, I dropped my keys to the ground. As I bent to grab them, Bueller shoved at me. "Leave them."

"But someone will steal my SUV." It was a stupid thing to say, but my brain had ceased functioning properly.

He snorted. "Won't matter." He pointed to his dark car. "Front seat. And don't do anything stupid."

"Stupid like kidnapping someone in a police station parking lot? Yeah, no, wouldn't dream of doing something stupid." So it figures that when my brain did engage again, it went for full-on sarcasm.

NINETEEN

I CLIMBED INTO the car. I gave my friend a look that read, "What the hell?"

He gave a tiny shrug.

"Rebecka. I'd say it's good to see you again, but getting kidnapped kinda shot that to hell."

"Shut up, bitch."

"Manners, too." I tugged the seat belt around me, clicked it into place.

"Sweets…" Levi's voice was shaking and all but begging for me to cool it.

"At this point, what difference does it make if I piss off the people with the guns? Do you think they're going to just let us go after they're done doing whatever it is they think they're doing?"

He looked at me like I'd lost my mind. Maybe I had. I didn't like having my life threatened. And as far as I knew I hadn't done anything to deserve it. This time. "To what do we owe this honor?" I asked Bueller when he got into the driver's seat and tucked the gun in his lap.

Something niggled when he gave me nothing more than his profile.

My brain flashed to the truck that tried to run me over the night of the fire.

"You were driving the truck." I let out a heavy sigh. "I don't know why I didn't realize it sooner."

"What?" Levi leaned forward and was shoved back

into his seat by the barrel of Rebecka's gun to the ribs. "Easy now."

"There's no need to be rough," I said to Rebecka. "You and your partner here are going to do whatever it is you have planned. You don't need to manhandle us."

"Partner?" Levi and Rebecka said in unison, though hers was less of a question and more surprised.

"You two were selling the handbags out of The Blarney Shop with Arnie."

Bueller glared over at me. "Where's the crate?"

"What crate? The one that Arnie moved the day he died?" I shook my head. "We don't have it."

"Bullshit. I saw the purse. The day we had lunch."

"That's why you abducted us?" I tightened the seat belt over my chest. The man was driving a little erratically. "I don't even have that bag. The police have it."

"Liar."

"She's telling the truth." The word *truth* squeaked out when Rebecka pushed the gun harder into Levi's side.

"You were in on it with Arnie," she accused him.

"No, I wasn't," he said slowly. "I wasn't in any kind of business with him."

"Not like y'all." I glanced over my shoulder at Rebecka. "But Arnie being Arnie decided to cut y'all out, started hiding all the crates on Levi's properties. And y'all got pissed."

"Sweets," Levi said through gritted teeth.

I looked at him and widened my eyes to say, "I can't shut up." I didn't know why I was pushing the pair. I should be scared spitless but I was angry and curious. A weird combination that fueled my mouth—which usually didn't need any extra help anyway.

"It was an accident, wasn't it?" I looked from Bueller to Rebecka and back. "You didn't mean to kill him, but he wouldn't tell you where he'd hid it."

"Shut up." Bueller smacked his hand on the steering wheel.

"Then y'all had to go and set fire to another property. With Poor Mandy Crenshaw inside. She knew you guys were the ones running the handbag scheme. She was going to turn you in. She just needed to find the crate Arnie hid. That's why she was out around asking questions. You were afraid she'd lead the cops back to you, especially if she was saying that Levi was innocent."

Rebecka narrowed her gaze at me. Bueller jerked the wheel a bit, then righted the car in his lane.

"Y'all killed two people. Over stupid handbags. Who does that?"

"Celeste Eagan." The harshness in Levi's tone was enough to get Rebecka to give him a quick side-eye.

"Your boyfriend thinks you need to stuff it, too." Rebecka's finger hovered near the trigger.

It was one thing to piss them off and maybe make them trip up somehow, but it wasn't worth getting Levi shot because the woman twitched at the wrong moment.

"Sorry, sorry." I held my hand aloft. But I couldn't stop. "No, I'm not. You two aren't going to get away with this." I waved my hands wildly at passing cars. "Hey. Look over here. We're being kidnapped. Hey."

"Shut up." Rebecka waved her gun at me. Levi leapt at her and wrestled with her for the gun. Bueller was stunned for a moment and seemed to be trying to figure out what was happening, but then you could almost see the gears clicking into place. He reached for his gun. I grabbed the steering wheel and yanked it as hard to the right as I could while I reached for his gun.

A loud blast echoed inside the car. My ears rang instantly. I wasn't sure which of the two guns went off. I waited a nanosecond to see if any pain erupted anywhere. Either adrenaline numbed any and everything or I wasn't hit. "Levi, you okay?"

If he answered me one way or the other, I couldn't really even tell as my ears were still abuzz. Then another, more muffled pop rang out and the back window exploded. I still had the steering wheel in a death grip and the car veered off the road and onto the curb just barely missing a parked car. The seat belt bit into my shoulder.

I smashed down the button to disengage the door locks. "Levi, get out. Get out!" I yelled over and over at my friend, who was still wrestling with Rebecka.

Bueller released his hold on the gun when the car slammed to a halt. I tucked it into the little pocket of the door—well out of his reach. Then I groped for the release of my seat belt. I pushed on it several times. About the time is came loose, Bueller snagged a handful of hair and yanked me back.

"Asshole." I slammed my fists against the hands in my hair just as my door came flying open. Two large meat hooks of hands came at me. "Stanley?"

Maybe I had a concussion. It was the only thing that could explain Gabriel's bodyguard reaching for me.

"Celeste?"

I could hear Levi, but between Bueller and Stanley both tugging me, I couldn't tell where he was. "Levi?"

"You stupid…" The rest of Bueller's words were drowned out when a siren neared. His grip slackened on my hair, and Stanley yanked me from the front seat. We ended in a heap, practically on the back bumper of the car Bueller hit.

"What are you…doing here?" My words came out between heavy breaths. It took a lot of effort to stop someone from kidnapping you.

"Saving you."

Two words. I'd never heard two words at the same time from the man. Then what he'd said sank in. "How'd you know I was in trouble?" I frowned. "You've been tailing me."

He gave a one-shouldered shrug as a police cruiser came to a screaming halt next to the wrecked car. "Stay." He dropped me unceremoniously to the ground and hopped over the hood of the car. The first thing I noticed was how well he moved for such a large man. Then I realized he was chasing after Bueller, who'd taken off through the houses across the street.

A squad car door flung open and Muldoon sprang out of the passenger side of the vehicle. He and the driver had their guns drawn as they approached us. Two more cruisers joined the fray.

"Celeste?" Muldoon rounded the end of the car. "Babe, are you okay?"

"Bueller's getting away." I pointed across the street. "Stanley took off after him. That way."

Muldoon called to one of the uniformed officers. He repeated what I'd told him and sent the man off after Bueller and Stanley.

I was still sprawled on the ground on my back. I rolled over onto my knees. It was only then that I saw Levi on the ground about ten feet away from me. I dove for him—crawling—my knees not quite sturdy enough to walk over with any dignity.

"You okay, hon?" I pawed at him, checked for bullet holes, and sighed with relief when I didn't find any.

"Fine." He swatted my hands away and checked himself for any stray holes. "You?" He gave me a cursory once-over.

"Okay. I think." Everything happened so fast I wasn't even sure if I was okay or not. My shoulder hurt a little and my scalp was sore. I rubbed the spot Bueller had grabbed onto my hair. I—thankfully—saw no red splotches forming anywhere. I got a little woozy just the same, but it was more for the potential of finding blood.

"I'm going to take a moment." Levi closed his eyes and laid back against the curb.

"I sure hope the officer gets to Bueller before Stanley."

"Stanley won't do anything." Muldoon gave a quick chuckle.

"How do you know?"

"If something happens to Bueller, everyone knows who was after him."

"Sure." I nodded. Ugh, my neck was getting stiff. "And Gabriel can't get his money back from a dead guy."

"It should sound strange hearing that kind of talk coming out of your mouth. But it doesn't. How messed up is that?" He shook his head. "Look at me. Are you okay?"

I tried to smile but it wobbled and tears filled my eyes. I held out my hand to him and he took it without another word and sat next to me. I leaned heavily into him, let my body relax for the first time since I got into that car. "How'd you find me?"

Muldoon looked away for moment. "Grady."

"Grady what?"

"He called me. Told me you were in trouble." He let out a long breath. "I thought he was trying to pull something. Then we got out to the parking lot and I found your keys under your Outlander. I knew you were in trouble."

"Again."

"I didn't say that." A small smile tipped the corner of his mouth.

"No, but you were thinking it. I could see it in your eyes." I leaned my head against his shoulder. "I think they killed Arnie Showalter. And Mandy Crenshaw. Because of the smuggling ring. Arnie was trying to cheat them." I shuddered. "They never quite admitted it."

"You got all that in five blocks."

"Yes," Levi piped up. "She wouldn't shut up. I almost wanted to shoot her myself." He peeled one eye open for a minute then snapped it closed again.

"Who are *they*, babe?"

"Guy Bueller *and* Rebecka Nylin." I frowned up at him. "Don't you have Rebecka?"

Muldoon shook his head. I sat up, or tried to, but Muldoon kept me rooted at his side. He nudged my shoulder. "Why did they grab you guys up?"

"They thought we had the missing crate." I swiped at a stray tear that snuck out and down my cheek. "Because of the purse I gave you. They thought Arnie had switched allegiances."

"Levi?" Muldoon tapped Levi on the knee. "You okay?"

"Peachy."

"Stanley was following me." I leaned back and looked at Muldoon. "Gabriel seemed to know where I was and who I was with. Because he had Stanley reporting back to him on me." But not every time. Maybe I'd seen too many movies—okay there was no *maybe*, I'd definitely

seen too many movies—but something felt slightly off.
I tried to stand again.

"Where are you going?" Muldoon tucked his arm
around my waist.

"I need my purse."

"Now?"

I looked up at him. "Yes, now."

"Where is it?"

"In the floorboard, I think." I motioned to the car.

"I'll get it. Stay put."

Muldoon snatched up my battered black bag. "Here
ya go."

I took the bag and turned it upside down, dumping
the contents on the cement beneath me.

"What are you doing?" Levi looked up from his perch
on the curb.

"Looking for something."

"Well, duh, I figured that one out all on my own.
What are you looking for?"

"He's been keeping tabs on me," I mumbled almost
more to myself as I pawed around inside the emptied-
out bag. "I've switched purses several times, but I always use the same wallet." I slid my fingers along all
the little slots and across the seams. Then I hit pay dirt.
"Gotcha." I used my thumbnail to dig at the little lump
in the corner of the change pocket. It took a minute or
two, but I was finally able to pry out the little device. I
held the damn thing aloft as if it were the Holy Grail.
"Asshat has been tracking me. Literally tracking me."

Muldoon took the thing from my fingers. "It is indeed
a tracking device."

"You've got to be kidding me." Levi sat up and looked
at my wallet like there might be another tracker just wait-

ing for him to discover it. "He always popped up when you'd just come in from your own surveilling."

I frowned at my friend. "I was not surveilling." I glanced from him to Muldoon and back. "I had a few innocuous, discreet meetings. There was zero surveilling."

"Yeah, okay." Muldoon chuckled. "Hey, the bus is here." He pointed to the ambulance that drove through the throng of onlookers and pulled up between two of the squad cars. "At this point, you know the drill." He looked pointedly at me.

I groaned. "I'm fine. Really. There's no need to—"

"Considering the spill you took not twenty minutes ago, it's not a bad idea."

"Spill? What spill?" Levi's blond brows slammed down over his narrowing eyes.

Muldoon pointed to the bandage on his cheek. "She caught me changing it."

Levi's brows relaxed and his lips pursed together. Probably to prevent a laugh from eking out.

"What've we got, ma'am?" The young EMT carried his black bag over between Levi and me.

"Hey, you. Long time no see." The young man had attended to me last year when my car exploded. I don't think he ever told me his name. I do remember him pissing me off ma'aming every time I turned around. It made me feel old. And I was old enough—almost, maybe—to be his mother. That was sadly not even the most depressing realization since I'd walked out of the police station and wound up kidnapped.

I frowned and looked down at my dirty trousers. I was a mess. Coming, going and even minding my own darn business. Why in the world would Muldoon want to put up with someone like me? When we'd met, I'd all but turned myself into his prime suspect, then the prime target. Now I had bad guy(s)—plural, which was something wholly unnerving and unexpected—chasing me for something I didn't even do. At least not that I knew of. I gave an internal chuckle. Maybe I was way better at all this sleuthing than I thought I was. I uncovered truths that I didn't know were covered. Which was why Muldoon was constantly gnashing his teeth and telling me to behave. And I never listened.

If I was him, I'd hightail it as far away from me as I could get.

I looked up at the man, who was speaking to the other EMT. He glanced over at me and winked. I was so very glad he was not me and had decided to stick around.

The EMT took my chin in his hand and shined a penlight in my eyes. "So you were in a car accident..." It took another ten minutes for him and his partner to clear Levi and me. We could have a mild case of whiplash. It could take a few hours for that to present, but otherwise we were in decent shape. Considering.

At one point, I thought I saw Stanley. He eased his way up to the edge of the onlookers, gave the mass of police officers a once-over, then headed off in another direction.

Did he have a vehicle nearby? He had to have had one to follow us. Was he just going to walk back to the bakery? It was a good ten-minute drive to the far side of Peytonville.

I sighed. Not my problem. Though I was ever so grateful he'd been following me today, I was going to have to talk to Grady about boundaries.

"I don't think Stanley found Bueller," I whispered to Levi.

"Why do you think that?"

"He just came and peeked over at us and didn't have blood or anything obvious that he'd just whacked a man."

"Whacked?" Muldoon asked from behind me.

I jumped. "What? It's a thing."

He shook his head and chuckled. I got that a lot from him.

"Y'all ready to go home?"

Home? Crap. "I left Paige up at the playhouse. Annabelle was kid-sitting for a bit." I looked down at my shoes. "So I could come talk to you."

"Did we cover what you needed to cover?"

"Pretty much. As long as we're good."

"We're good." He leaned forward and planted a huge smacker right on my mouth in front of God and everyone.

I don't know who was more stunned. Me, Levi or the herd of officers taking names from any potential witnesses. To my knowledge, Muldoon had never, ever, had a public display of affection. For sure not with me. And the way he'd been acting the past couple of weeks, I didn't think it would ever happen.

"Okay, then." I rolled back on my heels. "Will you drive me back to the police station so I can pick up my car? Then I have to go pick up Paige."

"You betcha. Levi?"

"I can use a ride. My car's still at my office. That's where the two jackholes scooped me up."

"You two lead the most interesting lives." Muldoon settled his hand on the small of my back and led me, with Levi trailing right behind, over to the cruiser.

"Shotgun," I hollered at Levi.

"I don't want to sit in the back. Again."

"At least you're not under arrest this time." I patted

his shoulder. "Get in, whiner." I held the door open for my friend and he reluctantly got into the barred-off backseat. "Did y'all find Rebecka or Bueller?"

Muldoon looked at me over the top of the car. "You're safe. We've already assigned extra cruisers to go through your neighborhood. And Levi's. And I seriously doubt Grady's going to leave you unattended if there's even the slightest chance they will show up."

"That's comforting."

"It is what it is." He ducked and got into the car.

My phone dinged in my pocket. I didn't even realize I had it on me. Everything happened so fast. I could have called for help myself, wouldn't have had to wait for the thug of a thug to come to my rescue after I sort of rescued myself.

I read the message, gaped at the picture. "This is all your fault."

"What? What'd I do?" He leaned forward and pressed his forehead to the metal cage separating us.

I turned the phone so he could see the picture my parents sent from Vegas. My mother was dressed up like a showgirl and my dad looked like a fifties mobster. "They're staying an extra week."

"That's good." Levi smiled.

I smacked the cage.

"Ow."

"I should never have to see my mother dressed like this. Ever. Maybe I should write a book. Who would believe any of this ever happened?"

"No," Levi and Muldoon said in unison.

TWENTY

"I COULD WRITE a book." I slunk a little lower in my seat and pouted. I just needed five minutes to myself—which would never happen. As soon as they picked up the pair of purse pushers, I could relax a little bit, then maybe… "Did you check the warehouse?"

Muldoon frowned over at me. "What warehouse?"

"I sent you a picture." I scooped up my phone. The message didn't go through. "It's the address from the crates at The Blarney Shop. The same one from the crate I saw at the Sagebrush house."

Muldoon pulled the car over. "Let me see it."

I handed him my cell.

"You're sure it's the same?" he asked as he reached for his own cell phone.

I nodded.

"That's the warehouse district." He paused and then mumbled, "Maybe ten minutes away."

"Then let's go." I clapped my hands together. "With lights and sirens we can be there in six."

He snorted. "I don't think so."

"They're going to get away," Levi said from the backseat.

"They'll be gone by the time you drop us off. Go." I motioned for him to drive.

"I'll call it in." He pushed a button on his cell.

I snatched my phone back. "They kidnapped us. We should be able to see the takedown."

"Bush, hold on," he said into the phone then turned his attention back to me. "Don't screw with me, Celeste."

"Come on."

"No." He held his hand out to me, palm up.

I clutched the phone to my chest. "Are you going to let them get away?"

Muldoon held my gaze, didn't comment or waver.

I huffed. "Fine." I slapped the phone back into his hand.

He relayed the information to Bush, then gave me back my phone and pulled the car back onto the road.

"You can drop us over there."

He glanced over at the strip mall to our right. "Here?"

"Yeah. I know you want to get in on it. I'll call Annabelle to come pick us up."

He hesitated. "You sure?"

I glanced back at Levi. "Yep." My friend looked confused but thankfully kept his mouth shut.

Muldoon pulled in front of the first business in the strip mall, a tailor shop. "You're sure?"

"Absolutely. Call me later when it's done. I wanna know what happened." I waved as the car departed.

"What the hell, Celeste?" Levi was practically bouncing on his feet.

The second Muldoon's car was out of slight, I turned and waved my arm wildly in the other direction. A black town car pulled up almost to the same spot Muldoon had dropped us off. As I suspected, Stanley hadn't been far behind. The opaque tinted passenger window smoothly rolled down.

I bent at the waist and peered into the darkened interior. "Can we get a ride?"

Without a word, the door locks popped open.

"Get in, Levi."

My friend stared at me with his mouth hanging open for a long moment before he finally slid into the back. I got into the front seat with Stanley. "We're headed to this address." I held out the cell phone so Stanley could read the address I'd given to Muldoon.

Stanley glanced up at me, narrowed his eyes, then tapped his fingers on the steering wheel.

"This is where Bueller and Rebecka are—or could be. Gabriel wants to know what's happening with them, doesn't he? What better way to find out than to go see for ourselves?"

"Celeste…" Levi warned from the back.

"What? Muldoon didn't say we couldn't go if we got our own ride."

"You know damn well the man will have a conniption if you just show up."

"Maybe he will, maybe he won't. We'll never know if we don't go." I stressed *go* and looked at Stanley but he sat somewhat immovable.

"If we get in the way and jeopardize this case…"

"We're the ones who put them on to the warehouse in the first place. They had an undercover in her shop and she didn't connect the two."

Stanley's thick eyebrow quirked upward in what was probably the closest thing he'd ever get to a smile. Still without saying a single word, Stanley had the car on the road and headed toward the warehouse district of Peytonville before Levi could register another reason it was a bad idea.

"Where is everyone?" Levi was leaning forward, his head between me and Stanley. We were about a block away from the warehouse. There was a stretch of five or six warehouses side by side. On a Saturday morning, the buildings were closed up and quiet.

We saw no signs of any squad cars. No Muldoon in his unmarked sedan. Not even a single soul out on foot— though the area wasn't really a foot-traffic kind of place.

"Did they go to the wrong place?" Levi asked.

"Did we?" I stated to ask, but Stanley gave me a look that said we were in the right place. "O-kay, then." I sucked in a slow breath. "Maybe they're all holding back, watching for them."

"Maybe they already nabbed them both and we missed it all."

"No way they could have gotten that done so fast and cleared up the area." I scanned the area again. "There'd be officers standing around. Crime scene tape with the area cordoned off."

Stanley snorted.

"What?"

"Nothing," Stanley said for the first time.

"So you think all those crates are here at the warehouse." Levi eased back slightly.

"I think Arnie was having things shipped to your properties, then having them shipped from there to his warehouse. It's probably how your stuff went missing. They grabbed the wrong crate from time to time."

"Why would he do that?"

"So your addresses, in your name, are the registered landing places for all the merchandise. Keeps him out of the loop," Stanley supplied.

"Then why would he try to get me to partner with

him? That would put him square in the middle of my business."

Stanley stared at him for a long moment. "Were you really considering partnering with him?" He and I turned in our seats to look at Levi.

"I, uh, well, maybe." Levi toyed with the seam of the seat. "Not really. But I didn't want to piss him off by outright saying no."

Stanley rubbed his jaw then pointed at Levi. "But it gave him access to you and your properties while you entertained the idea."

"I guess."

"Arnie and Bueller were already partners," I said. "And Arnie, like he did with everyone else, screwed him over. Probably started moving the crates around until he could unload them himself."

Levi nodded. "Bueller got tired of it and cut his losses."

"But there was still one crate left." His reaction when I met him for lunch. "Bueller thought we had it when he saw the handbag I found with Arnie's body." I was watching the warehouse. Not a single body had moved anywhere near it since we parked. "I don't think they're coming here."

"Where else would they go?"

"Anywhere." I shrugged. "They tried to kidnap two people in broad daylight. They killed two people. Would you have expected that from Bueller?"

Levi shook his head.

"She was a little bit unhinged." Something niggled the back of my brain. It first hit me when we were at The Blarney Shop. Something familiar about Rebecka.

Then again when I got in the car. My adrenaline was so ramped, it'd faded into the background.

Levi tapped me on the shoulder. "What is it?"

"I know that woman from somewhere. Or at least her voice." The anonymous caller. I snapped my fingers. "She called me at work."

"Rebecka?"

"Yeah. A couple of days ago. Told me to meet her at some address if I wanted some more info." I shook my head. "That was even before we figured out Bueller was in on all this."

"What's the address?"

"I don't remember." I rubbed my temple. "I wrote it down, but then I threw it away. I wasn't about to show up at some strange house."

"That's a first," Levi said almost under his breath. Louder he added, "Do you think they would lure you to their own property?"

"There's only one way to find out." I tilted my head and batted my eyelashes at Stanley. "The address is at the playhouse."

STANLEY PULLED THE town car to the curb and let it quietly idle three houses down from the one we were watching.

I'd run into the playhouse and grabbed the address out of my trashcan. Annabelle and Paige had both peppered me with questions, but I just ran right back out, waving the paper in my hand. "Later. Promise."

No one spoke on the short ride across town to the Flagstone address.

"There's movement inside." Levi clapped his hands. "Should we call the police?"

"And tell them there's a house that has movement in

it?" I scoffed. "Sure. They'll bring out SWAT for that. We don't even know if it's them inside."

"Then let's go scope it out." Levi reached for the door handle, but there was a loud click. "It won't open."

"You two, stay put." Stanley opened the driver's door and stepped out.

"He does this for a living, so yeah. Probably better we let him go." Levi examined his cuticles.

"I should call Muldoon." I tapped the little green phone icon and called him.

"Did you get a ride?" he asked in lieu of hello.

"Yes, we did. How's it going? You still waiting for them to show up?"

There was a pause. "How do you know we're waiting? Did you come to the warehouse?"

Busted. "Maybe."

"But you're not here now?"

"No."

"Where are you?"

"Right at this moment?"

"Celeste…"

"We might have driven to an address that may be where Rebecka and Bueller are."

"What?"

I explained about the strange phone call and that after the kidnapping attempt I realized it was Rebecka.

"Why didn't you tell me sooner?"

"I wasn't going to go, so I didn't think it was pertinent."

"What's the address?" He sounded harried as I rattled it off, then he said, "Do not go anywhere near there."

"Levi and I won't. We're sitting in the car. Listening

to the radio." I punched at several buttons until a soft jazz song filled the inside of the car.

"Who picked you up?" I could almost see his face, his brows crushed low, his mouth turned down.

"From the strip mall?"

"Yes, Celeste. Who picked you up from the strip mall and then drove you over to your attempted kidnappers' location?"

"Stanley."

"Where is he now?"

"Checking out the—" A loud round of unmistakable pops sounded.

"Someone's shooting," Levi yelled as he ducked down in the backseat.

"Who's shooting?" Muldoon demanded.

"I don't know. I can't see anything. It sounds like... It's Bueller." Guy Bueller ran out the front door of the house and over to a green-and-brown clunker. "Levi, here." I tossed my cell phone into the backseat. "Talk to Muldoon."

I had to crawl over the console between my seat into the driver's seat where Stanley had been sitting. It was not easy, let me tell you. When I finally swung my legs over, my left foot smashed down on the gas pedal for a moment and revved the engine. It was loud enough that Bueller turned in our direction. I didn't think he could see into the car and tell that it was me, but he hurried, shoving things into the back of his car.

"Tell Muldoon they're trying to get away."

Levi relayed the info.

"What should I do?"

"Nothing." Even from a seat away, I could hear Muldoon's retort as he yelled into his end of the phone.

"But…" I glanced into the rearview mirror where Levi was holding the phone away from his ear as Muldoon cursed up a blue streak. Then I shifted my gaze back to Bueller. That son of a bitch killed two people over freaking handbags, then tried to kidnap me and Levi—which would have surely ended in our deaths, too. No way in hell was I going to let him drive away.

I settled myself into the driver's seat prepared to go when I realized my feet were nowhere near reaching. I had to shift my butt to the very edge of the seat in order to touch the pedals.

"Hold on, Levi."

Bueller hopped in his car and started backing out of the driveway as I shifted the town car into gear and floored it.

It all happened in slow motion. I could hear Levi's "No-o-o-o" as the town car seemed to move frame by frame toward the other car. In the driver's seat, Bueller's gaze shot in my direction and his mouth slowly formed an exaggerated O.

There was a horrible screeching noise of metal on metal as the town car plowed into the passenger side door, pushing the crappy vehicle completely off the driveway. Almost instantly a white pillow exploded in my face and knocked me back into the seat. My nose clogged up. White powder went into my mouth and I could not stop coughing. My head was spinning a little and I could hear bells—no, it was sirens.

Sirens?

Bueller.

The powder-dust was floating all over the front seat as I pushed the airbag down and away from me so I could get out.

"You okay, Levi?"

There was a moan followed by a colorful curse I wouldn't repeat even to Naomi. Levi was fine.

I got out of the car in time to see Bueller heading for me.

"You crazy bitch." He took two steps, then disappeared from view.

"What the…" I moved closer but before I could round the end of the car, two large arms circled me. I opened my mouth to scream when I heard Muldoon say, "We got 'em."

He guided me over to the curb and sat me down. An officer pulled Bueller to his feet and dragged him over to a squad car.

A bottle of water materialized in front of me with a gruff, "Drink this."

I complied, rinsing out my mouth quickly before I took several swallows. My throat was dry and scratchy. Once my throat was a little better, I croaked out, "Déjà-freaking-vu."

Muldoon chuckled from behind me. "I should have known you'd catch them before we did."

I'd almost swear there was a little bit of pride in his voice.

"Did we win?" Levi crawled over to where I sat. His hair was sticking out in every direction and he was still clutching my cell phone tightly in his hand.

"Did we?" I asked over my shoulder.

Before Muldoon could answer, Stanley came around the corner. He had Rebecka by the arm and handed her off to an awaiting police officer. He had an armful of handbags that he handed to another officer, then he turned toward us. He raised his hand with a thumbs-up, gave me a quick once-over and frowned.

As I'd guessed, the pair'd come back to the house to load up on what they could carry and they were going to hightail it out of town. But not with all the bags. They still didn't have the shipment Arnie had hidden. "Levi, have you been to all of your properties lately?" If Arnie put crates at some of the properties, maybe he put them at all the properties.

He scrubbed at his head, his eyes still glued to the two vehicles crumpled together in the street.

"No."

"Which one haven't you been to?"

"The one in Old Town Peytonville. I don't plan on starting on it 'til the middle of next month. Why?" He turned toward me, his eyes widening slightly, and pinched his lips together.

"Muldoon." I yanked on his sleeve. He was talking to a police officer decked out in tactical gear. "Hey. I think I know where the missing crate is. I think it's at Levi's house in Old Town. I think Arnie was playing keep-away with the crates. He was moving them around Levi's properties, trying to keep them away from Bueller and Rebecka."

He nodded slowly. "Okay. I'll send someone out there to check it out. How are you feeling?"

"Like I was in a car wreck. Twice." I coughed again. "I think I got that powder up my nose. It's all stopped up."

"Uh-huh."

"Why are y'all all looking at me so strangely?"

"Sweets, your, um…" Levi waved his hand in a circle around his face.

"Do I have some of the powder on my face?" I reached up and winced as my fingers lit on my nose. "No, no, no, no, no." I stood on shaky legs and hurried over to the side mirror. "Shit, shit, shit." My nose was swelled up and already turned all sorts of lovely shades of purple. "Damn you, Marcia."

We finally pulled back into the PPD parking lot, a couple of hours after I left it. Muldoon was thumping the steering wheel as we neared my car. "You have company." Gabriel's shiny black Beemer was parked right up next to my little SUV.

"Just drop me off. I'll get him to leave."

"He did send the cavalry after us," Levi piped up from the backseat.

"Because he Lojacked me."

"Lojacking that saved us. Just saying."

"Promise me you won't do anything." I looked over at Muldoon.

"What could I possibly do?" His unbandaged eye ticked.

"His lawyer is just looking for a reason to sue the department." I set my hand on his arm. "I will talk to him, he'll leave and all will be well."

Muldoon grunted but didn't comment any further as he pulled to the opposite side of my car.

"Can you drive Levi back?"

"I'll just get a ride with you." Levi reached for the door handle but couldn't open it from the backseat.

"I think it'll be better if Muldoon drives you."

"She wants us to leave so I don't smack the guy. Again." He reached into his shirt pocket and pulled out my keys. He held them close to his chest for a moment before he finally held them out to me.

"I kind of want to see that," Levi said under his breath.

"Thank you." I leaned over and kissed Muldoon's cheek.

"You will owe me one."

"Absolutely." I beamed up at him then climbed out of the car. "See you later." I blew him a kiss and watched the car until it left the parking lot.

"You had some excitement," Gabriel said as he stepped away from his car. His nose was sporting a bandage and he had dark circles under his eyes. "We match." He didn't seem the least bit surprised when he pointed to my swollen nose. Stanley must have given him a report the second he was out of eyesight of the police. Gabriel gritted his teeth and balled his first at his side. "Does it hurt?"

It was the first time I think I'd seen him truly mad. It was not something I ever wanted to see again.

"It'll be fine." Eventually. At the moment it throbbed like a sonofabitch. "I guess I should thank you. If you didn't have Stanley watching me—oh, and the tracker I found in my wallet—things could have gotten really uncomfortable for me and Levi."

"You're mad." Gabriel tilted his head and eyed me.

"Y'think? It was a total invasion of privacy." I slammed my hands on my hips.

"That saved you."

"A coincidence."

"That saved you."

"If you keep throwing that out there, it's going to make it more difficult for me to stay pissed."

His smiled broadened. "That was the plan." His smile

fell and he stepped forward and ran his hand over my cheek. "Are you okay? Stanley told me everything."

"Stanley was a big help." I stepped back out of his reach. "I'm sorry about your car. I didn't think, just reacted." I swallowed heavily. "I hope my insurance will cover that."

Gabriel waved away my comment. "Don't worry about that."

"Well, if you need me to talk to your insurance agent or anything…" I gave a half shrug.

"You're looking out for my welfare now?"

I scoffed. "Hardly." I said the words, but I could tell by the look on his face that's exactly what he thought. I was never going to shake the man. Maybe brutal honesty—if stretched out just a wee little bit—would work. "You realize that I'm with Muldoon, right? Like me and him."

"For now." He eased back into his car.

"For now?" I asked, but he'd already shut the door and revved the engine. "Seriously?"

LATER THAT NIGHT, Muldoon walked me and Paige to the front door. We'd had a quick meal—it was our first date in months. If you counted having Paige and Colby along a *date*. Which I was. It was wonderful, even if the sullen teen stared daggers at me half the night. We finally made a truce of sorts, Colby and I. Actually, once Paige was done touting my heroics, he'd looked at me with more curiosity than contempt. I called it a win. "So go ahead," I said when Paige went into the house.

Muldoon paused midstride. "Go ahead and what?"

"Ask me what Grady and I talked about earlier. You've been dying to."

"I wasn't…" He toyed with the collar of his shirt.

"Yeah, you were, but you didn't want to bring it up with the extra little ears sitting there with us." I gave Colby a finger wave as he squirmed in the backseat of his dad's sedan at the curb.

Muldoon opened his mouth, started to argue, but grinned. "What did you and Grady talk about this afternoon?"

"He pretty much told me to thank him for saving me."

"That man is so full of himself." He narrowed his eyes. "But it's true."

I toyed with the doggie bag in my hand until I just blurted out, "I told him that I wasn't the least bit interested in him. That you and I were together."

A slow smile crawled across Muldoon's face. "Good." He bent down and gave me a sweet, gentle kiss.

I wanted to lean forward and take more, but his cell went off at the same time as Colby started blaring the car horn.

Muldoon chuckled. "Well, at least we got through a whole meal for a change."

* * * * *

Get 2 Free Books,
<u>Plus</u> 2 Free Gifts –

just for trying the *Reader Service!*

Get 2 Free Books,
Plus 2 Free Gifts—
just for trying the
Reader Service!

◆ HARLEQUIN
INTRIGUE

Get 2 Free Books,
Plus 2 Free Gifts—
just for trying the Reader Service!

♦ HARLEQUIN
ROMANTIC suspense

Get 2 Free Books,
Plus 2 Free Gifts—
just for trying the
Reader Service!

✦ HARLEQUIN®
Paranormal Romance

YES! Please send me 2 FREE novels from the Paranormal Romance Collection and my 2 FREE gifts (gifts are worth about $10 retail). After receiving them, if I don't wish to receive any more books, I can return the shipping statement marked "cancel." If I don't cancel, I will receive 4 brand-new novels every month and be billed just $25.92 in the U.S. or $28.96 in Canada. That's a savings of at least 13% off the cover price of all 4 books. It's quite a bargain! Shipping and handling is just 50¢ per book in the U.S. and 75¢ per book in Canada.* I understand that accepting the 2 free books and gifts places me under no obligation to buy anything. I can always return a shipment and cancel at any time. The free books and gifts are mine to keep no matter what I decide.

237/337 HDN GLW4

Name	(PLEASE PRINT)

Address	Apt. #

City	State/Prov.	Zip/Postal Code

Signature (if under 18, a parent or guardian must sign)

Mail to the **Reader Service:**
IN U.S.A.: P.O. Box 1341, Buffalo, NY 14240-8531
IN CANADA: P.O. Box 603, Fort Erie, Ontario L2A 5X3

Want to try two free books from another line?
Call 1-800-873-8635 or visit www.ReaderService.com.

*Terms and prices subject to change without notice. Prices do not include applicable taxes. Sales tax applicable in NY. Canadian residents will be charged applicable taxes. Offer not valid in Quebec. This offer is limited to one order per household. Books received may not be as shown. Not valid for current subscribers to Paranormal Romance Collection or Harlequin® Nocturne™ books. All orders subject to approval. Credit or debit balances in a customer's account(s) may be offset by any other outstanding balance owed by or to the customer. Please allow 4 to 6 weeks for delivery. Offer available while quantities last.

Your Privacy—The Reader Service is committed to protecting your privacy. Our Privacy Policy is available online at www.ReaderService.com or upon request from the Reader Service.

We make a portion of our mailing list available to reputable third parties that offer products we believe may interest you. If you prefer that we not exchange your name with third parties, or if you wish to clarify or modify your communication preferences, please visit us at www. ReaderService.com/consumerchoice or write to us at Reader Service Preference Service, P.O. Box 9062, Buffalo, NY 14269-9062. Include your complete name and address.

PARA17R

Get 2 Free Books,
Plus 2 Free Gifts—
just for trying the Reader Service!